Midnight Ruin

Moira Kane

This book is dedicated to every reader who knows how to silently carry the burdens of others.

This book is also dedicated to my sisters. I would burn the world for you.

Sensitivity Warnings

Hello again,

Thanks for reading Midnight Ruin. Before you begin, I want to inform you that this is the darkest of the Dragon Brides books thus far. By no means is it a *dark* romance, but the following triggers should be noted for sensitive readers:

Physical and emotional abuse

Scars/scarring

Non-consensual sexual acts (mentioned but not depicted)

Violence and gore

Depictions of PTSD

Dubious consent

Religious fanaticism and purity culture

Pregnancy and Childbirth

PS.

It's pronounced like Owen. You're welcome.

SPEARTIP BREACH
DISTANT SHORES
RYDAR
ESKALI FJORD
ESAKLI CITADEL
STARBORN GLADES
WAR CAMP
STARBORN
SILVER ORE PORT
BURIE'S SECRET
SILVER SEA
SILVER COAST
CAPE OF CASTREL
GAZAR
GREY JUNGLE
GAZARI PORT

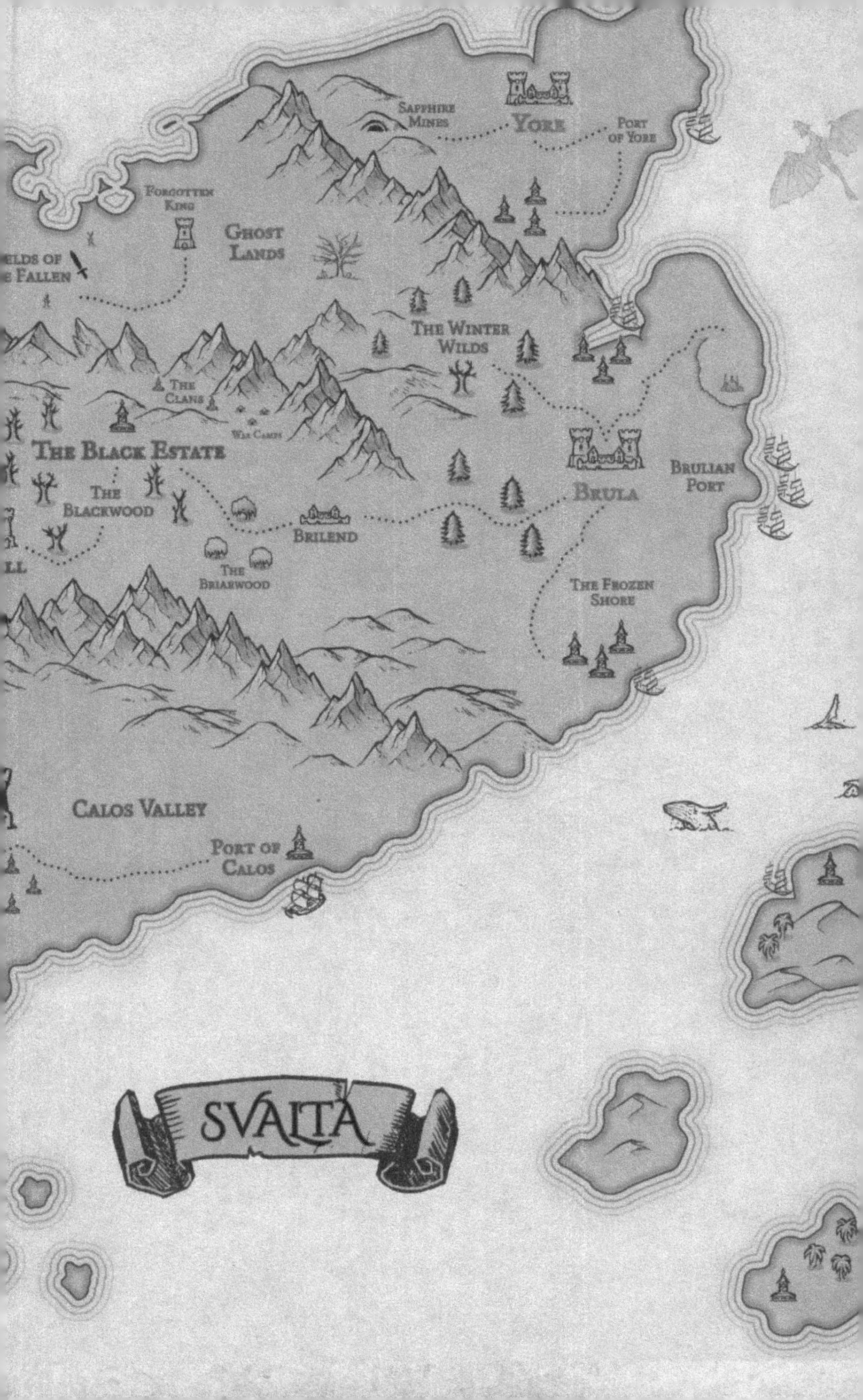

SAPPHIRE MINES
YORE
PORT OF YORE
FORGOTTEN KING
GHOST LANDS
FIELDS OF THE FALLEN
THE WINTER WILDS
THE CLANS
WAR CAMPS
THE BLACK ESTATE
THE BLACKWOOD
BRILEND
THE BRIARWOOD
BRULA
BRULIAN PORT
THE FROZEN SHORE
CALOS VALLEY
PORT OF CALOS
SVAITA

Chapter 1

Eoin

E oin was racing midnight, his breaths so rapid they were daggers of air swiping in and out of his lungs. The muscles in his legs were burning. They were molten, melting away from his form.

When he finally collapsed onto the leafy earth in the Blackwood, Eoin would come apart.

Then he would be reborn as darkness.

An obsidian nightmare.

An indomitable force of death.

It happened abruptly, dropping him to his knees with a roar of pain. Father taught him that it wasn't supposed to hurt. The change should be a gentle wave washing over him, a brief flash of heat as he stretched and contorted. To be a *drakonmein* was a gift from the Gods and a gift should not be a source of distress.

Eoin thought maybe it was a curse instead because what he was, what lived inside him, was the source of his greatest agony. If he were merely a man, he could swallow it down. Recall flashes of war in horrible nightmares, but wake up assured the destruction ended when his sleep did.

Instead, Eoin bolted upright in his bed, never sure if the room would be ablaze. Pillows shredded to feathery remains. In his worst moments, he woke fearing there would be blood on his hands.

That was why he was here, battling the serpentine dragon trying to emerge from beneath his skin. The creature was mad, mind warped by bloodshed, and if Eoin allowed it free reign, the dragon would destroy everything he loved.

Right now, his sole focus was on the one person he cared for the most. It was all Eoin could do to get himself away from the Black Estate, putting miles of space between his family home and himself in hopes of distracting the dragon with easier prey.

It never worked. Even if he ran a hundred miles, it would seem a short distance to a monster hellbent on collecting the treasure he believed was his.

Eoin knew better. She would never be his. There was no happy ending for a *drakonmein* destroyed by war. He was death incarnate, a vicious ghost of battle, and he would ruin everyone around him in time.

The dragon ripped free in a spark of light and Eoin was gone, nothing more than a murmured voice deep in the recesses of a purely primal brain. It wasn't always like this. Once Eoin and the dragon that shared his being were equals. Two souls entwined into one.

War had ripped a jagged hole right through the middle of him, creating a rift so wide between him and his dragon that Eoin feared one day the creature would leap from his skin and escape into the Blackwood.

Except it wouldn't flee like some caged animal set free. He stood now under the thin ceiling of newly budded leaves, absorbing his surroundings, calculating the distance between where he was and where he would find his prize. The sweet scent of early blooming blackberry vines tangled with the heavy smell of moisture and decay. Winter and spring clashing in whirls of green and grey.

The Blackwood was alive with the sounds of night. Crickets set a tempo for the midnight chorus of nocturnal birds and screeching animals. Somewhere distant, where the wood met the mountains, a wolf howled. Another answered, closer to the Black Estate than wolves were usually heard.

Like any animal, they were deterred by the presence of the Beast of the Blackwood, keeping a healthy distance between themselves and the Black Estate where the beast made his territory known. That was before last autumn when a runaway princess stumbled into the Blackwood and the beast—Eoin's older brother Gannon—claimed her as a mate.

Months went by and Gannon scarcely set foot in the Blackwood, too focused on his new bond to care about what happened outside of his bed chamber.

Eoin's other two brothers, Davin, and Amos, had been present at the Black Estate since the untimely maiming of the king—also Gannon's doing—left the country in disarray and the army with no orders but to return home. There was no coin to pay soldiers and no one to lead them.

Not that Davin or Amos needed an income. They had inherited two lifetimes of wealth from their father, as Eoin had.

But Davin and Amos didn't care to stalk the woods as Gannon did. The estate was their home, but not their territory. They had no interest in keeping the worst types of predators at bay, be they human or animal.

Selfish, as far as Eoin was concerned, but he supposed he could understand. Davin and Amos were young, and they had nothing to lose.

They didn't grasp the true risk.

When the urge came to shift, Amos would wander high into the mountains, where no mortal man could find him. Gods only knew what Davin would do, foolish lout that he was. Probably flying recklessly low to neighboring towns, searching for a new woman to harass or ruffians to brawl with.

As for Eoin? He was part of the problem. His nightly sprints into the Blackwood did little to scare away bears, wolves, and the worst kind of men. If he were like his eldest brother, stomping around, killing all manner of prey, leaving a trail of blood and gore in his wake, Eoin might have an impact. With a dragon as violent and ruined as his own, it should be instinct to do exactly that.

The bounding of deer and the spoor of frightened prey did nothing for him tonight, nor any night, because his dragon had his sights on larger prey. One creature in particular.

A divine creation, tall with a lush waist and ample hips. Her caramel skin was always buttery soft, no matter how hard she worked herself. It was her eyes that stuck in his mind when he was on the prowl for her. Toasted chestnut, bright with boldness and beauty.

Boldness and beauty. Yes, that was her. Striking not only in her unrivalled beauty but in the way she carried herself. Fierce as any warrior, composed amidst the shouting and ill-tempered Black brothers she was loyal to.

She was close, close enough that he could almost taste the spicy cinnamon scent of her. He need only rise above the treetops, beat his leathery wings, and carry himself across the Blackwood to the estate. His treasure would be waiting for him there, had been waiting for *years* too long. There was such an urgency in his need for her, a building anxiety that warned him that his time was running out.

A mate should not go unclaimed.

For months at a time, he had left her behind, *left her* to be propositioned by other males. Left her unprotected. Without his mark.

He would not live another day with his mate unmarked.

The dragon could feel her as a weight in his chest, drawing him first up into the sky and then down, down to the sprawling Black Estate. A single candle burned in a third-story window, the sole light in the sharp, jutting black structure that Eoin and his brothers had always called home. She called it home too, and he would make sure she could *never* leave.

A narrow balcony stood out against the black stone walls that made up her chambers. Small, much smaller than the great balcony to the baron's chamber. That balcony was designed for dragon landing, built by his grandfather so he could come and go as he pleased. Dragons of the Black line were beasts of the night. They preferred to fly unseen against the star-studded heavens.

It was in darkness that they became their most lethal. A Black dragon was a cunning dragon.

Just as Eoin's dragon was now, carefully assessing the width of the black iron balustrades and whether the ornate spear-like metal would puncture his scales. Not if he was quick, graceful as a serpent, slithering his way into the outer door propped open to let in the breeze.

She never closed that door, even in the winter, he remembered. Her hatred of enclosed spaces far outweighed her desire to be warm. The first winter that she stayed in the Black Estate, Eoin dragged every feather blanket he could find up the stairs, insisting she use them, or he would bar the balcony door shut.

That, he learned, had not been a wise choice of words. His mate was not a woman that handled threats well and if he'd been an ordinary man, he would have taken a candelabra to the head.

The dragon approved. He liked her ferocity.

He could just make out her face through the crack in the door, smooth and sweet in sleep. The untamed waves of her brown hair spilled across her pillow, tumbling in the wind from his beating wings as it pushed the door further inward. He was almost there. He simply had to find his way through that narrow opening, and he could *sink his teeth into her.*

No! A voice struck him like an arrow, jolting his body so violently he nearly dropped from the air.

NO! It was louder now, ripping through him, pounding his head like a hammer.

The dragon crashed against the balcony, scrabbling to take hold of the metal railing. It groaned under his weight, leaning perilously toward the garden below. With a shimmering flash, his body broke apart, rebuilding itself into the smaller form of a man. Eoin managed to tuck and roll at the last second, catching himself on his knees as he tumbled into Elsie's bedroom.

Naked, filthy, and panting.

The sound of legs shifting under sheets spurred him up from his awkward crouch. If she woke and found him like this in her room she would think him a madman, at best. At worst, she would curse his name and never let him within a hundred feet of her again.

Perhaps he should let her wake to see him like this then. It might resolve the issue if she hated him.

The dragon thrashed inside of him, tearing him apart internally. *He* didn't care if Elsie hated them both. There was nothing he wouldn't do to have her, even stealing her away and holding her captive until she loved him above all else.

Even marring her flesh with his teeth so no other male would covet her again.

In a quiet shuffle, Eoin darted from the room, hurrying up the stairs to the far corner of the west wing where the house was on the verge of decay. Dust puffed up from the rug as his feet kicked along it, leaving him in a fit of sneezing when he finally made it into his room and closed the door. The space was dark as pitch, the curtains drawn and not a single candle burning.

Eoin liked it that way. Both he and the dragon were less likely to destroy something if there was nothing visible to destroy. Even the sharp night vision of a dragon was useless in total darkness.

No amount of darkness, of isolation, or sending himself madly into the Blackwood was helping anymore.

This wasn't the first time the dragon had made it to the estate. It wasn't even the first time he tried to get into Elsie's room. But he'd never come this close to succeeding.

Usually if Eoin ventured far enough into the Blackwood, whittled his energy down until he was exhausted, the dragon couldn't make it that far. Their energy reserves were shared and if Eoin kept himself shaking with exhaustion, his hope was that the dragon would be unsuccessful in his hunt.

Clearly, that was not true. The dragon was too determined.

It was easier when his stay was brief. A few days back home for a holiday or important family business was not an impossibly long time to keep the dragon contained. But Eoin had been here for nearly half a year, and it was growing harder than ever to resist the temptation.

Nearly impossible as he remembered the warm scent of her up close, the flavor of her skin. The way her figure had grown from the scrawny girl he found on the road all those years ago into a woman, soft and supple against him. The cinnamon sugar taste of her was burned into his tongue. It didn't matter what he consumed, he tasted only her.

One weak moment five months ago and Eoin was ruined.

Gannon was in a fury, his mate gone without explanation, and Elsie put herself in the middle of it, as always. She was brave, and she was foolish. Eoin was at the other end of the manor when their argument began. Even with his preternatural hearing, he should not have overhead the confrontation, but he did.

Somehow, Eoin knew that Elsie was in distress.

Though they weren't bonded, it was as if a whisper of a bond had formed anyway, growing the way a delicate and fragile flower might in the shade. There wasn't enough water or light, and the soil was poor, but still, it persevered.

Eoin flew up flights of stairs, careened around corners, crashed through hallways until he reached the baron's chamber. It didn't matter that it was his brother, or even that he hadn't laid a hand on Elsie. The dragon calculated the risk to his mate, and his ability to overpower Gannon, and the decision was made.

Gannon had to die.

Anyone that so much as spoke a harsh word to Elsie would die.

Then Elsie intervened, and the dragon found another target, only this time he wasn't out for blood. Her skin burned hotter than dragon fire, scalding his lips as he skimmed the column of her neck. That sole moment of intimacy, the barest touch of flesh on flesh, destroyed years of composure.

That was why he stayed away, even when the war was over. It was why he was dedicated to a position he didn't want in an army he hated serving in. He'd known that a weak moment was inevitable. A man only had so much willpower.

A *drakonmein* within touching distance of his unclaimed mate had even less.

Eoin felt his will cracking. Any day now it would shatter, and he would do something reprehensible. The beast inside of him was too unpredictable now, too damaged by the horrors of war. Too ruined by the violence he witnessed.

The violence he committed.

He glared down at his roughened hands, cursing them. Then he cursed the King of Dunhill for starting useless wars. The Gods too, for their part in it all.

Lastly, he cursed himself. Damn him and his naivety. Damn his need to do what was honorable, no matter the cost to himself.

And damn him, because he would do it all again, even if it destroyed him tenfold. When whispers of war travelled across the countryside, the families of Dunhill holding a collective breath, Eoin knew what he had to do.

Gannon was working closely with Father to take on the responsibilities of the Black Estate. Amos and Davin were barely more than children with so much life ahead of them. Even if Nigel's arms were thicker than his middle back then, Eoin worried for him too.

For all the hairless boys that would be called to arms by their king should the war not go in their favor. Innocent lives forfeit for wealth they would never see and land they would never own.

Who better to turn the tides of war than a *drakonmein*?

Weeks later, his parents were dead, and Eoin was riding home from the training camp to mourn their loss when he encountered a delirious, bloodied young woman on the road. That was the irony of it. Had he not enlisted as a soldier, he never would have discovered Elsie.

Elsie would be dead.

Anxiety became a cool fist around his throat at the thought of what might have been. By now, he should know better than to entertain the possibilities of the past. They were nothing more than ghosts haunting his every waking hour.

Eoin knew more ghosts than he cared to.

At least he wouldn't be alone when he finally found the courage to admit what he'd known for months. It was time to leave the Black Estate for good.

Chapter 2

Elsie

IT TOOK SEVEN YEARS for Elsie to stop dreaming of home.

Dreaming wasn't the right word for it. Dreaming implied fantasy, an enchanting world beyond this reality. The visions that tore through her quietest moments couldn't even be called nightmares. Nightmares, at least, were fictional.

She could wake from a nightmare, feel the sheets cocooning her in warmth, and laugh at her own reaction.

It wasn't her father's actions that made him so frightening. It was the anticipation. Never knowing which version of him would come stumbling through the door at any hour of the night. Never knowing if he was alone. If any number of rough men passing through their village would follow at his heel, leering and muttering about how many minutes they would pay for.

It was Mother's unnatural silence as she scrubbed her hair in a bucket of frigid water the following morning.

Seven years before the dreams faded. Bittersweet because even as she relived every wretched moment of that man's life, she relieved every moment of her own, too. The golden shimmer of Mother's hair as it dried in the afternoon sun. Chicory blue eyes and the lines that crinkled her baby sister's nose as she giggled.

Irene was so unlike Elsie. Her hair was pale, as Mother's was, her eyes bright and colorful. Elsie was carved in her father's likeness so accurately that there was a time she couldn't stand her own reflection.

Seven years to wash his poison from her mind.

Seven years to wash his blood from her hands.

Seven years to earn her freedom and now he had returned like a phantom to stir her from sleep and whisper malicious warnings in her ear.

To believe herself free of him was foolish. No one was ever free from their past.

There was the illusion of growth. Even if she wasn't born into status and wealth as the Black brothers were, Elsie could still make a name for herself. Here she was, managing a household fit for fifty people, not five. In days long past, when there were servants bustling through these halls, she instructed all of them. A fork was not polished without her say so.

Ah yes, polishing silverware. That was her grand adventure. Her claim to legend. A better fate than her mother was ever given, and yet at the end of the day, Elsie didn't feel any different. Somehow, this house had become a prison. The stone walls pressed in on her, making her claustrophobic.

Like she was still that scrawny girl stuffed under her bed, covering her mouth so as not to make a noise.

For a decade Elsie was given the chance to play make-believe, to think herself better than that girl. Changed into someone stronger, more resilient. One act of kindness from a stranger on the road had warped her expectations so thoroughly that she believed her life would carry more meaning than marriage to a baron's footman.

That fantasy was easy to play out when he was gone. Eoin Black, her savior. The first man to offer safety. To keep his word.

The first man to take her heart.

The first man to return it.

When he was at war, earnestly answering her every letter, waxing poetic the way only a man at war could, Elsie believed there was more. Buried between every line of broad ink strokes was the love he would not plainly speak. Eoin didn't care where she came from. Who she was born to. What evils she committed in her past.

Or perhaps, Eoin simply didn't want to be alone in his suffering. Could she blame him? Writing to her as if she were a lover waiting for him at home. Stringing her hapless heart along for the sake of his own sanity during battle. Any desperate man would do the same.

Any desperate man except Eoin. There was too much goodness in him to deceive her.

It was Elsie that deceived herself. Saw what she wanted to see. Believed that despite her stained history, she had earned the love of a man that was not her equal. Eoin never treated her like a servant. None of the Black brothers did.

But she *was* a servant. A glorified maid. Certainly not fit to be the bride of a baron's son. Not even to be the lover, it turned out, because the baron's son was not a mere man but a *drakonmein*.

He would love only one woman in his lifetime, and it was not Elsie.

That realization struck her for the first time this morning as she lay in bed, trying not to remember her father's bloated, red face. For nearly half a year Elsie had been waiting, as if the timing simply wasn't right. Giving Eoin a chance to gather himself. Emotion came unsteadily to him, and it was often at the least expected times that he would blurt his feelings about one issue or another.

No admission came. No admission came and Elsie ruthlessly convinced herself it hadn't come *yet*, but that was a lie, an expert denial of the obvious truth, and suddenly she could see it clearly.

Eoin didn't love her. Eoin never would love her.

The very foundation of her world was built upon the delusional idea that one day he would come home to her. Not simply come home, but come home to *her*. Every decision that brought her to this point came into question.

Elsie loved the Black brothers. She loved Gannon and his tempers, Amos and his riddles, Davin and his mischief. Eoin and the gentle peace he brought into every room. They had become like family to her and yet, they weren't her family.

A cold burst of air finally forced her from beneath the weight of feather blankets and across the cool wooden floor. Elsie pushed the balcony door against the wind, pausing halfway as she noticed the balcony sat at a new angle, one corner dipping toward the garden.

This house really was falling apart.

Gannon couldn't put off his hunt for new help any longer. There had to be trustworthy staff in Dunhill. Some families searching for room and board in exchange for work. The western side of the estate would crumble to pieces if Elsie and Edgar were left to maintain it on their own.

With that, Elsie temporarily forgot her own pain. A list formed in her mind, longer than Gannon would want to deal with but all more urgent than he was willing to admit. Though it wouldn't be Gannon discussing summer plans for the estate. It would be Mara, the Baroness Black, lady of the house.

Mara who so graciously accepted Elsie's lists and requests. Mara who was patient and gentle, whereas Elsie was terse and rushed. At first Elsie blamed Mara's behavior on her upbringing as the only princess of Dunhill, but she'd come to know Mara like a sister. Kindness was her nature. Softness an aura that followed her through the halls.

And just as swiftly as she'd forgotten her, Elsie was thinking of Irene again. Another sister made of softness and kindness.

What did Irene look like now? Would she still be that same quiet, happy girl, or had the world hardened her the way it had Elsie?

She wanted to believe she prevented that, skimping on her own needs, and avoiding luxuries so she could send every coin she earned back home. That was the cowardly way of looking after her sister, and clearly Irene and Mother agreed. No letter was ever returned, yet no response was sent back either.

Someone was receiving Elsie's hard earned income. What if it wasn't Mother? What if Irene and Mother had left Brilend when Elsie did and they were in some distant town, or even in the neighboring country of Brula?

The sudden desire to see her sister again struck her so swiftly it was brutal. A wound in her middle weeping fresh blood.

Seven years to stop dreaming of home, and now her mind was fixated on it. Drawn to it.

Perhaps *this* was her fate. Not waiting for a noble man that was too kind to break her heart. Not marrying the next servant that wandered into Gannon's employment.

Returning home.

Making amends.

Facing her sins.

⬥

A GIGGLE ON THE other side of the study door told Elsie that she had at least a fifty percent chance of walking in on something she'd rather not see. That was always a risk with Gannon and Mara, even if they were in public parts of the house. A weedy sprig of jealousy sprouted in her heart at the sound of the happy pair.

Five months ago, Mara had arrived on their doorstep—dropped in the garden by a dragon, actually—bruised and terrified. She was a wayward bride and a princess at that, desperate to find shelter from her cruel family and to escape her impending marriage to a man she didn't love. Fate was clever with Mara, sending her straight into the home of a *drakonmein* that would do anything to protect his mate, which she soon proved to be.

Their courtship was quick and turbulent, ending when Gannon was captured by Mara's father, the King of Dunhill. The king intended to use Gannon as a weapon, a dragon to fight wars that men alone could not. A stupid plan that went gloriously wrong when Gannon's brothers joined Mara in setting Gannon free. It ended with the king roasted and half dead, and Mara presumed dead by the court of Dunhill.

Half a year was long enough for the two of them to forget their tragic beginnings, it would seem. They were floating on a blissful cloud, smiling dumbly at all hours of the day, and sighing pitifully whenever they weren't together. It was a lovely turn of events for them. Gods knew Gannon deserved happiness after all he'd been through, and Mara did, too.

Elsie only wished the happiness of others didn't leave such a bitter taste in her mouth.

She decided against barging into the study as she used to, instead taking the time to knock. At least Mara would have a chance to get her skirt back down.

"Enter!" Gannon's deep voice called.

Mara was scurrying from his lap as Elsie stepped into the baron's study. She pushed her shoulders back, her spine snapping straight, her doe eyes dropping to her toes. It was remnants of her old life, years of abusive training to shape Mara into a perfect, poised princess. Elsie understood how hard those old habits died. Especially the ones that were beaten into you.

"Your eyes are far too beautiful to be hidden, Mara," Gannon said quietly, his irises a glowing green as the dragon within him came alive. He could be an idiot sometimes, but he'd learned well when it came to his mate. Mara was not as fragile as she looked, but like a wounded animal, she needed some coaxing.

Mara smiled down at Gannon. Her smile turned to another giggle as he yanked her off her feet and plopped her onto the desk in front of his seat, her legs resting in his lap with her back to Elsie. The baron's desk was a massive piece of mahogany and provided a little too much room for them to get comfortable. Elsie always made sure to clean the surface if Mara spent the afternoon in the study with him. Ridiculous, besotted fools.

"What can we do for you, Elsie?" His smile was relaxed and genuine. Gannon had been a broody bastard for such a long time she'd nearly forgotten he was capable of smiling.

Elsie approached the desk, her hands on her hips. Standing before them, the words suddenly stuck in the back of her throat. Her gaze flitted about the room, staring at the copper sconces, the matching mahogany cabinet on the far wall, the window overlooking the open gates at the front of the estate. Her foot kicked at the edge of a maroon rug with gold filigree, making a mental note to take it outside for beating now that the weather was warming.

Only, she wouldn't be here to do that, would she? She wouldn't be here to cut blooming roses from the hedge maze or watch the apple trees blossom in late spring. There would be no raspberry picking along the border of the Blackwood, no opening up the estate to let in the crisp spring air and chase away the dusty shadows of winter. All her rhythms, routines, and comforting tasks would be gone.

Mara twisted around to look at her sweetly, and it was almost enough to bring her to tears. Was she truly going to make this choice?

"I've come to tell you that I am finally accepting your offer," she pushed the sentence out stiffly.

Gannon frowned. "My offer?"

"To leave your service."

Painful silence fell over them as his frown deepened. "Elsie, I told you to leave when I thought I was going mad." Gannon leaned across Mara's thigh, hands steepled. "Is it the house? I can hire more staff if you need help. Tell me what you want, and I will get it for you."

"I've never struggled to manage this house." Though it was a burden some days. "But you will need more staff. Someone to oversee the cleaning. You'll need a crew of men for the west wing. It will fall right into the garden if you don't do repairs this summer, Gannon." Elsie swallowed tightly. "I won't be here to manage them."

Mara stood, fidgeting with the belt of her dress before finding the courage to ask, "it's him, isn't it? You're leaving because of Eoin."

"Yes." No use lying if they already knew.

"That witless bastard."

"Gannon," Mara chided. "He's your brother."

"All the more reason to call him an idiot when he's being one."

"It's not Eoin's fault." Elsie wanted to blame him, but how could she? "He can't help his nature. And I cannot wait for a man that will never love me." Those words burned with shame as she finally spoke them aloud.

"He does love you," Gannon insisted, rising from behind the desk and putting out beseeching hands. "He's just...lost."

"Aren't we all?" Elsie sighed. "I won't be gone forever, but I need time."

"Where would you go?" Mara blinked sadly.

"Home."

Gannon's eyes widened. "Why would you go home?"

"I've wondered about my mother and sister for years. I'd like to know that they are well." She wanted to know if her sacrifice was in vain. Mother was resourceful, but it was always Elsie who provided what father's schemes could not.

Really, she should have gone home years ago. How long would anyone search for her father's killer? If they did at all. Father was a good-for-nothing drunk on his best days. On his worst days…Elsie shuddered.

That was why she hadn't returned home. It was too painful. Even now, she wondered if she could do it, or if she would find herself on a familiar road mere miles from her childhood home and falter.

Here in the Black Estate, life had been easy. The work was hard, of course, but it was better than she was accustomed to. And she had the brothers. Edgar and Nigel, too. So quickly they became like her own brothers, the strong men she'd never had in her life when she needed them most. She could flit about the house, bringing order to chaos, giving instruction to the staff before they eventually abandoned the estate.

On the best days, she spent her evenings with Eoin.

He wasn't a man of many words, even before he went off to war, but when he did speak, she sat in silent reverence. There was something old about him. Not in the intellectual way of Amos or the authoritative demeanor of Gannon. It was deeper than that, as if his soul had been around much longer than his body.

Elsie exhaled, realizing that whatever Gannon said had slipped right past her. "Pardon?"

He rubbed his jaw, studying her with those too sharp eyes. She'd never met the previous Baron Black—his father—but sometimes Gannon was the spitting image of the painting that hung just over his shoulder. A crisp, angular face with a harsh jaw. The black wells of his eyes and the slicked back locks of raven hair only added to his cool and commanding appearance.

"You should leave."

"What?" Mara gasped. "You can't let her go."

Gannon conveyed something to his mate with a look Elsie couldn't interpret. "It's the right choice for her."

Mara chewed her bottom lip, eyes clouding. "It is, isn't it? Perha ps..." Tears tracked down her face as she stepped around the desk and collapsed into Elsie. "You must be very careful, Elsie. A woman alone on the road is not safe."

Elsie embraced her weeping friend. "Sweet Mara, you worry too much. It is *me* who is the danger on the road. Gods help any man that tries to steal my horse."

Mara laughed through her tears. "I will miss you."

"And my days will be lonely without you. But I must go."

Their gazes met, and she nodded. "I understand."

Perhaps Mara was the only one who could understand. She fled the Black Estate six months earlier and returned to her terrible family to protect Gannon. In a way, Elsie was doing the same. She was protecting Eoin from guilt and saving herself from misery. Her love for him was strong enough that she would step away.

Today, Elsie was letting him go.

CHAPTER 3

ELSIE

Eoin's shoulders tensed in time with the click of the door latch. A common response during the rare moments Elsie was alone with him. This wasn't meant to be a confrontation. This wasn't meant to be *anything*. In fact, she scarcely remembered walking down the hall to the spare study where Eoin busied himself with *responsibilities*, whatever those might be.

He was a soldier without orders. Shouldn't he be reveling in his newfound freedom? Enjoying the fresh air and the early blooming roses that his mother painstakingly planted among the hedge maze?

Elsie wanted to tell herself it didn't matter to her anymore, but she'd spent too much time lying to herself. Soon the lies would be so great that she wouldn't be able to tell the difference between truth and fiction.

Like the fiction that was spurring her on now, that last little glimmer of hope that told her he needed *one more chance*. One more chance to prove her wrong. One more chance to make her stay.

"You've been avoiding me." *Again*, Elsie added silently.

Laughter rang across the breakfast table this morning. Forks clinked, bacon crackled, and the scent of whatever sweet Nigel was baking for Gannon's insatiable appetite for dessert wafted through the dining room. And at the end of the table sat a vacant chair, a ghost haunting their revelry.

When had their tightly knit friendship unraveled? Elsie was scarcely more than a girl when Eoin brought her here, but she'd grown into a woman she was proud of. A woman she thought he would be proud of.

Eoin travelled home as often as he could during those early years, spending the evening sharing stories of his time in the mountains, the clansmen he met, the myths he learned. Once he even let Elsie wield his sword. There was nothing she wouldn't tell him. He was the only one that knew all her secrets.

Then war came, and he was gone for so long. A lifetime, or maybe an eternity. Those years of wondering, waiting for a letter with news, were excruciating. Realistically, Gannon assured her, he was the safest man on those battlefields. To kill a *drakonmein* was no simple feat. That knowledge did nothing to ease her worry.

After the treaty was drawn up and the soldiers sent home, the distance became worse. Elsie imagined there were a great many horrors that he witnessed in battle. That shouldn't have turned him away from her. She would never ask of them if he did not wish to divulge. If anything, she could distract him, help him to remember the joys of life again.

Eoin would have none of it. They were as good as strangers.

"I haven't been avoiding you." He didn't turn away from the window, gaze locked on the dark forest that rimmed the estate. "Gannon is distracted, so I have been fulfilling some of his duties while he enjoys being newly wed."

It was true that since discovering his mate last autumn Gannon—the oldest Black brother bearing the title Baron Black—had been preoccupied. That distraction meant nothing. There were no consequences for unfulfilled duties to a useless, dying king.

As for managing the wealth of the Black Estate, that was equally pointless. The Black family could buy the entire country of Dunhill, perhaps all of Svalta, and still have coin leftover. They were far wealthier than the royal family and the many investments Baron Black Sr. made paid dividends whether Gannon was overseeing them or not.

Their father was wise in many subjects, but his wisest choices had always been where he put his coin. It was his intention to leave his sons with more than a living. He wanted them to have bountiful lives with wealth to shower upon their own families.

"I'm aware of Gannon's duties. I've been helping to fulfill them in the absence of his family." Bitterness twisted the word *family*. Something that, without the Black brothers, she might not have anymore. How could Eoin take such a blessing for granted?

"Are you suggesting that we've abandoned him?" Elsie could hear the pretentious arch of his brow.

Yes, and me as well. "I'm only pointing out that I know how busy one should be when aiding the baron."

Silence. Long, irritating silence.

Elsie sighed and dropped onto the edge of a chaise lounge. It was the only seat in the room, further proving that this study of his was simply an excuse. How was he sitting at a desk with no chair? A desk that had a layer of dust an inch thick.

She was going about this the wrong way. Time to stop skirting around the true issue. Either he could admit to her that he loathed her, or he could stop this nonsense and cleanly break her heart so she could carry on with her miserable life.

"Do you not find me beautiful?"

That earned his attention. "Don't be ridiculous. Of course, you're beautiful."

"Objectively." *If you don't look too closely at the scars.* "Is it because I'm not ladylike, then?"

He roughed up the side of his short black beard. That was a new addition to his appearance. As a soldier Eoin was expected to keep himself clean shaven. "Free of visual obstruction," he always said. She mourned every time she saw him with that thin blade in his hand, scraping away every thread of beautiful raven hair.

Now it curled from his scalp, framing the harsh lines of his forehead, softening them. The beard was a shadow for his angular jaw, making the square, stern shape of it more apparent. He looked less like a commanding captain now and more like the son of a wealthy baron. Regal posture, confident demeanor, fierce handsomeness that intimidated as much as it invited a soft caress.

"What are you talking about?"

"Or perhaps it's because you know what I've done. You know my sins."

"I do not judge you for your past. The Gods know I have committed far worse acts than you, and for far worse motivation."

"I see." She rubbed a circle on the pad of her thumb with her index finger. "I'm simply not the right one. Not *her*."

Eoin finally turned around, his eyes black as the early afternoon sun shone through the window behind him, shading his face. "Speak plainly, Elsie."

"I've had suitors, you know. During the years that you were away, I received three marriage proposals."

"Why—" He cleared his throat. "Why didn't you accept any of them?"

"I've had offers for far less virtuous acts too."

The side of his upper lip twitched. "I see."

"What's the matter? Aren't you going to ask if I accepted any of those offers?"

"Did you?" The question was a vicious stab across the room.

"Never." She stood, moving to the narrow fireplace to poke at the coals. "I was waiting for you."

"You shouldn't have." Eoin's tone and words were a contradiction, a mingling of relief and irritation.

"But I did." Greedy bits of flame rose to gnaw at the slivers of unburnt wood as it surfaced from the bottom of the fireplace. "Fate is so terribly, terribly cruel."

"Lady Fate gives blessings and curses in the same breath."

Elsie swallowed, stoking her courage as she stoked the flames. She didn't want to be a coward anymore. The inevitable pain of rejection couldn't hurt any worse than her aching desire.

"She has given me both. For I am blessed to know you and cursed to love you. I will wither away while you remain young and whole forever. At least until you find *her*. Then I will watch from afar as you grow older and happier with the years. If I am lucky enough to see it in my lifetime, anyway." Elsie placed the poker back into the stand and hugged herself. "You will be fulfilled, and I will be alone. My love for you will become a poison, corrosive in my veins, eating away at my heart until there is nothing left to give another. There will be only hollow space within me."

"Elsie..."

"I cannot blame you for it. Your nature is not your choice. But I can wish that it were different. It is misery to have you here in this home again and feel invisible under your gaze."

"I am not the man you remember, little sparrow." His words tickled her nape, the weight of his body suddenly close enough to press into her. He didn't, of course. That would be too close.

"And I'm not a little sparrow anymore. I'm a woman grown. I have seen everything that happens in this home, and I have never looked away."

"You are so soft, Elsie. I can't be soft for you. I cannot give you the tenderness a woman needs from a man. Seek out someone sweet, someone easy to speak to."

Elsie whirled, her palm cracking against his face so hard it burned. "Now you insult me. I'm not the girl you brought here years ago, and your memory must be false because that girl was never *soft*."

Her back hit the wall before she could make sense of his movement. Hues of yellow and orange coalesced in his obsidian eyes, irises aflame with his dragon. "You want to bond with this?" Eoin opened his mouth wide to reveal teeth sharp as knives.

Elsie met his gaze unflinchingly. "Yes."

"I'm a product of war, Elsie. War makes men brutal."

They flew across the room, her palms landing on the desk as he slammed her into it, bracing her body with his. "If I was to claim you, I would take you right here." His pelvis thrust forward with the final word. "I would lift up your skirts and take you with no care about who might barge in through that unlocked door." Too sharp teeth grazed the back of her neck just as a hard length pressed into her backside. That motion alone brought her to the very edge of ecstasy. She was on fire, burning with years of unsatisfied need.

"And I wouldn't care if the whole house heard me begging you for more."

Cold encircled her, ice in comparison to the scalding temperature of his skin. The door bounced against the frame with a thud, the only sound signaling that Eoin had made a swift retreat.

Elsie rubbed her palm along the back of her neck, feeling the phantom touch of fangs. That was all it was though, a phantom. A shadow of the moment she so desperately wanted.

Instead, she was alone. Bleakly, utterly alone.

CHAPTER 4

EOIN

"**W**HAT DO YOU MEAN 'no?' That wasn't one of the options." Davin swaggered into the kitchen, where Eoin was trying to sneak food from Nigel after missing another meal.

In a house this large, it should have been easy to avoid company. There were two dozen unoccupied rooms, an entire wing where no one but the rats traversed, and somehow this was his third unwanted encounter since this morning. First it was Edgar waking him with the dawn, claiming he was trapping pests and hadn't realized Eoin was staying in that particular room.

Then it was Elsie, who came to rip out his heart. There was not a word for the grief he felt as he fled from that study.

"My love for you will become a poison..."

It already was, and Eoin was so desperately trying to bleed it from her veins. She was right, though. How could he when she was never free of him? Always under his watchful gaze? Shadowed by him constantly?

Eoin didn't have the chance to ruminate on those questions, or complete his plans for departure, because his pestering little brother had found his hiding place and was clearly not keen on keeping his head.

"No is always an option," Eoin grunted, hand curled around a wooden bowl of mashed peas and pork broth. It was cooler than peas were meant to be eaten but he wasn't particularly fond of peas in the first place. Like most meals, he would shovel it down as quickly as possible, doing the minimum necessary to keep himself from withering away.

Nigel barked a laugh, obviously already more than a few sips into the flask he kept stashed in his apron. The old cook was getting drunker by the day. Someday he would set the whole kitchen on fire. Deep in the oldest rings of memory, Eoin thought he recalled Nigel sober. He was a younger man then, the bald sheen of his scalp still tufted with springs of dark hair. The beard was the same, prematurely grey and disguising the bottom half of Nigel's face so well that Eoin doubted he had a chin.

"Careful, Eoin," Nigel warned. "You'll find yourself bound and tossed onto the back of a horse. Elsie was given the same threat."

Eoin betrayed himself, turning too sharply to glare at Davin. "Elsie is coming with you?"

Davin's lips tipped into a mischief making grin. With his clean-shaven face and shoulder length hair, he had a boyish appearance that only added to the wickedness gleaming in his dark eyes. "Perhaps I should have led with that." He clapped Nigel on the shoulder, sharing a secretive look with the cook, having forgotten that Eoin was sitting right next to him.

Gannon. That bastard couldn't keep his mouth shut. Davin knew about Elsie—what Elsie was to Eoin. His brothers had always teased the two of them, but there was an edge to Davin's expression now, a quiet viciousness Eoin didn't trust.

"Elsie is going to the Braying Jack for a drink. Amos, Edgar, and I are accompanying her, out of pure chivalrous intent, of course. Can't let a beauty like that go prancing into a tavern unaccompanied." Davin shook his head, feigning indignation. "No telling what kind of rabble would try to snatch her up."

Nigel snorted an objection. "Get a drink in her and she's the rabble. The last tavern nearly burned to the ground after the fight she started. Walking trouble, that one."

"Elsie started a tavern fight?" Eoin couldn't even picture her in a tavern. Then again, he'd missed the better part of a decade with her. In truth, he had no idea what she got up to anymore.

"Don't act so surprised, brother." Davin waved dismissively at Nigel. "Are you coming, or aren't you?"

The answer was obvious. A crowded, stinking building with foul-mouthed drunks was the last place he wanted to be. Already Eoin could feel the press of bodies, his skin tightening around him until he was close to rupturing.

His bowl clacked on the small table in the corner of the kitchen. Eoin swung his foot over the narrow wooden bench, wincing when one of the legs groaned ominously. He turned his back on his brother, shoveling cold slop into his mouth as if it required extreme focus. He could tell without looking that Davin was glaring at him, mouth agape in bafflement.

Eoin didn't care what Davin thought. Davin had a childish heart to match his looks, problematic at times but also innocent. He didn't know what Eoin lived through, couldn't fathom the cruelty he'd seen. It was only because Eoin believed peace was guaranteed that he ever allowed his younger brothers to train with him up north. They needed to pass the time and selfishly, Eoin needed them near. They were pillars that held him upright.

Now he would leave them behind, as he would leave Elsie, and everything else he knew. Eoin swallowed tightly, almost choking on a flake of pork.

Be strong, he reminded himself. *Be strong for your brothers. For her.*

Those words were the reason he made it through the war. The constant reminder that he had a reason to keep going, to bring himself home from the battlefield.

Ultimately, they didn't save him. He was strong in body but weak in mind. The weight of death crushed in on his psyche, splintering logic and virtue and leaving dark, hollow madness to take its place. What was the point in being strong for his brothers when they didn't need him? When he was only a burden to them?

No, not a burden. A threat. A pot on the verge of boiling over. Oil creeping closer and closer to a lit match.

Eoin should not have returned here. He should have left Gannon to his wallowing and princess thieving and found a cave deep in the mountains to bury himself in so that—

"Eoin!" Davin clapped a hand on Eoin's shoulder.

Eoin whirled, slamming an arm into Davin's middle, and sending him flying across the kitchen. The half-empty bowl of peas tumbled to the floor, splattering Eoin's legs with green mash. He was too fixated on the blood trickling from Davin's head to notice.

"Dammit, Davin!" The gash was superficial but only because his brother was like him. *Drakonmein* took wounds well and healed quickly. It was why Eoin believed he was fit for war—fit for war!

No man was fit for war.

If Davin had been Nigel, he would be dead. Skull caved in after smashing against the stone wall.

There was a reason the late Baron Black, their father, was choosy about the help they allowed into the estate. There was a reason Gannon had sent most of that help away. *Drakonmein* were not the safest company under the best of circumstances. These were the worst of circumstances.

Eoin needed to leave. *Tonight*. No more lingering.

It was Davin groaning on the kitchen floor because he was imprudent, never mindful of giving others space.

Elsie was imprudent too.

It could have been her. Eoin's wayward instincts could have killed her.

His spine tingled, hands itched, joints ached. The dragon making himself known beneath the skin. Blood stirred the creature, bringing to life a horrid fascination. In his dreams Eoin could smell it, taste it on his tongue, and sometimes...

Sometimes he enjoyed it.

Leave. Get out of here before you hurt anyone else.

But Eoin's horrified retreat to the west wing was blocked when an angel descended the staircase. Her hair was carefully braided down one side of her head, gleaming like shined mahogany. The rose-colored gown draping down her shoulders was nothing like the modest wool dresses she wore around the house. It revealed the dips beneath her collar bone, the soft slopes of her shoulders.

Elsie was never ashamed of herself and the scars she bore, but Eoin had never known her to put them on display, either. The white line beneath her left eye was impossible to hide, but he didn't expect her to sport the matching stripes along her upper back with such grace and dignity.

Realization hit him like a stone to the gut. This was what she intended to wear tonight. To a tavern. Where dozens of men would leer at her beautiful figure.

Eoin was the only man to have seen those scars once.

Fire flared in his chest. He needed to kill someone. Many someones.

Either Elsie didn't notice him, or she didn't care about his presence enough to acknowledge it after their tempestuous interaction this morning. Her eyes immediately flicked to Davin, still hunched on the floor with an angry glare marring his bloodied face. Elsie crouched beside him, carefully brushing his floppy black hair away from his forehead and cooing.

"What have you done to yourself now, you lout?"

Davin clapped a hand over his heart and whimpered, "blaming the victim? It was that cruel brother of mine. I need a beautiful woman to kiss it and make it better."

Elsie rolled her eyes but only after smiling at Davin, eyes warm with affection. Eoin's jealousy fueled the flames until they licked at his throat, causing him to growl. Nigel, still standing stunned and slightly terrified against the stove, raised a wooden spoon as if to defend himself from the raging dragon ready to fill the kitchen with blood.

The growling stopped only momentarily when Elise shot a scathing glower in Eoin's direction. She quickly returned to ignoring him, instead wetting a towel, and dabbing at Davin's forehead. She lifted him onto his feet with one hand, using the other to steady his balance. Already the bleeding had slowed, and the color was returning to Davin's skin. That didn't stop his brother from making a show of clutching his head and moaning.

Elsie didn't remove her hands from Davin. Those strong, slender fingers trailed up his back, stroking gently.

Eoin watched those fingers, saw the exposed line of her breast as the fabric in her gown dipped, and envisioned another scenario.

"I've had offers for far less virtuous acts."

Was Davin one of those offers? His brother didn't care for his future mate or the sanctity of their bond. Eoin had seen him chase all class of women.

Was Elsie one of them?

Had Davin—

Red. Eoin could see nothing but red. Those flames arching up from inside of him to dance in his vision, blur anything but the image of his mate, exposed, soft and supple, giving herself to someone else.

Because you allowed it. All but insisted on it.

Didn't matter. She was his, and he was going to kill his brother to prove it.

Eoin roared, clutching the sides of his head, and slamming his body into the door that led from the kitchen to the garden. The cool air did nothing to quell the hideous jealousy unfurling inside of him. Blooming roses twirled their sweet scent around him, and it incited him further, bombarding him with more images of Elsie and roses and hands that were not his own.

The tingle in his spine became pain, excruciating, burning pain. Eoin tried to run, but he knew it wouldn't be enough. Not this time.

"Edgar!" He howled, stumbling to the stable, and praying his oldest friend was there. "Edgar, I need you!"

Edgar appeared from the shadows of a stall, white hair glowing in the afternoon sun. His skin was alabaster, eyes as blue as Brulian ice. In front of him, Edgar's hands waved back and forth as his fingers carved out words from a language few spoke. At the same time his mouth moved, pink lips trying to make the sounds that would never come from his mute tongue.

"The chains," Eoin hissed, collapsing onto his knees. "I need you to ready the chains."

Edgar's already pale complexion became transparent, his eyes wide with urgency.

This was a burden he wished he didn't have to place on Edgar. But Eoin and Edgar shared secrets that none other in the Black Estate knew. If anyone could save Eoin from himself, it would be Edgar.

Once, when they were boys, Eoin had stumbled upon Edgar and his mother practicing their craft in the Blackwood. Wickedness, the temple would call it, but being born *drakonmein* made him understand there were aspects of the world the temple didn't understand.

Edgar's mother was born a world away, across the sea. It was there that she inherited her magic, there that she learned to cast spells in a language none but her ancient gods spoke. Father knew of her kind when he took pity on her and her mute son, taking them into his service and offering Edgar an education in exchange for work.

It was a secret he'd taken to his grave, and one Eoin intended to die keeping as well. There was a reason there were no more witches in Svalta. A dreadful, tragic reason.

"Chains," Eoin begged again, barely upright as the pain ate at him.

Edgar nodded gravely, dragging Eoin into the back of the stable and through the feed storeroom. There he chained Eoin's hands and feet to a metal platform bolted into the floor, carefully moving bales of hay to hide the sight of Eoin writhing against his binds.

He didn't know what it was about these particular chains that worked to hold the dragon back, only that Edgar's mother had crafted them for the late Baron Black.

A man with four sons destined to transform into fire breathing monsters needed to have security measures in place.

Father had never needed them and so Eoin knew nothing of their existence until Edgar suggested them this winter. Using them too frequently was dangerous, Edgar claimed. Resisting the change so thoroughly so often might completely fracture his connection with the dragon. Meaning the next time the dragon barged into Elsie's room, Eoin wouldn't be able to stop it.

There were nightmare tales of *drakonmein* that broke the connection with their dragon. They were the reason stories were told of man-eating beasts that haunted the skies and burned entire villages. Eoin never intended to become that. He simply needed...time. More time to figure out what he was doing.

But there was no more time, was there? And he already knew what needed to be done. He'd been selfish and foolish and now he was here, again. Trapped by his own nature. Destroyed by it.

The pain of holding the shift in became so great that his vision blurred. Edgar swam before him, rapidly waving his hands in signs Eoin could barely decipher.

He blinked, understanding only, *"this is the last time,"* before blackness swallowed him up.

❖

EOIN WOKE TO RAUCOUS laughter and overlapping voices. He blinked against the darkness, trying to judge his surroundings. Chains clattered onto the floor, Edgar moving over him and unhooking the shackles that kept the beast at bay.

As always, the creature was unnaturally silent after being denied his freedom. At first, Eoin used to think the dragon was being dramatic, and this was a fit. Now, he understood it was something graver. Feeling completely void of the dragon had nothing to do with the dragon and everything to do with the magic that held it at bay.

The beast was in there, Eoin simply couldn't hear it.

He rubbed at his wrists as Edgar propped him up and tipped a cup of water to his lips. Eoin drank greedily, gasping for air when the cup was drained. Edgar dipped his chin sadly, moving his lips and mouthing words he couldn't speak.

"I know," Eoin murmured.

Edgar shook his head, white eyebrows creasing into a scowl. His creamy hair was pulled back from his face, and he'd changed from his usual working clothes into a plain shirt and leather pants. His hands came up to form shapes in front of his chest, telling Eoin everything he didn't want to hear.

"You need to tell her."

"No, I won't do that."

"I cannot help you anymore."

"There has to be another way." It came out as a pleading question more than a statement. "You must know some other way to—to fix me."

Edgar pressed his lips together, squinting in annoyance. *"I've told you the way."*

Yes, he had many times. *"Tell Elsie and the rest will fall into place,"* he claimed. Eoin didn't believe that for a moment. It was too easy, and the Gods had not destined him for easy. The dragon was becoming louder and clearer every time he shifted, hellbent on one thing: hurting Elsie. Claiming her in the most brutal way to prove that she was his.

They'd gone too long without a bond. That alone could drive the beast to madness. Add to that a penchant for violence and a disturbing passion for gore and the dragon was downright unhinged. Too dangerous to be near Elsie anymore.

He'd already made the decision. Days ago, he accepted the truth. Today only served to solidify his resolve.

But amidst the talking on the other side of the feed room Eoin heard a familiar feminine lilt, and a tiny, traitorous voice in his head whispered, *one more night.*

CHAPTER 5

ELSIE SAT STIFFLY ON her horse, trying to ignore the feel of Eoin's deep scowl behind her. What right did he have to be foul? It wasn't as if they'd strong armed him. Well, if she was being fair, Davin probably did pester him into coming. That was Eoin's problem, and he should keep it his problem. She had no interest in entertaining his poor mood.

What was wrong with him, anyway? This morning she'd poured her heart out to him, and he fled, *fled* like some fearful boy. Then he pummeled his brother in the kitchen only to run out again. Eoin reappeared as they were mounting their horses, sweating, scowling, still covered in mashed peas, and climbed onto his stallion without a word.

Tonight was meant to be a night of merry making, one final and joyful farewell to her friends, not a night of cracking skulls and stomping about. She couldn't understand what was happening with Eoin. Maybe she didn't want to.

Thinking of him was exhausting, and she'd done nothing else for days. Months. *From the moment they met.*

She was weary and heartsick, and she wanted a single night to enjoy herself before she was gone.

Then Eoin had to join them and ruin everything. How was Elsie to be free when she could feel the shackles of Eoin's gaze holding her still?

She wasn't herself around him, too conscious of the way she moved, spoke, existed. To have him at her back now was driving her mad. They hadn't even arrived, and she was already considering turning back and flopping into her bed instead.

"Chin up, Elsie." Davin pulled his reins and slowed his steed to match pace with hers. "You're starting to look like my ogre of a brother with a grimace like that."

"You know, I've always thought the two of you looked the most alike." Elsie pursed her lips. "Don't speak to me of your brother."

The mirthful sparkle dimmed in Davin's eyes. He tried to hide it with a half-smile but they both knew it was false. "He'll find his way. I know he will."

Find his way to what, though? Elsie didn't care anymore. Eoin was her friend, her dearest friend. If he had no interest in their friend-ship—or more—she couldn't control that. Wouldn't try to. People deserved the freedom to make their own choices without judgment, even if those choices hurt the hearts of others.

"I'd like to find my way to a drink and a good round of cards."

His smile turned genuine. "Sweet Elsie, a gambler? I'm scandal-ized."

"You don't know the half of what I can do." Elsie obeyed Davin's earlier order and lifted her chin, smiling confidently. With a tap of her heel and a click of her tongue she sent her horse into a gallop, leaving the others in the dust.

⚬◦❖◦⚬

THERE WAS ONLY ONE tavern in the town where Elsie grew up. The second floor was an inn—for those with low enough standards—and below it a portly man served three-day-old stew and ale so foul that piss smelled delightful in comparison. Elsie passed that awful place every time she hauled water from the well. As a girl the sounds inside frightened her. When she grew old enough to understand why her father disappeared in there for hours, sometimes days, she resented it. Stared at it and wished her hatred alone would burn it to the ground.

Her father was dead for seven years before she found the courage to step into another tavern. The one Nigel and Edgar dragged her to was nothing like his old haunt. Clean—clean enough, anyway—with kind and lively patrons. The ale was smooth and earthy, the music uplifting and cheerful. Elsie didn't love the way men hovered around her, nor was she fond of the filthy rambling of drunks. But lately the Black Estate felt more like a tomb than a home and leaving to find a few hours of merriment reminded her that she was still breathing. Not buried alive under dust, decay, and despair.

It was better with the Black brothers at her side. Their imposing height and obvious muscle made every man in the room shrink away from whatever advance they planned when Elsie stepped up to the taverner and ordered a round of drinks. Davin jabbed her side with his elbow as he made a bet over a pair of dice. Amos told her about the local architecture, explaining something to do with spring flooding and irrigation that went over her head. Edgar's hands worked quickly to make jokes at Davin's expense.

Davin never was good at reading Edgar's hand signals, and it bothered the youngest Black brother immensely when he wasn't in on the secrets.

Elsie tried not to glance across the room at Eoin, sitting alone on a stool at the end of the bar, glaring at the back wall as if it had insulted him. Once he would have sat beside them, shaking his head reproachfully whenever Davin made mention of the sword in his trousers.

He didn't care for jokes anymore.

As the night wore on and Elsie gulped down a second mug of ale, she found her thoughts growing more distant from Eoin. She could forget him for a night, focusing on the deck of cards in front of her and the friends prying laughter from the hollow in her chest that had been stagnant and quiet for months.

This might be the last time she shared in their laughter.

"A tortoise!" Davin shouted proudly.

"A tortoise doesn't have five points, you numbskull." Edgar flipped his hands in rapid response.

"Tortoise doesn't have..." Davin mouthed slowly. "It does! A head and four legs. That's five, count 'em." He made a show of counting on his fingers in mockery of Edgar's gestures.

Edgar offered him a more universal, and offensive, gesture instead.

"I've forgotten just how terrible they are at riddles," Amos murmured to Elsie as she finished the contents in her cup.

"Davin has gone nearly ten minutes without saying the word 'cock.' That alone is a feat worth celebrating."

Amos started to stand. "Should we continue celebrating?"

Elsie was about to agree that yes, they should celebrate until they were drunk and dizzy, but her attention was diverted by a gust of cool night air as the door swung open.

It wasn't the temperature change that caught her eye as much as it was the young woman that caused it. Confidence oozed from her, not the prideful kind noble born women often floated on. The angles of her face were striking, a dangerous beauty. Even more dangerous was her attire, a tunic, and leggings to outline a trim waist and slim figure.

The path she took was straight and focused, leading her to the stool where Eoin was hunched over an untouched drink. When she spoke to him it was not as a stranger. His head slanted in her direction, muttered words drowned out by the din of revelry, but Elsie knew instantly that they were words spoken with too much familiarity for this to be a chance encounter.

Elsie set her mug too roughly onto the table, glaring at the tall, well-built beauty that had an eye for the most unapproachable Black brother. After only a moment of whispered exchange they dropped from their stools, Eoin taking the woman by the upper arm and leading her quickly from the tavern.

Someone was throwing knives. They had to be. Elsie felt them pierce her heart, one, two, three, in quick succession.

She pushed back from the table abruptly, ignoring the questioning voices of her companions. In a daze she stumbled out of the tavern, hissing at the damp night air.

Eoin left with a woman. A woman he knew. A woman that was obviously not his mate.

Now she stared stupidly, helplessly as Eoin disappeared into a narrow alleyway across the road with that woman glancing over her shoulder at him, face eager. Sickness crawled up from her belly and Elsie had to swallow to keep her drinks from rising in her throat.

She'd once heard from Davin that there were pleasures a *drakon-mein* could find with a woman that didn't bind her to him. She simply hadn't thought Eoin would partake.

It seemed his vehement refusal of her had nothing to do with loyalty to his future mate and everything to do with...*her*.

Elsie was the problem. Eoin couldn't see her as anything more than that skinny girl he found wandering the road. A poor creature that deserved his pity. A farmer's daughter, a maid. *Beneath him.*

Elsie was the problem.

She was the problem.

Not ladylike. Too brazen with her words. Too quick to join in with the roughhousing and debauchery.

She wasn't charming.

Imprudent and rugged and outspoken.

Too much for a man like Eoin. A man with his upbringing and expectations.

Too much.

Those were the words that stuck in her mind, repeating themselves, making laps around her brain until she was clutching her temples in agony.

Lower lip trembling, Elsie found her way to the stable where they'd left the horses. She fumbled with her purse, handing the stableboy a coin, and hoping it was the right one as she leaped onto the back of her horse.

Tears blurred her already perilous journey. It was dark, and she was alone. Robbers could be waiting on the road. Or even a pothole that could break her horses leg and leave her crushed beneath the beast.

Elsie didn't care.

She wanted to get away from him, from these wretched thoughts.

Too much? Damn him! She wasn't too much.

If not for her boldness, the Black Estate would be in ruin. If not for her pluck, she wouldn't have lasted a day with his family.

There was not a delicate, ladylike bone in her body, and she was *glad* of that because the life she led was never delicate nor gentle and her bones had to be unbreakable.

She had to be unbreakable.

And she was.

She was.

Eoin Black would not destroy her, any more than the men of her past. Elsie wouldn't let him.

CHAPTER 6

EOIN

"**Y**OU HAVE BEEN IGNORING my correspondence, Captain Black."

Eoin dropped his eyes to the brazen woman standing before him with fists planted on her hips. Her eyes were an unusual shade of green, like one of the deadly snakes known to inhabit the Gazari jungles. Lia was tall—taller than any woman he'd ever met—and wrapped tightly in cords of lean muscle.

The tunic she wore cinched at her waist, revealing more of her built physique. If he were an ordinary man, Eoin did not doubt that Lia could have him on his knees, begging for his life in a matter of seconds. Twin daggers sitting indiscreetly on either hip reminded him of that.

They'd met three years before. Lia was from one of the northern-most clans in Dunhill, tucked on the windward side of the mountains between Dunhill and Rydar. It was those settlements that saw the worst destruction during the war, not because of the battles them-selves but because they lost a great many sons, fathers, and brothers.

All of them, if Lia was reliable.

Eoin fought beside many of the men she named, watched them die on muddy slopes only to be forgotten about, left for the carrion creatures. They were the strongest mortal men he'd ever known. The clansmen swore they were blessed by a goddess, given an extraordinary gift that they kept hidden in their mountain home for hundreds of years.

The gift of shapeshifting.

"It's Eoin now. I'm no longer in service to the crown."

"Because there is no crown! The king is as good as dead and while the nobles squabble amongst themselves, trying to decide who might take his place, the clans are being ravaged. " Lia threw her hands up. "Our men are dead. We are but mothers and elders now. Our blood is old and strong, but our numbers are small, and they grow smaller every day."

Eoin swallowed down the images his mind conjured with her words. He knew what war-ravaged villages looked like. He'd been the one to do the ravaging more than once.

"What kind of thieves and marauders would travel so far north for little more than meat and mead?" Unless news of the king had already spurred the border war back to life and the treaty was broken.

"I can handle thieves and marauders." She tapped her daggers to demonstrate. "The phantoms that haunt our nights are not plucking chickens and stealing cloth. They are organized. Controlled. And they are from Dunhill."

The watery plea that followed physically pained him. "Please, Captain. We need aid."

"As I have reminded you, I have no command anymore. There is no army standing behind me." He rolled his shoulders, itching to end this conversation and go back to his miserable vigil. Gods knew what kind of trouble Davin was getting Elsie into without Eoin supervising. "I am not unsympathetic to your plight, but I don't know what it is you expect me to do."

"I require only you, Captain."

"I am one man."

"You are *drakonmein*!"

Eoin clapped a hand over her mouth, pressing her into the wall of the alley and growling, "I do not appreciate your carelessness."

"I do not appreciate watching innocent people die!" Lia slapped his hand away, glaring fiercely. "We are kin, Eoin Black."

"So, you say." He'd heard myths of dragon men deep in the northern mountains. Their bloodlines were old, the most concentrated populations of dragon shifters in Svalta at one time. Just because they had a distant relationship and the misfortune of carrying monsters beneath their skin did not obligate him to help her.

He was in no shape to help anyone.

"I'm sorry for your troubles and whatever part my family has played in this." Gannon, the eldest Black brother was responsible for the army being disbanded since it was he that scorched the King of Dunhill. Despite the growing turmoil it was causing, Eoin didn't blame him. Gannon's mate was the daughter of the king and from what Eoin gathered, he was not a doting father.

Mara still flinched whenever someone set a teacup down too swiftly.

There was also the part where the King of Dunhill damaged Gannon's wings and kept him in a menagerie of exotic animals for nearly a month. The Black family had an extremely complicated relationship with the crown, and they were at fault for the political unrest in this country.

Well, partially at fault. The politics in Dunhill were already troublesome and the raids on Lia's beloved clans were happening *before* the king was disfigured. He simply didn't care because he was too busy making Gazari alliances and planning for his next war. Eventually raids would give him an excuse to break the treaty and they would be right back where they started half a decade ago.

Only now Lia was claiming the raids were not enemy soldiers. Another scheme. More men with dark motives using innocent people to achieve their goals.

Eoin flexed his fists, resisting the urge to flee from the alley and the way the tall brick walls made him feel confined.

"Please, Eoin." Lia placed her palms on his forearm.

Eoin quickly shook them free. "It is not wise to touch me."

Lia dropped her hands and held them at waist height in a placating gesture. "Dragon fire would do what a hundred soldiers could."

More death. More killing. When did it end?

"You don't know what you're asking."

"We will die! Every last woman and child. It is not a matter of if but *when*. We cannot retreat any further into the mountains. The melting snow has made the journey south too perilous. We are trapped. There is no one left to help us." Tears shimmered in her viper eyes.

His teeth bit into the skin inside his lip. Eoin was planning to leave the Black Estate, and he had nowhere to go. The only plan was to get as far from Elsie as possible. North was very, very far from her. Too far for the dragon to fly in one night.

But more killing would ruin him for good. He knew it. Eoin was a fractured piece of glass and one more impact would shatter him, his sanity flying into a thousand piercing pieces.

"Very well," he exhaled. "I will help you, but I have a condition."

"Yes, anything." She clasped her hands together, suddenly looking younger. Lia was young, Eoin realized. Barely more than a girl.

"When it's done, you will kill me."

The hopeful light sank from her eyes, replaced with a knowing sorrow. "Can it be done? By me, I mean. I have the old blood, but I am not..." she caught herself before she blurted the word again. "Like you."

"I will instruct you how."

Gods, forgive me. Eoin closed his eyes against the pain of the dragon lashing inside of him. *Elsie, forgive me.*

———◇———

EOIN RETURNED TO THE tavern last night with every intention of sitting quietly in a dark corner and waiting for the rest to be done. He didn't want to be there, but he was also compelled to stay as long as Elsie did. When he'd woken in the barn earlier that evening, dazed and ill, he managed to pull himself up from the ground only because he heard Elsie leaving with his brothers. He couldn't stomach knowing she was out with them yet not knowing what she was doing.

His strategic plan was obliterated when he walked up to the table next to Amos, trying to inquire about the empty chair where Elsie should have been seated. Amos was known for his peaceful nature, the calmest of the four brothers. Well-read, reasonable.

There was nothing reasonable about his behavior when Eoin approached him. For a heartbeat he stared at Eoin, head tilted, nostrils flaring. Then the dark of his irises bled a deadly red, and all hell broke loose.

Amos was a gentle soul. His dragon was not. That *thing* in him was a demon. Truly. Unlike his brothers, Amos had never enjoyed an amiable relationship with his dragon. When he shifted it was as if he was purely primal, no trace of humanity inside of him. Amos's desires meant nothing to the dragon. It was why he ventured so far from everyone when the time came to shift. There was no telling what the demon would try to do.

Even so, Amos had excellent control. He didn't have a choice. Otherwise, he might end up chaining himself to the floor the way Eoin did.

Apparently, that control vanished after a few pints. Amos was all fists and fury, beating Eoin as mercilessly as he could with multiple hands trying to hold him back.

Edgar and Davin both helped Eoin to wrestle Amos from the tavern. It was convenient that they'd been seen drinking enough ale to knock a mortal man unconscious. Tavern patrons would assume Amos was a rowdy drunk being dragged out by his companions.

Eoin wished his brother was sloshed and not on the verge of slashing everyone in sight to bloody ribbons. They could hog tie Amos and carry him all the way home on the back of their horses, and it wouldn't make a difference if he shifted.

They made their way to the same alley where Eoin had met with Lia. Somehow this incensed Amos more, and he tackled Eoin, landing a dozen punches, splitting Eoin's lip and bruising his eyes until they swelled. They were facing the worst-case scenario, two *drakonmein* out for blood.

Eoin's dragon wanted him to rip his brother limb from limb. Tear his fists off for daring to use them against Eoin.

He kept the dragon in check with one focused thought: *Elsie was gone.*

The entire confrontation began when Eoin came searching for her.

Amos finally collapsed against the brick wall, breath heaving, eyes fading to his usual dark color, his knuckles a bloody mess. Black strands of hair plastered to his forehead as he rested his head back. The stink of copper and sweat was all Eoin could taste as his own body leaned heavily on the other wall of the alley. For once the Gods were merciful, and his dragon wasn't grappling to escape and murder everything. That pulsing need to locate Elsie kept him distracted.

"Do either of you want to tell me why you're flogging each other?" Davin stood with Edgar at his shoulder, both of them looking disheveled.

"Amos?" Eoin waved impatiently at his brother. "Are you going to go mad again or can I leave?"

"You smelled like—" Amos paused to spit a mouthful of blood. "The scent of you made me see red."

"Right. So, you tried to kill your brother because he smells offensive. My faith in you has been restored." Davin tapped his foot.

Eoin said nothing. It was easy for him to deduce why Amos was furious. Eoin had the same experience every day. Whenever one of his brothers approached him with the scent of Elsie on them, even the tiniest whiff, he felt homicidal.

Now was not the time to worry about why Amos was reacting to the scent of Lia on him. He had more important concerns.

"Where's Elsie?"

The three men glanced around as if they'd only now noticed she was gone.

"Dammit!" Eoin snarled, storming out of the alley, and heading back for the tavern.

"She left when you did," Davin called, hurrying to catch Eoin by the shoulder, then thinking better of it. "We thought she was with you."

Edgar waved to get Eoin's attention, lifting his hand to sign, *"she's gone home."*

"How can you be sure?"

"She watched you leave with a woman."

Eoin recalled their earlier conversation. The way Elsie confronted him. Admitted her feelings to him, only to be pushed away.

It didn't matter if Eoin was a dragon or man, he couldn't keep himself from hurting her.

He didn't say a word to the others before fetching his horse and riding home. He didn't have to. Everyone was in on his secret, it would seem. It was only to protect Elsie and her dignity that they hadn't harassed him constantly. For that small mercy, he was grateful.

Eoin didn't even make it to the stable. He leapt from the back of his horse, trusting the animal wouldn't venture too far from familiar ground in the dead of night.

He burst through the front door, startling Gannon and Mara as they enjoyed a glass of wine in front of the sitting room hearth. His feet thundered up the stairs, down the hall, and further until he reached the wing where Elsie kept her room. As he neared the door he slowed, quieting his footsteps in case she was asleep.

When he pressed his ear to the door, he was relieved to hear that she was within. Safely returned home. Then he heard a sniffle, and he could do nothing but crumple to the floor, his back against the door, knees to his chest.

He wanted desperately to barge in there and take her hands, begging her to forgive him for hurting her. He wanted to tell her that her love for him was not poisonous, it was life giving. That knowing she was here, nurturing love for him, saved him when he was on the battlefield. That her love was the only redeeming thing he had left.

But Eoin couldn't do that. He could only clutch his chest, trying to quell the throbbing there. The unbearable pain of having the life he wanted dangle in front of him endlessly, never to be his. Regret swelled inside of him, a drowning wave that choked the air from his lungs.

These were the consequence of his choices and still he couldn't stop thinking how unfair it was. Not only that he had to live with those consequences but also that she did.

Elsie would always be hurt by his choices. The least he could do for her now was remove himself. Draw him from her skin like a thorn and let the festering wound he'd left her with heal. It would take time, but he hoped that one day soon, she would find happiness. Even if it killed him to envision it, he wanted a better life for her.

When he was gone, she would finally be free to find it.

CHAPTER 7

EOIN

EOIN WOKE WITH A vicious growl, skin blistering and damp, body aching from the change that was attempting to break him apart and make him into his monstrous half. He didn't have to glance at his arms to know they were coated in scales. They always were when he woke from a dream of her.

No moonlight penetrated the thick, dusty curtains that covered the sole window in his room. Even with his keen night vision Eoin could scarcely make out the shape of his hands in the darkness. He liked it that way. He picked this room at the furthest end of the west wing because it was as dark and isolated as the Black Estate could offer. No one ventured here in their daily lives. Eoin was safely cocooned in blackness and misery for as long as he chose to stay here.

But today he chose to stay no longer.

Months had passed since that fateful moment with Elsie outside the baron's chamber and Eoin had not recovered. His confrontation with her yesterday proved that he was no longer capable of handling himself. One more word from her mouth and he would have taken her right there, just as he threatened. He would have bound them irrevocably without her knowing the full truth.

Eoin nearly doomed the only woman he would ever love because he couldn't control his baser desires. It was completely unacceptable.

It was a sign that he needed to remove himself from her life.

An easy choice to proclaim, not an easy one to act out. It wasn't only Elsie that kept him anchored here longer than he intended. Though Eoin struggled in their presence, he could admit that he was pleased to have his brothers together again. They were always the foundation for him, his driving force when he was clashing with enemies in faraway lands. Eoin wanted a better world for his brothers. He wanted to see them happy.

None of them would be happy if he stayed.

The hard sole of his leather boots thumped rhythmically down the long hall leading to the baron's study. Each step was measured, precise, and intentional. Despite months away from the training camp, Eoin hadn't been able to rid himself of the rigid structure of being an army captain. He rose before the sun and worked his muscles in a punishing routine. Even the way he walked, talked, and ate was controlled.

He'd only stopped scraping the black stubble of hair from his scalp because he knew Elsie was fond of the way it curled over his forehead as it grew. It was a petty change, one tiny pleasure he could give her.

He needed that control now more than ever. Coming home was a horrible, painful idea and he should never have given in to his brother's moods. It was Gannon that brought him back here, Gannon that sent a cryptic letter claiming he was on the cusp of dangerous madness.

Ha! What did Gannon know of madness? His dragon wasn't mad, only bored after years of Gannon pitying himself for choosing the wrong woman.

Eoin tapped his knuckles on the door to Gannon's office exactly three times.

"Enter!" Gannon didn't raise his head from the paper he was scribbling on, nor did he drop his quill when he said, "you took longer than I anticipated, brother."

Eoin halted the gruff sentence ready to leave his mouth and frowned. "What do you mean?"

"You're here for one of two reasons." Gannon placed the quill back into the inkwell and folded his hands. The expression on his face was inscrutable. "Either you're going to tell me that you're leaving the estate—returning to camp to needlessly train soldiers or some other nonsense—or you know, and you've come to reconcile your mistakes."

Ice crystallized his blood and Eoin wasn't entirely sure why. "Know what?"

"That you're a fool and you've lost your only chance at happiness."

Elsie. His beast let out a guttural sound.

"Do not play games with me, Gannon."

"It's you who has been playing games, Eoin. You're an idiot, you know that? I always admired your strength, even that pesky obedience of yours. But I was blind and selfish, and I hadn't realized how much suffering you caused."

"Where is she?" Eoin snarled, suddenly filled with such intense anxiety he felt his heart might climb up his throat and choke him.

"Gone." It was Mara who responded. Eoin whirled, finding the princess hovering in the doorway behind him. Her eyes were bloodshot, her shoulders hunched forward. "Elsie's gone. I hope you're pleased with yourself."

Mara was not the woman Eoin met six months earlier when his brother had hidden her away from her abusive family, but she wasn't that different either. She had moments of boldness and bravery that grew more common all the time. Still, Eoin didn't miss the timid way she skirted around him and how pointedly she avoided meeting his gaze. A meek thing like her could sense the predator inside him and knew how broken and wild it was.

Today, she didn't seem so meek. Her eyes flashed when they locked on his, fists clenched in anger. "You are a cruel man, Eoin Black. Perhaps when you return to us from your cowardly retreat, you will finally have found your heart."

Not possible, because his heart was somewhere outside of this estate. *Gone*, as they vaguely put it.

"Where. Is. She?" Eoin repeated harshly, sharp, serpentine teeth bared.

The next few moments were chaos even Eoin had trouble tracking. Gannon moved faster than should have been possible, his fist flying over and over as he pummeled his brother away from his mate.

Eoin would never have lost ground to his brother under normal circumstances, but he was too caught off guard by his fear for Elsie to react in time. Or at all. In truth, he deserved each blow that sent him tumbling to his knees.

"You keep that beast of yours away from my mate." Green eyes burned into him, a pinprick pupil sizing him up. Gannon loved his brothers, and would lay down his life for them, but Eoin understood that he was just as ready to take Eoin's life if he became a threat to Mara.

He knew the vicious fury coursing through Gannon better than anyone. Anything that tried to harm Elsie would become ash in his fingertips.

"Gannon, tell me where she is," he pleaded this time, willing his dragon to quit writhing beneath his skin. For once, the beast obeyed, understanding it was the only way to gain the information he needed.

"So that you can do what?"

"Go after her!"

"Why?" Mara spoke up, peeking around Gannon's protective stance.

Eoin swallowed thickly. No answer found purchase on his tongue.

Why would he go after her? To bring her back to this estate so she could wither away on her own, grieving his disappearance for the rest of her days?

Well, yes, that was what he wanted. He was a greedy, selfish creature beneath all the lies about honor. The darkest days were bearable when he knew Elsie was only a ride south. Waiting for him, wanting for him, cherishing every simple moment they had together before he was gone.

If she left the Black Estate, Gods knew what would happen to her. Danger was his greatest concern, but it was closely tailed by the fear she would find the happiness he wished for her only hours before. Another to embrace her strength, to warm her bed. To build a family with.

Elsie deserved happiness and he would never be able to give it to her. Soon enough he would be gone, and someone would need to look out for her.

Eoin hadn't given much thought to that part of his plans. He assumed his brothers would take care of Elsie. They always did. She was as good as a sister to them, and they cared for her. It never crossed his mind that Elsie might leave. She never did. She was always here.

Always waiting for him to return.

The sudden slap across his face was far more unexpected than Gannon's assault. Mara stumbled back as Gannon wrapped his arms around her waist, pulling her away from Eoin before she could provoke the monster.

"Shame on you!"

"Mara—"

She cut Gannon off with a huff. "It's the least he deserves!" Then she stormed down the hall, the heel of her boots clacking angrily.

Gannon quietly studied Eoin, an annoying smirk tugging at his lips. "I do so love that woman."

"I don't care. Where the fuck is Elsie?"

That made him scowl. Gods, Eoin was going to strangle him. "She's gone home."

"Home?" What did he mean she'd gone home? This was her home.

"To Brilend. She left to look after her mother and sister."

"Mother and sister?" He'd scarcely remembered she had either.

He really was a heartless bastard.

"She has a life outside of this estate, Eoin."

"You think I don't know of her life outside this cursed house?"

"Temper," Gannon tsked, his casual demeanor only incensing Eoin more. "You never used to have a temper."

He lifted back onto his feet to tower over his brother. Gannon might be older, but Eoin was taller and broader. "How is she traveling? Who is with her?"

Gannon almost looked pleased when he answered, "she took her mare."

"Alone."

"She didn't ask for company."

"She shouldn't have to ask! Elsie took care of your every need while you wasted your life away for ten years, brother. The least you could do is send an escort to assure she arrived safely. You unbelievable bastard!"

Gannon stepped around his desk, returning to his seat as if they weren't beating each other a minute earlier. "I thought you would take her, but you obviously have more important tasks to attend to."

Those fletched words were a direct hit, slicing straight through bone and cartilage to strike the most tender muscle in his body. Eoin clutched his chest, swaying on his feet.

What have I become? He called himself a monster for the broken creature that lived under his skin, but really the monster was him. A tainted soul that tormented the ones he loved because he was too involved in his own suffering to see theirs. Elsie was right there, a hallway and two flights of stairs down. For half a year she was there, feeling as if he'd abandoned her while they were standing in the same room.

Eoin slipped out of Gannon's study in a rush to get back to his room. His bag was already packed, waiting neatly on his bed. Fifteen minutes more to prepare a horse and he would be ready.

Gods, what was he thinking? Go after her and then what? He wasn't fit for her anymore. He couldn't force her to stay here only for his peace of mind.

But she was alone on the road. Gannon let her ride alone to prove a point, meddling bastard. Anything could happen to her. At the very least Eoin would bring her safely to where she was headed.

And then he would take his leave. There was no other choice for him.

"Whatever it is," Gannon leaned against the doorway to his study as Eoin passed, face serious., "it's not as bad as you think."

Eoin was frozen in the hall, hands tight at his sides. "You have no idea, Gannon."

"I have some idea."

"I—" He couldn't bring himself to say it, to admit his weakness. His dragon was broken and nothing he'd done could fix it.

"Lady Fate chose a mate for you knowing the life you would lead. She does not pick wrong. Don't forget that."

Those words echoed in Eoin's head as he swung his bag over his shoulder and bounded down the stairs two at a time.

She does not pick wrong.

But how could Lady Fate have known he would become this awful creature that he was and still bind Elsie to him? It wasn't *fair*.

It wasn't supposed to be, was it?

Capricious Gods and their games. If Eoin was cruel, fate was evil.

She does not pick wrong.

No, she didn't. Even now Eoin could feel the pull of Elsie from somewhere distant, a rope tied to his sternum, tugging heavily.

Would Elsie feel it snap, he wondered, when Lia drove a sword through his neck?

CHAPTER 8

ELSIE

ELSIE WAS BEGINNING TO hate birds. Always twittering happily, bouncing from branch to branch, and fluttering about as if they didn't have a care in the world. She'd turned her attention to those feathered fiends to distract herself, only to realize they were highlighting her bitterness.

She was supposed to be noticing how the sweet scent of sun kissed berry blossoms clung to the air and not the way an invisible chain pulled mercilessly at her ribs the further she travelled from the Black Estate. Their floral breath was accented by that weedy grass smell Elsie loved so much in the warm seasons. Traveling east away from the Black Estate, the foliage shifted from dark and foreboding old growth. Fir and cedar trees gave way to oak and birch, their trunks bright and narrow, their branches opening to let the sun dapple the road.

It was too bright. Her eyes weren't accustomed to sunlight and vibrant colors anymore. Elsie already missed the gloomy haze of the Black Estate.

How would they fare without her?

One part of her wanted them to be well. Another felt such sadness at the idea that they would be fine without her. The Black family would forget her, swiped away like another irritating cloud of dust gathered across books and untouched gowns.

When she said her final farewell to Edgar and swallowed down the threat of tears, Elsie promised herself she wouldn't spend another minute wallowing in thoughts of the past. That promise was already broken. How could she keep it when every uneven ridge of this dirt road was scattered with bittersweet memories?

It was on this road that Eoin found her. On this road that she nearly died trying to escape what she'd done.

Elsie had no concept of direction then. She'd never left the small village where she grew up, hardly knew east from west unless the sun was rising or setting. Even the road signs were nonsense to her, symbols she couldn't read, arrows pointing toward destinations unknown.

The air was so heavy. It shouldn't have been possible for air to have weight, but it did, seeping heavily into her lungs and making her breathing labored. Or perhaps that was the mass of her body, curling in on itself in exhaustion and making every inhale an excruciating effort.

Death was imminent. Elsie remembered the injustice of that realization spurring her onward as she withered and crumbled under the hot summer sun. Her only skills—skills to keep a home—were outright useless now that she was without one and she would have cursed her father and his soul, wherever it was damned to, would it not burn her dry throat to speak.

Water. She needed water desperately.

The sun scorched the earth, drying the grass and evaporating the thin streams that once trickled along the side of the road. Any water that ran off from the fields and farms was polluted by manure. She was smart enough not to drink but watching it run down the low slope on the far side of her dusty path each morning as the farmers watered their crops was torture of the greatest kind.

When Elsie dreamed of breaking free from the cruel grip of her father, she thought it would be easy to find her way. There were other villages and towns between here and the capitol. But the farmers and traders that travelled to them had carts and horses, means of transportation *and* the resources to get there. Elsie had nothing but the filthy dress hanging from her weak body, still painted with her father's blood.

It was delirium that prevented her from hearing the pounding steps of the animal whose shadow pooled over her. Elsie squinted up, seeing nothing but darkness blocking the glare of the sun. A misshapen darkness that was too tall and wide to be a bear come to eat her and yet, too large to be a man either.

Except, there was a man's voice echoing around her. It was deep and rich, refined in the sharp syllables that rang out across the road.

"Gods, what has happened to you?"

A solid hand wrapped around her shoulder, large enough to cover it. Large enough to squeeze and break her with minimal effort. A man's hand, heavy and rough. Elsie knew that she should rebel at such closeness, run the other way like the feral creature she had become.

Except the weight of his hand was somehow lightening, soothing the burden she'd dragged with her down this Gods forsaken road until she was nearly floating off the ground. Elsie blinked up, her unfocused vision sharpening in time to see the strangest hallucination.

A man of impossible height loomed over her, forcing her chin to tilt upward until her neck strained. Black curls tumbled over his forehead, and his eyes were the perfect match. Pale skin created a sharp contrast, those inky curls like a whisper of midnight clinging to the day.

Then he inhaled roughly, his eyes whirling with color. Shades of yellow and orange coalesced into black until they overtook it completely, leaving nothing but a pinprick pupil. He reminded her of a snake, moving silently toward her, poised to strike.

She should fear his poison, as she feared the poison of all men. The lot of them were snakes, dangerous in their trickery. Disguising themselves as innocuous items until she overstepped and suddenly found herself being strangled like a pitiful little rabbit.

Elsie was not afraid as his other hand propped her upright. Her fingers wrapped in his clean tunic, clinging to him desperately because somehow, she knew—knew with all of her being—that she was safe now. A haven opened before her, a dark angel come to carry her away from the consequences of her own treachery.

"It's really you," he whispered.

Elsie tried to smile at him but the skin on her lips cracked and bled. She parted them to speak, to say anything that would convey to him her great need for him, but she could not find her voice. Molten sunset swam in her vision, slowly vanishing back into darkness.

This darkness was not the stunning obsidian of her midnight angel. It was an endless black, the hungry maw of the underworld coming to eat her up for an eternity in punishment for what she'd done.

⚬

"IT'S ALRIGHT, LITTLE SPARROW. It's going to be alright."

That voice. Elsie couldn't understand why she knew that voice. It was so familiar, so soothing, that she blinked her eyes shut and snuggled deeper into the soft cushion of her bed. Let this angel murmur sweet promises to her until she was lost to sleep for the remainder of her days.

Suddenly cold liquid splashed down her chest and Elsie jerked up, spluttering and scrambling backwards.

She was not in her bed but on the forest floor, shaded from the glaring sun and dripping with water. A man hovered over her, cradling a water skin, and staring at her as if she was a phantom and he couldn't quite believe he was seeing her. Elsie felt the same.

His eyes were black, so very black, and she worried that if she continued to look at them, she would be lost in them forever. Hypnotic power radiated from those eyes, and it quieted the voice within her that screamed to be wary.

Never trust a man. Especially not a man such as this.

He was powerful, carrying more muscle than even the youngest and strongest men she'd known. The width of his shoulders was double hers, his arms so thick that they threatened the stability of his tunic. Elsie would be helpless in his grasp, crushed beneath him if he tackled her.

He didn't look as if he planned to tackle her. Moving with all the caution he would toward a spooked horse, the man reached the water skin out to her. Droplets pooled on her neck and in her knotted hair. She could almost taste the sweet coolness on her tongue.

Instinct overrode fear and suddenly Elsie was gripping the skin with both hands, gulping so wildly she choked. When her coughing fit was over, she returned to the drink, tilting the skin to the sky until every last drop was gone. She ought to feel guilty for her greed, but she was *so thirsty* that it had incited madness in her.

"Do you need more?" he offered softly.

Elsie glanced around, as if she would see a river sparkling behind him. "Yes," she rasped.

The man rose to his full height, stepping over to the horse that Elsie hadn't even noticed in her bleary state. If ever there was a horse fitting its rider, this was it. He was bigger than even a draft horse, broad shouldered, heavy hoofed, and a sleek black that blended with the black of her savior's springy hair.

Elsie swallowed a hungry moan when he returned to her with a second water skin and a small, hard loaf of bread. He placed both on a smooth rock beside her, followed by a wrapped package of cheese. With a bow of his head, he stepped back again, settling onto his knees far enough from her that even his long arms couldn't reach her.

Was it that obvious that she was frightened? Elsie readjusted herself on the ground, finding she was perched with her back to an oak tree. Beneath her was a soft cushion of moss.

The thoughtfulness of such a simple act—placing her where she would be comfortable—made her eyes burn. No amount of desperate blinking kept the tears at bay. They were the first she'd shed in years, since she was old enough to understand what they represented.

Weakness.

Now she was bearing her weakness to this stranger. Elsie swiped helplessly at her face, but her panic dissolved into more and more tears. They wouldn't stop. How was it even possible to cry when she'd been so dried out and thirsty only moments ago?

Shame brought her hands to her face, covering it completely as she wept. Such a childish display was unlike her. Though, she supposed she was allowed a moment of heart break after what had transpired over the last four days.

Her father was dead. Her home gone. Mother and Irene were gone too. It hadn't occurred to her until this moment that she might never see them again. Everything that was familiar, that was *hers*, was lost to her.

Had it been selfish to do what she'd done? Elsie told herself it was to protect her sister, to save her mother from the cruelty father enacted upon her. But it was Elsie's own pride that made her plunge the blade into father's chest.

She wouldn't allow him to use her for his gain. To destroy her the way he'd destroyed mother.

Elsie could almost laugh at her naïveté. Even in his death, he still had the last word.

Elsie was destroyed in every way that mattered. She had nothing left. That hateful, devilish man had taken it from her.

"You're safe now." *His* voice startled her from her spiraling despair. "No one will hurt you anymore."

Hands dropping to her lap, Elsie blinked at him. Salt crusted her eyelashes and withered her already dry cheeks. Her shame had vanished though, and she no longer cared what state he saw her in.

She believed him. Wholly and unequivocally. Below her ribs a wisp of instinct unfurled, a tiny, fragile voice that echoed this trust. Her mind wanted to deny it, to tell her heart that it was foolish and impulsive.

She could not deny it.

So, Elsie turned her attention outward and gripped the offered food. It was all she could do not to moan in delight as she licked the oils from the cheese off her fingers. She'd never eaten so ravenously, and she never dreamed that dry, days old bread could taste so delicious.

When she finally glanced back up, it was to a soft smile. That subtle expression was transformative on the sharp angles of his face. He seemed a man that frowned often, his brows thick and square. The jut of his chin should have made him harsh. Instead, he seemed solid, an unbreakable wall of stone that for some reason, was erected around her.

"Thank you," she whispered.

"You owe me no thanks, little sparrow. Only the Gods deserve thanks for delivering me to you." His smile grew, brightening his dark eyes and provoking her own.

Elsie dropped her chin, twisting her hands in her lap as her cheeks heated. They were filthy hands. Her dress was tattered at the hem, caked in dust and blood. What a vision she must be.

"What is your name?"

"Elsie."

"Elsie," he repeated, as if the name meant something to him. "I'm Eoin Black."

"Eoin," she repeated his name too.

It didn't go unnoticed by her that he shared his family name. Names were only important to men of good breeding or notable wealth. By the look of him, he was both. That proud posture, crisp speech, and the tailored cut of his clothes.

Yet, he didn't present as a nobleman either. Not that Elsie would really know. There was a hardened quality to him, the callouses on his hands and the steel edge to his voice when he asked, "whose blood are you wearing?"

Elsie swallowed, clasping her palms over the brown stain on her chest as if she could make him forget the question.

"How do you know it doesn't belong to me?"

"You're uninjured. I checked."

She gaped at him. "What kind of scoundrel—"

"Come now, Little Sparrow. Your feigned offense does not sway me." He pressed his knuckles into the loamy earth, crouching to meet her gaze with a ferocious intensity that had her thinking of snakes and other dangerous predators. "I'm not asking because I intend to see you punished. I'm asking because I need to know if there is a man waiting to be impaled upon my sword."

Several silent heartbeats passed before Elsie fully grasped what he was saying. "You would—but what if—I can't—" She swallowed her stumbling words, asking, "are you mad?"

"You do not yet know me, Elsie, so you cannot understand the value of my word. Someday, you will." Eoin moved closer, daringly close. His breath mingled with hers, his eyes catching the sunlight and tricking her into believing that unnatural orange glow was returning. "So long as I live and breathe, you will be safe from harm. No one, man or beast, will bring you pain."

His thumb caressed the thin wound that cut across her eye and left her cheek pink and discolored, Father's parting mark. "I am a man of my word, Elsie, and you have my word that anyone who dares to lay a hand on you will have to beg forgiveness from the Gods after I send his soul from this earth. If that makes me a mad man, so be it."

Of all the reactions that warred for freedom within her, laughter was the least expected. Her chortling stunned them both, catching that spark in his black eyes and sending bursts of color through them, only for them to vanish as she searched for them. The edges of his lips curved in a true smile, drawing out a dimple in his clean-shaven face.

The hard, aristocratic air left him and suddenly he was just a handsome man, making promises that should push her to her quivering legs to flee from him. Elsie laughed louder, letting the heat of his hand lingering on her cheek sear this moment into her memory.

That was ten years ago. Eoin didn't smile at her anymore. It was true that he was a man of his word. He proved it countless times, steadfast in his loyalty to his family, to the men that served with him.

Over the years Eoin had forgotten his promise. Or else he hadn't included himself when he swore no man would cause her pain.

Elsie was so deep in her memory that she was surprised by the sudden appearance of men on horseback in her peripheral. Four of them bounded past her, kicking up dust, and making her horse shake her head nervously. The last man slowed his horse, eyeing her openly with a sour twist to his lips.

It wasn't uncommon to see travelers on this road since it forked two miles before Brilend, leading north toward the neighboring country of Brula. Suspicion nibbled at Elsie regardless as she returned the man's hostile expression.

Grey. That was the detail sticking in her mind. All four men were garbed in the same grey fabric, like soldiers in uniform. Their hair was neatly trimmed, not as a soldier but shorter than men in Dunhill were known for.

What did it matter to her? If they weren't thieves, she would pay them no mind.

Ignoring the next traveler proved difficult. An old man passed with an overloaded cart, his mule sweating with the effort of hauling it. Covering his wizened frame was the same grey fabric. Wool, perhaps, because the man was sweating more than the mule.

His eyes speared her with accusation until Elsie was out of sight.

She was a woman alone on the road, wearing men's riding pants that she stole from Edgar. That warranted second glances.

Both Edgar and Nigel wrestled with her determination to set out on her own. The king was dead, the road full of thieves and ruffians. Couldn't she wait for one of the Black brothers to escort her home?

Their solemn faces belied their true motive.

They wanted her to wait for one Black brother in particular, be-lieving that despite the chasm between them, Eoin would still march by her side one final time.

To them, the outcome of Eoin and Elsie's fractured relationship was ridiculous. Nothing a private moment on the road couldn't repair.

They didn't know the truth, couldn't see what Elsie was beneath her bold tongue and brazen manner.

A killer. Violent in the face of torment. Bloodied by her own pride.

Ultimately, her motivation for taking her father's life didn't matter. Whether she sacrificed years with her sister to protect her or simply stabbed him to set herself free, the outcome was the same.

Elsie proved herself like a vicious animal when cornered. Fit to sit in the kitchen and mop up the scraps of noblemen but never trusted enough to lay by their hearth.

Eoin was too kind to turn her away when he saw the whole of her, but he was also too proud to associate himself with the likes of her anymore.

There was no love for killers in this world. She was unworthy of it. Though she hadn't set foot in a temple for over a decade, she recalled even the Gods offered no forgiveness for slaying your own kin.

Elsie would have to make her own amends. Redeem herself the way she had at the Black Estate, through sacrifice and toil. She would find her mother and sister, whether they were in Brilend or not, and she would care for them the way she should have before.

Shower them in the coin she'd saved working for Gannon—he paid her more generously than any housekeeper dreamed of—and give them the life they deserved.

Perhaps then Elsie would feel clean again. Perhaps then she would feel worthy.

Another rider passed, sporting grey clothing and unkind eyes. The sun was tickling the treetops as a second cart bumbled by too. A hunched man drove the tired animal faster than the poor creature deserved. Seated beside him was a young woman, hair wrapped tightly in grey cloth. Body buried beneath the same.

Was there a raving new fashion trend Elsie was unaware of?

Or was it more sinister than that?

Sinister seemed a silly word for matching clothing, yet it hung over her as she guided her horse off the road and into the trees. Even the dusk was grey, the trees blotting out the watercolor sunset.

That was for the best. Even sunsets reminded her of Eoin and the pale orange of his dragon eyes.

Her need to avoid the memory of him was so great that Elsie stubbornly refused to continue six miles on, where a sign suggested the inn still stood. She'd slept there once, frightened, and exhausted, wearing oversized clothes that Eoin had purchased off the innkeeper's wife.

The warmth of the hearth there would never penetrate her skin. Cold, swelling loneliness would leave her stiff and tired.

Besides, she wasn't a wealthy traveler, despite the size of her hidden coin purse. She was a housekeeper. Not the wife of a baron's son, as she once envisioned herself, but the servant to one.

She could sleep on the ground as the rest of them did.

Dark settled in, and Elsie felt fear creep in with it. Her horse too was nervous, chuffing and stomping her feet.

Let robbers come for her. Let the wolves open their hungry maws. They would regret meeting a woman like her.

Everyone did, eventually.

CHAPTER 9

EOIN

ELSIE WAS UNAWARE OF the shadows at her back. By the look of her, she was scarcely aware of the horse beneath her. She rode with her chin dipped, eyes fixed on some destination only she could see.

Eoin wasn't surprised that she didn't take notice of his presence. He *was* surprised she hadn't seen two poachers drop their kill at the edge of the Briarwood and slip through the trees to follow her.

He wanted to be proud of himself for not killing them, but dusk was falling, and they were still pacing behind her like hungry dogs, which meant there was still a fair chance Eoin would rip their heads from their shoulders.

There was always a chance the dragon would force his way out and make his own scene. Eoin distracted himself from that potential by mentally mapping familiar terrain.

The road between the Blackwood and the northeastern border of Brula wasn't previously a well-travelled one, but in recent years a new route had been carved through the forest. Unlike the Blackwood, the Briarwood was thin and open, giving cover for only ordinary predators like bears and wolves. Brooks weaved in and out of the bright white trunks of birch trees, adding a serenity to the forest that belied even the most obvious threats.

With more foot traffic and more pelt hunters, there were fewer predators in the Briarwood and the surrounding villages than ever before.

That was, until the king became charcoal, and laws were a matter of choice. Eoin never cared for the gossip of soldiers, but he was always careful to listen to their news from home. What happened between the Briarwood and the Blackwood was also what happened near the Black Estate, and he wanted to be the first to know if there was danger.

The last he heard, poachers were murdering pelt hunters as often as they were killing bears and bucks. Thieves hid in the shadowy borders of the forest and waited for easy prey—like women travelling alone with a heavy coin purse and a meager dagger.

There was also talk of rebels to the crown, religious zealots that believed the Gods had punished the king with dragon fire because he was not the rightful ruler of Dunhill. Lia's account of the attacks on the clans added weight to these rumors. Who they believed *was* the rightful ruler of Dunhill, no one knew. Perhaps they thought the Gods would plop someone righteous and worthy on the throne.

In Eoin's experience, it was often men of the very worst breed that became outspoken about the Gods. Any man that had true honor cared not for power or prestige, unfortunately. They saw the corruption in it all and fled. Just as Eoin would have fled the army, had he not signed a contract. There was no honor in brutality. No respect for soldiers and no glory, either.

They were whipped into a frenzy by noble born generals that preached like high fathers, speaking of blood and battle as if it was a divine dance. An act of the Gods.

None of those men ever took up arms. They never ran blades through the fragile chests of innocent boys, ripped from their mother's arms only to become pawns in a pointless fight for wealth and land.

Wealth and land that those mothers would never see a scrap of. There was no compensation for losing a child.

Eoin could do nothing about that. He couldn't beg forgiveness from the families he had broken or return the dead to be buried in their holy ground. That didn't make him powerless. For all the terrible deeds he'd done, his last act on this earth would be a good one. Eoin would guarantee the safety of the remaining clans in the mountains. He would come to Lia's aid and save her people.

It might not be enough to earn him a place in service of the Gods, but at least he would die with his conscience lighter.

Night fell as he pondered about Gods and their divine scales. They'd passed several travelers, each of them more wary and unfriendly than the next. Their demeanor had his hackles up and he couldn't pinpoint why. Then again, most people put him on edge. It was possible he simply didn't like anyone anymore.

Anyone but *her*.

Her was who slipping into the woods with only a sliver of light left, two poachers creeping after her. They'd fallen behind, even with the slow pace Elsie's horse kept, but if they were determined enough to follow her this far, they surely wouldn't give up until they caught up to her.

What did Elsie think she was doing?

Eoin dropped from the back of his horse, patting the animal, and sending him off to graze on the short grass at the edge of the road. Valor was built for war, massive shoulders and legs that could crush a man with ease. If a daring wolf happened upon him, the horse would stomp the animal to pieces without mercy. A thief would get the same treatment. Most days, Eoin let the horse wander as he pleased. He always came back when he was called.

Without his horse he could be silent, boots sliding across a mat of decaying leaves. His bag rustled faintly on his back as he avoided the thorny underbrush these woods were known for, but it was not enough noise that someone with an untrained ear would notice.

Elsie had her back to a tree, eyes closed as she chewed. The sight of her transported Eoin to another time, a sweltering summer day where she leaned wearily against a tree in this same forest. She was barely more than a girl then, so underfed that she hadn't grown into the womanhood she carried so boldly now.

When she fainted in his arms, there was a horrifying moment where he believed her dead. His mate, coated in blood, clinging to him, dying in his arms only minutes after finding her. Eoin wouldn't allow that. He decided it and so, he carried her tenderly, depositing her against a tree and willing her to wake up. To live for him.

Ten years later and he was willing her to live without him.

After a long pause to assess the surroundings, Eoin dropped his bag and turned back the way he'd come. It took half an hour for him to identify the sound of feet blundering through the briar. If their stomping didn't alert Elsie to their presence, the hissed argument would.

"I'm tellin' ya, she went this way."

"Wolves have surely eaten our kill, all because you wanted to chase a pretty lass on a horse," the second man retorted.

"A pretty lass with fine leather boots and a saddle to match. The horse alone will fetch more than venison." A yellow grin reflected across the moon dappled understory, pinpointing exactly where Eoin's prey was. "And she was pretty, wasn't she?"

The song of steel and leather was loud in the fading evening. Both men halted, their ragged breaths making them sound like frightened animals.

"Did you hear that?" one whispered to the other.

"Shhh," the second shushed.

"Would you rather I cut off your heads, or drive my sword through your heart?" Eoin boomed into the darkness.

Both men swiveled their heads, searching the low light and missing his silhouette as he hovered behind a birch. It would be justice to kill them. Elsie wasn't the first traveler they'd followed, he was sure of it. Not to mention the moral corruption of poaching game and charging a hefty sum to starving families for mere pounds of meat.

Already Eoin's vision was growing sharper, the shadows thinning as his pupils absorbed fine strands of moonlight. Peering out of his eyes, the dragon saw only two things: a threat to his mate and a new source of amusement.

First, he would defile one for even thinking of defiling her. Then he would pin the other in place as he tore his companion apart one string of muscle at a time. There was no sweeter sound than the screams of his enemy.

An enemy that was now fleeing through the wood, tripping, and tumbling over each other in their haste. Claws curled around the hilt of his sword, and he nearly dropped it as scales hardened the surface of his skin.

Eoin ground his teeth, biting back the dragon with all his might. He should have sent Amos. Even Edgar would have been a safer travel companion.

His brothers thought they were helping by sending him after Elsie, believing he simply needed a moment alone with her for a change of heart. They had no idea what the real danger was.

Because he refused them. Every time they tried to dig into his heart, he shut them out, steeled himself out of fear and pride.

That pride was the reason he'd almost hurt Elsie a dozen or more times.

Elsie.

Eoin used that singular thought to focus himself.

Elsie was alone and there were other predators about.

The night was cool, and Elsie didn't have enough bedding to keep her warm.

The food in Elsie's bag would only last her a day, and she could wake up hungry tomorrow.

His legs were stone weights, but he lifted them anyway, sheathing his sword as the sound of retreating poachers vanished. Obsidian scales glittered across his forearms. Inside him the dragon writhed with indecision, wanting to bleed his enemies but also agreeing with Eoin's assessment.

Eoin crept from his hiding place between two birch trees twined in their growth, leaving his bag, and dropping to a crouch beside Elsie. She was curled on her side, lying on the hard ground and covered by nothing but a thin blanket. She didn't stir when he brushed the hair from her face, no uneven breath as he settled next to her on the cold soil.

He wrapped his arm around her, moving close enough for the unnatural heat of him to seep into the fabric of her blanket. He was too close, *dangerously close,* and he could feel the puppy-like excitement of his dragon at the contact. Eoin would have to be careful not to let himself rest too deeply, lest the beast wrestled control from him and got his maw around Elsie as he so often fantasized.

Instead, Eoin distracted himself with his own fantasies, imagining a life where this was not an exception. Not a silent goodbye.

Once he was a young man, grieving and alone, until he found Elsie stumbling down this very road. Her lips were dry, eyes bleary, and it was clear she hadn't eaten in days. And whatever she had been eating? It wasn't enough to satisfy the needs of a young woman.

Her thin shoulder snapped back, sharp, shallow face turned up fiercely when she heard his horse approach. She was half-starved and wearing a torn, bloodied dress, and she looked like she planned to unmount him and fight him to the death.

Eoin still remembered her like that. Fragile, yet unbreakable. She was a force of nature. Her beauty and ferocity struck him right down to his soul and in that one breathless moment, he was lost. Lost to her eyes like polished wood. Lost to her stubborn chin and the way she planted her hands on her hips when she was angry. To the way she collapsed in his arms, nearly dead from exhaustion, when he finally convinced her to climb upon his horse.

She knew she was safe. Knew that she truly was invincible now, that nothing in this world could touch her as long as he was there.

But then he wasn't there. All his silent promises to her, to protect her, to build his world around her, were broken.

She needed him and he wasn't there.

And with that crushing reminder, his fantasy shattered, and Eoin was left to watch her sleep peacefully in his arms for the very last time.

CHAPTER 10

ELSIE

A PLACE COULD CHANGE and somehow stay the same. Brilend was tucked neatly between the forest and the pastures, giving beautiful sunrise views over the fields of sprouting alfalfa and corn, and creating the perfect shady place to rest among trees.

There was never much rest to be had, of course. Too much work to do in the fields. Animals to be fed and let out to pasture. Fences to be mended.

The scent of horse and hay carried to Elsie on the wind. Cows murmured to each other in their deep bovine voices from the safety of a barn somewhere nearby. It wasn't a particularly pleasant smell, but it was a familiar one. Comforting in a way only memories could be.

Once Elsie was happy here. Before she understood the circumstances of her family and the inconsistencies of her father. Once this was home.

Now it could be again.

She rose before the sun that morning, feeling surprisingly rested after sleeping on the hard ground. In her dreams she was cocooned by roaring flames, a hearth large enough to warm her head to toe. No wolves came to devour her in the night after all.

Elsie was almost disappointed. That brand of excitement would have made a welcome distraction. The potent concoction of emotions whirling in her belly at the thought of returning to this wretched place was nauseating. A thousand potential encounters played out in her mind.

Would she be confronted for the disappearance of her father?

Would she return only to find her mother and sister gone?

Would she get to the edge of the village and feel compelled to turn back?

With a gentle nudge of her heel, Elsie urged her horse forward. There was no turning back now. She had amends to make, a family to reunite. Besides, this place didn't seem so wretched anymore.

Smoke curled from the chimney of a nearby cottage on the perimeter of a cow pasture. Grain silos stood sentinel in the distance. Chickens sang their morning song to each other, bounding through the grass on the hunt for worms.

Without the filter of childhood, Brilend didn't look nearly as dark. The sparse collection of homes at the westernmost end of the village looked cleaner and better kept than she remembered. Brown and white stones were embedded in the road, making it clean and smooth where once there was mud and deep holes.

The morning light was tepid and gold, and Elsie found the worst of her anxieties fading.

Until she cleared the Briarwood at the top of the slope and saw all Brilend laid out before her, and realized her earlier assessment was wrong. This place was not the same. Not at all.

Rooftops stretched as far as the eye could see, the red and brown shingles obtusely bright in the morning sun. Large wooden buildings lined the road from the base of the slope all the way to the old inn. Elsie could barely make out the familiar shape of it beyond the overcrowded square.

Ten years ago, that square housed only a small temple, a bakery, and a tailor. She cupped a hand over her eyes, squinting into the distance to see grey shapes meandering between buildings.

What was once a tiny settlement was now an expansive town. It would explain why she'd seen so many travelling the eastern road. Elsie felt a little shock of joy to think perhaps the Gods had smiled upon this place that so needed it and granted them abundance in the darkest times.

The hooves of her horse clicked pleasantly as they navigated down the hill. Elsie was tempted to charge into town, exploring every new corner of Brilend on the hunt for her sister. Instead, she opted for caution, guiding her horse onto a dirt path, and approaching a nearby barn. The family that owned this barn used to accept travelers and their horses when the inn was full. Perhaps they would still welcome a stranger.

On the outside Brilend had changed. That didn't mean there weren't still scavengers hiding in plain sight.

A willowy boy with shaggy brown curls dropped down from the loft of the barn as she dismounted. Elsie shouldn't have been surprised that he was clad in all grey. His eyes rounded as he approached her, staring openly at her dress and all the places it hugged her figure. He was on the cusp of manhood, broad shoulders, and long legs, and so she could hardly blame him for admiring her.

The expression on his face didn't suggest admiration, however. Stunned, perhaps, and a little uneasy. The dress really wasn't that showy, was it? This morning Elsie had changed from her riding clothes into a fresh dress. It was modest with three-quarter sleeves and a high neckline, but the color was a brighter red than she would have chosen for herself. Mara insisted she take it, wanting Elsie to look her best for a reunion with her family.

Now Elsie was second-guessing Mara's wisdom.

"M'lady?" was all the boy managed to mumble as he blinked dark eyes at her.

Elsie snorted a laugh. She wasn't *that* finely dressed or even that clean after a day of riding. "I'm not a lady. Does your father still welcome travelers in exchange for coin?"

"My—my father?" His mouth fished open. "My father is dead."

Elsie could relate to the haunted, hollow expression that followed his blunt statement. Not all fathers chased the nightmares away. Some became them.

"I am sorry for your loss."

The boy nodded too briskly. "We can take travelers, m'lady."

"Call me, Elsie, please."

"Elsie," he repeated, fidgeting with the hem of his shirt. "Are you traveling alone?"

Elsie stepped back into the shadow of the barn, eyeing him thoughtfully. "I am."

"A woman ought not to be alone in these parts."

She refrained from rolling her eyes. He meant no harm, even if it irritated. "I'm perfectly capable on my own."

"You been to Brilend before?"

"I was born here. I came to look for my mother and my sister."

He gnawed anxiously at his lip, looking side to side as if the horses might later gossip about their conversation. "S'not safe here for a woman like you. Best to move along quickly, m'lady."

"It's not safe for a woman anywhere in this world." She tapped the dagger hilt hidden by the ornate piece of leather hanging off her belt. Intricate flowers and vines were carved into the hide. A gift from Eoin, given to her a lifetime ago. "I know how to look after myself."

And where to stab a man to inflict the most pain and damage.

She didn't think it was possible for his eyes to become any larger, but they did. "Did you know the king is dead?"

"Incapacitated, not dead."

"They say he's dead now." More fidgeting. His nerves were making her horse jittery. "Things are different without a king. People are different."

Elsie took her time tying the rein of her horse to a nearby post, stepping away from the animal, and gently asking the boy, "will you speak plainly with me?"

"I—there are words I'm not supposed to speak."

"Who doesn't allow you to speak them?"

"The Gods."

She pressed her lips together to disguise her smile. "Did they ask you to personally keep their secrets?"

"The High Father..." He cleared his throat. "The High Father has brought the Gods to us."

Ah, so the people of Brilend had finally found their faith. Perhaps that explained his nervous appearance. Some members of the temple believed it was inappropriate for unwed men and women to be within speaking distance of each other unchaperoned. "As I said, I'm looking for my sister. Her name is Irene. Do you know of her?"

"Irene..." he shifted on his feet. "There's Irene the baker's wife."

Wife. Of course, Irene would be a wife. She was only four years younger than Elsie. In her mind, Irene was a child, a fragile girl with big blue eyes, and that golden hair so like Mother's.

"Thank you," Elsie whispered, too afraid to speak louder lest her voice break.

Surely it couldn't be that easy. Surely Irene wasn't waiting down the road, only miles from where Elsie last saw her ten years ago.

"M'lady," the boy murmured, taking the reins of her horse as she untied them and handed them to him. "Don't linger in Brilend."

"Why?" She reached into the pocket of her dress, pulling out double the coins the boy would expect for boarding her and her horse.

"This is too much." He tried to hand it back.

"Extra for your kindness," she explained.

"The Bastards," he hissed, stuffing the coins into his pockets. "Stay away from the Bastards."

He hurried off with her mare before she could ask another question, leading the horse to the back of the barn where the sun hadn't penetrated many of the shadows yet.

Elsie gave her dagger another reassuring pat, trying to shake the vague warning off. It was true what she'd said. Women were not safe in Svalta, nor anywhere in the world, so long as there were men that would commit terrible deeds. That didn't mean she would cower and hide.

Irene was here. *Her sister was here.* No bastard, whoever he may be, was going to keep her from her family.

◆

G REY NEVER STRUCK ELSIE as an unusual color. There were half a dozen grey dresses in her wardrobe. Plain, easy to disguise dust and other stains. On its own, grey clothing was innocuous. When an entire town was clothed in grey, it began to seem suspicious.

Why was *everyone* wearing grey? Why were they staring at her as if she'd grown a second, grotesque head?

Women with grey scarves wrapped tightly about their heads hurried gawking children along as Elsie marched by. Men leaned against alleyways and loitered in front of storefronts, watching her with too much interest for her liking. The squirrely warnings from the boy clung to her, sparking her own nerves and making her wary.

This wasn't the Brilend she remembered. There were dozens and dozens more people than a town this size could house. Were there more homes on the east end of town, tucked in the woods where Elsie's own childhood home stood?

The uniform clothing, hair, and expressions reminded her more of soldiers waiting for orders than it did farmers hurrying to work.

Though, based on the size and cleanliness of the new structures in the square, there were far better opportunities than farming. There was a tailor, a shoemaker, a butcher, and a blacksmith. The scent of fresh baked bread sweetened the air. It should have been lovely.

Instead, Elsie felt unsettled.

Her heart was thundering when she finally found the bakery. It still stood in the center of Brilend, adjacent to the temple, but the building had been expanded. The second story room where the baker and his family used to live was now twice as wide, offering ample living space.

The changes to the bakery were nothing compared to the temple. Elsie's feet skidded on stone as she stopped to gape at the monstrous structure. A narrow bell tower jutted up above the arched doorway, bronze bell on beautiful display. Stained glass gleamed in the rising sun, bearing every color imaginable, depicting scenes with winged men driving swords through the bodies of mangled, demonic depictions.

The contrast between the bright hues and violent imagery was disturbing. The most devout always did like to go on about demons and devilry.

A vast courtyard surrounded the temple with carefully trimmed hedges, lush grass, and a series of statues depicting the five High Gods. There were nearly twenty Gods and Goddesses in the faith, each bearing varying importance and roles in the making of the world. All of them were children of the High Gods, the five creators.

That was the most Elsie could recall from her days at the temple. Her mother dragged them to the ramshackle place for every worship day, forcing them to sit stone still in the hot, dank corner and listen as the ancient High Father prattled on about faith and sacrifice.

That High Father was likely long dead, and the new one had wildly different taste.

Elsie shifted her attention back to the bakery, sucking in a breath for bravery and pushing open the door.

A sweet little bell tinkled as she entered, eliciting a soft feminine voice to call out from somewhere out of sight. Hot air rushed to greet her, along with the delicious scent of bread, sugar, and butter. For all the dark memories in Brilend, this bakery was not one of them. The baker's wife was always kind, measuring extra flour for Elsie without charging her, offering for her to take home bread that was too stale to sell.

They had a son, younger than Elsie but not by much. He wanted to be a knight, she remembered. He was always waving loaves of bread around like a sword and getting swatted for it.

The room was divided by a massive table, along with a display case filled with cooling loaves of bread and pastries. Pale light sliced through the windows, revealing clouds of fine flour dust that danced and shimmered up from wood floors. A woman appeared from a doorway on the other end of the room, clad in a long grey dress that covered her all the way to her throat. It hung loosely over her gravid belly.

Elsie couldn't help the small smile that formed on her lips. It wasn't often that she saw a woman with child—not after Gannon sent all the servants away from the Black Estate—and it was even less often that she saw children.

Her gaze lifted to the matching grey scarf wrapped snuggly over the woman's head, shielding everything but her plump face. This was the second woman she'd seen wearing one of those scarves. What was the purpose? The weather wasn't nearly cold enough.

It was only after a moment of study that Elsie startled with recognition. Pregnancy and age had changed her features, but the freckles and chicory blue eyes were unchanging.

"Irene?" Elsie nearly shrieked, hurrying across the space, and leaning over a table filled with loaves of bread to grasp her sister's hand. "Gods, it really is you!"

She was still here, right here where Elsie left her.

"Elsie?" Irene blinked, snatching her hand back, mouth agape. "What—what are you doing here?"

"I came home," Elsie whispered tremulously.

"Why?" she questioned, staring as if Elsie was some apparition that wanted to steal her soul.

"For you," she reached her hand out again, desperate to touch her sister, to know that she was truly here. "For mother. I came to find you."

"Find us?" Irene shook her head, arching away from Elsie's touch. "We weren't lost. We haven't gone anywhere."

It was only fair for Irene to be angry with her, Elsie admitted. Her greatest regret in this life was leaving Brilend and not taking her sister with her. She glanced at Irene's full belly and wondered what kind of life she'd led with Elsie gone. Had she married young? Did she have more children? Where was her husband?

All questions she could ask once she'd made her amends.

"You're right. It was me who left. Who abandoned you. I should have taken you with me, Irene. I didn't, and I will carry that regret to my grave." She clenched her fists, holding them at her sides to give her sister space. "But I've come home to make amends."

"Make amends?" Irene placed a palm over her heart. "You can't *amend* what you did!"

"I know," she murmured, "I know. I came to offer more than an apology. I came to give you and mother the life you deserve."

Irene's round face twisted with offense. "*Give us the life we deserve?*" She gestured at Elsie's dress. "Did you find yourself a wealthy husband and now you feel guilty for how you left us? Without coin, without protection. Is he still alive, or did you kill him too?"

Elsie stumbled back, physically wounded by her sister's words. "Without protection? *I* protected you. From *him*." And never once had she done it with the intention of holding it over her sister. Elsie would have thrown her body in front of Irene's a hundred times because that was what she was meant to do. As the elder sister, *she* was the protection. Not the man that bloodied his fists with his own family's flesh.

"And what about the letters I sent? The coin? Were you so destitute even after I provided for you?" She sounded bitter and superior, and she hated it, but Elsie couldn't swallow the words back even if she wanted to. She'd given up her life here to save her sister, and this was not the welcome she expected.

Perhaps it was the welcome she deserved.

Irene's anger faltered. "What letters?"

"The letters I sent every season. I knew mother wouldn't be able to read them, but at least the coin would keep you fed," Elsie explained. The courier she paid to deliver them for her cost more than what she put in the envelopes. She was afraid that a man of lesser value would simply steal the contents and disappear without a word.

"There were no letters," Irene hissed. "There was no coin. There was no one to provide for us except Mother, and Gods forgive her for what she did to put food on the table."

That wasn't possible. For ten years Elsie had sent more than half her earnings home. It was all she could do from so far away.

"I—I don't understand." The courier promised they were delivered, her only assurance that Mother and Irene were alive.

"What is there to misunderstand? You *killed my father*, and now you dare to show your face again? To walk in here as if you're some savior!" Irene was shouting, drawing a man from the back doorway. His face was white with flour, his apron caked with flecks of dried dough. The hand he placed on Irene's shoulder was familiar. Intimate.

This must be her husband.

The baker's son. Hamish, was it? Henry? Elsie couldn't remember anymore. She wasn't going to find out.

"What's going on here, Irene?"

Irene didn't have the chance to answer. The bell above the door jingled. Elsie didn't look at the newcomer. Every person in Brilend was a potential thief, stealing the money meant for her mother and Irene, and she wanted nothing to do with them until they were proven innocent.

Whoever it was, both Irene and her husband recognized them. Their faces hardened, gazes dropping to the bread table as her husband called out, "Gods be with you, brothers. How may we serve you today?"

Curiosity got the better of Elsie, twisting her head to stare at the two men crowding the entry to the bakery. Unsurprisingly, they were cloaked in grey, though their fabric seemed cleaner and neater than what Irene was wearing. Something softer and more luxurious than wool. Their brown hair too was identical in style, close cropped and neatly combed to the side, making them difficult to tell apart.

Or perhaps it was difficult because their faces *were* the same, right down to the arched ridge of their noses. Twins, or at the very least, brothers.

"Gods be with you," the men echoed in unison. They spoke like holy brothers, but they looked like ruffians. What kind of religious nonsense was going on in this town?

One of them stepped forward too eagerly for Elsie's liking. "We're just here to give a proper welcome to travelers."

Elsie turned back to Irene in time to see her visibly swallow. Welcoming a traveler wasn't a good thing, apparently.

"I've had a warm enough welcome already, thank you," Elsie answered coldly.

"Not yet, you haven't," one spoke. "You have to speak with our father."

"The High Father," the other added. "Our High Father welcomes every man, woman, and child that walks within the borders of Brilend. It is his duty to the Gods and standing before him is an honor."

"I've no interest in stroking a man's ego this morning, High Father or not."

The brothers approached in unison. Elsie's fingers twitched toward her dagger. She stayed her hand at the last moment, deciding now was not the time for a confrontation. Not with Irene pregnant and unarmed. Not in a confined space with two opponents that outweighed her. Eoin taught her to use her size to her advantage—escaping as soon as she saw an opening—and to avoid a fight in tight spaces. She would never have the upper hand against a man, so she would need to use her head.

Right now, her head was telling her this was a losing battle. Better to appease these men and find her chance for escape when she was out in the open.

Only, she wasn't expecting them to touch her. Elsie kicked out when strong hands wrapped around her upper arms. It was an instinct, one born of years of mistreatment, and she wasn't ashamed when her foot connected with a shin and sent one man stumbling back. Again, she wanted to reach for her dagger and forced herself not to think of it. They didn't need to know she was armed.

"Don't fight them, Elsie," Irene murmured pleadingly. Her husband shook his head, urging Irene not to intervene.

For the first time, Elsie wondered exactly what she'd walked into when she came down the hill this morning. Not all was as it seemed in this town.

She wrenched from the second man's hold, stepping as far back as she could out of their reach. Elsie glanced at her sister, at her round belly and the bewilderment on her face. She had done the unthinkable to protect her sister once. Giving audience to an overzealous High Father and his band of ruffians was nothing compared to that.

"I've removed a man's hand for less," Elsie warned, chin raised haughtily. "Take me to your High Father so I can inform him how unwelcome his welcoming party has made me feel."

They escorted Elsie outside with matching sneers, walking close enough to make sweat bead between her shoulders. The hair on the back of her neck tingled and internally she was screaming. This was wrong. It was all very wrong. She was still reeling from her conversation with Irene, and she felt too off kilter for whatever madness she was approaching.

As her welcoming party led her through the square, past the temple and toward a grand home she hadn't noticed before, Elsie felt her unease shift to fear. The strange air she'd detected among the people and the town itself was radiating from these men like a stink from a dog and she knew, deep down in that knowing place, that there was something insidious at play.

For the first time since leaving the Black Estate, Elsie had to admit that she was in over her head.

CHAPTER 11

I T WAS TRUE THAT high fathers didn't always represent the modest and laborious lifestyle they preached. Elsie had passed more than one holy man wearing expensive silks and sparkling gems during her rare outings to the capitol with Edgar. Temples received generous donations, even from those that didn't have the coin to afford it. A cruel scheme that played on the devotion of righteous people and stole from the needy.

She expected nothing less from the slippery men that lived in the Dunhill capitol. A city like that bred wickedness. Many high fathers took the title simply to receive free coin in exchange for babbling nonsense during the worship hours once a week.

After leaving the bakery, Elsie was dragged to a house seated at the back corner of the temple courtyard. Delicately trimmed hedges and more stone statues depicting the five High Gods lined the path leading to the home. It wasn't a manor, necessarily, but it made the neighboring houses appear cramped and plain.

Smaller, more subtle stained glass windows decorated the bottom floor. The brick walls were painted a rich green, and the door was made from thick cedar, polished to a shine. The roof too was clean and new, and a narrow balcony jutted out from the second floor.

When she entered Elsie wasn't surprised to find decor that exceeded the craftmanship found in Brilend. People here built their homes and the furniture within to be practical. Wooden bedframes and chairs meant to withstand time. There were no loose cushions and soft velvet lounges. No fine beading and elegant stitching decorating the sofas in the sitting room.

No one even had sitting rooms.

This passive display of wealth wasn't why Elsie judged the new High Father. A man was allowed to enjoy his wealth if he'd rightly earned it. She had no grievance with the Black family and their enormous estate. What bothered her was the way the temple spoke ill of the rich, demanding men and women give up their income to pay tribute to the Gods, while their High Father enjoyed luxury.

What bothered her was an entire village cloaked in grey while their High Father lived in a sparkling palace of color.

A testament to the egos among holy men, as clearly, they were the ones benefitting from such tributes. Elsie had seen a man of true divinity and this High Father, whoever he was, could not match him.

The two men that delivered Elsie stood like sentinels at the front door, watching her pace around the seating room as if she was a venomous snake that might slither over and bite them. She was feeling venomous after being waylaid and held captive, and she intended to make it known.

First, she needed to understand why she was here. Second, she needed to know why this High Father had such a stranglehold over the people in Brilend. Third and finally, she needed to free herself from his scrutiny so she could convince her sister to come back to the Black Estate with her immediately. Her husband could come too if Irene wanted to keep him.

Elsie would forget making a home here. Whatever this place had become, it certainly didn't feel like home. Elsie wanted no part in religious drivel.

Footsteps tapped quietly down a hallway, just out of sight. Elsie whipped around, stationing herself away from the door, close to the hearth. She'd seen a fire poker on the stand and would use it if need be. Holy man or not, Elsie would not be held prisoner.

Whatever battle plans she was devising tumbled from her mind and disintegrated like ash when a figure shuffled through the open door, eyes fixed anywhere but on her. When they finally forced themselves to meet Elsie, gazes clashing, she almost couldn't see through her own tears.

"Mother," she gasped.

"Elsie," her mother answered with biting coolness.

Her hair, once pale and lovely and long, was mostly covered by a dull grey scarf. The color was almost a perfect match for the few thin strands on display, accented by shocks of white at her temples. The absence of her flowing curls, along with the deep lines carved around her mouth, made her already dark expression severe. Bitter and unkind, as the years had likely been to her.

Neither of them moved to embrace the other. Elsie was suddenly paralyzed, too terrified of reaching for her mother and being rejected. There was no warmth in her eyes. As a girl Elsie had always thought of them like twin cornflowers, glowing brightly even during the longest winters. She wasn't sure if they'd lost their luster before or after Father's death.

"Why have you returned here?"

Elsie should have expected this reception after her encounter with Irene. Somehow, she hadn't. She thought surely there was some confusion and Mother would clear everything up.

"I came home to look after you, but it seems someone else beat me to it."

"You came to look after us? *You?*"

Elsie steeled herself, not giving an inch as her mother took a menacing step forward. "I was rather good at it as a child, or don't you remember?"

Mother's laugh was brittle, circling past Elsie and twisting to stare at a stained glass sword. Only a red lounge separated them and yet, they were worlds apart. "How could I forget? How could I ever forget what you did to us?"

Her mouth flew open. "You mean how I liberated you? Sent you pouches filled with more coin than you've seen in your life? Forgive my own lapse in memory, Mother, but what have I done to earn such hostility?"

Mother said nothing, so Elsie continued, feeling a childish sort of desperation take hold of her. After all this time she still wanted her mother to recognize her, to dote on her, to comfort her.

"I never meant to stay away for so long, Mother. I wanted to come back for you. Both of you. I found a good life for myself away from here, but I was afraid my presence would become complicated. Put you at risk." Elsie stepped around the lounge, approaching slowly. "You did receive my letters, didn't you?"

"Yes, we received your letters. I burned every one of them."

Elsie stared in absolute disbelief. This was the woman that bore her into the world. The woman that cradled her as she cried. Suddenly, every one of those memories was tainted. She recalled the blank expression on her mother's face as she murmured a lullaby or repeated soothing words. They were meant to comfort and yet, there wasn't any true feeling behind them, was there?

She'd blamed that distance on Father, on the horrible things he expected of mother, but now Elsie didn't know. Was it him or had she always been this empty person?

The night her father died, mother was frantic, sending Elsie out of the house with nothing but her bloody dress and a scarf to cover herself. She always believed it was fear that drove Mother to chase her away. Fear for her eldest daughter and what would become of her if she were discovered to be a murderer. Recalling the memory now, Elsie could just as easily see vitriol in place of terror.

Perhaps motherly instinct was the only barrier that kept her from snatching the knife out of Father's chest and plunging it into Elsie's.

"And the coin I sent with them? Did you burn that too?" Elsie spat, refusing to be the monster in this nightmare. If Father stood before her now, she would kill him all over again. That wicked man deserved death. She would never feel remorse for defending her own honor when no one else would. "What fine fabric you're wearing, mother. And that necklace, where did it come from?"

Elsie stumbled back as her mother's palm connected with her cheek.

"You disgusting, vile—" Mother raised her hand again and Elsie braced to block the blow that never came. Instead, Mother lowered her hand, staring at it strangely, before placing it onto her shoulder and closing her eyes. She hummed softly to herself and whispered, "you were always a snake. Even in my womb, I could feel the darkness in you. A serpent suckling at the breast. I should have ended you then, before you could take him from me. I loved him more than you will ever dream of being loved and you took him from me.

"Gods forgive me for giving life to a murderer. A killer. Gods forgive me." Her eyes remained tightly shut as she shuddered and mumbled to herself. Half of the words she spoke were nonsensical, throaty gibberish.

Elsie no longer had tears for the pain she was experiencing. She was too shocked to cry. Too confounded by the words her mother—her own mother—hurled at her. This woman was mad. She'd been too young to see it, or perhaps too naïve, but Mother was as cruel and mad as Father.

As if on cue, a second figure stepped into the room, answering the question that had been lingering at the edge of Elsie's mind. What was Mother doing in the home of the High Father?

The newcomer examined her with chilling blue eyes. Elsie didn't flinch, instead raising her chin and making her own inspection obvious. A man was only a man. She'd faced off with a dragon and walked away unscathed.

At first glance, the High Father of Brilend was void of obvious greed. Grey robes draped down his body, covering everything but the tip of his boot and the sinking skin on his face. If Elsie had been another poor farmer, she would never have noticed the intricate stitching on the soft young leather of his shoes. She might have overlooked the chain around his neck, mistaking it for copper rather than gold.

But Elsie had spent the last ten years carefully maintaining the fine wardrobe left behind by the late Baron and Baroness Black and she was quite familiar with the craftsmanship of these items. His hands too were not the hands of a working man. Though a holy man wasn't expected to work the way a farmer would, he was still responsible for his own home. Chopping wood, tending animals, and keeping a garden left their mark in the roughness of a man's palms. Even she had callouses from the menial tasks of life.

Why then, were this man's hands so clean? Soft and plump like a child's, bearing no marks except for several circles of pale skin where rings once sat. His nails were clean and blunt.

Perhaps she was looking for evidence of something sinister that wasn't there.

Or perhaps after all these years she still had a sense for a man that couldn't be trusted. A man that was capable of secret cruelty.

His rigid posture was too practiced for a dour high priest in a town on the outskirts of Dunhill. He reminded her of the pouty lords and courtly men that came calling to the Black Estate after Baron Black died. They would fuss and drone on about tragedy, hoping to gain favor with Gannon and fool the new young baron into giving up some of the sizeable estate he'd only recently inherited.

The years on his face were obvious, and yet he had that tender look to him that most lords did. A face that hadn't seen the elements. A face that knew nothing of suffering, except that which was inflicted by his own hand.

Elsie glanced from the shining surface of his nearly bald head to his wobbling chin and asked, "High Father, to what do I owe this displeasure? Do you often send ruffians to kidnap travelers for you?"

The High Father ignored her question, coming up behind Mother and placing a gentle hand atop hers. Her fingers were digging so deeply into her skin that she was wincing. When the High Father touched her, he murmured some kind of prayer, and Mother dropped from her rabid trance, turning to him with a delighted smile.

"Thank you, sire."

"Finish your prayers in private. I will handle this."

Mother placed a soft kiss on the High Father's cheek, then another on his left hand. She curtsied low to him before leaving the room without a second glance at her estranged daughter.

The High Father paced around the lounge, giving his back to Elsie without a care. "You've made quite a stir with your arrival."

"As have you," she replied. "I've never met a High Father that has soldiers at his beck and call."

"They are not my soldiers. They are the Soldiers of the Gods. It is their divine right to take up arms in the name of our creators."

Elsie stomped around to the fireplace, close enough that she could smell the thick stench of incense wafting from his robes. "Who are you taking up arms against? Women that dare ride alone on the road?"

The High Father smiled for the first time, indulgently as if she were a clueless girl. "We are taking up arms against the wicked. Wickedness can hide in the most unexpected places, as you well know."

"Why am I here?"

"That is precisely the question I brought you here to answer."

Elsie crossed her arms, her fingers tapping lightly against the hidden hilt of her dagger. A comforting reminder. "Why is my mother in your home?"

"Sara is my wife."

She glanced down at the floor so he wouldn't see her surprise. Given the life that Mother led before Father's death, Elsie was surprised a High Father would even look at her. It wasn't fair for a woman to be judged for such actions, especially if they were committed under duress, but that was the way of this world.

The temple preached purity. A woman was meant to keep her body and soul clean. Did the High Father know of Mother's indiscretions, or was that yet another lie?

"Then you must know the pain she endured at the hands of my father."

"Indeed," he answered gravely. "I know *every* dark and wicked act that has been committed in this town. That is why I began my work here. Wickedness must be weeded out from every tiny root of the tree if we are to bring a new era of divinity to Dunhill."

There was an accusation woven into those words. Mother *had* told him everything. Or at the very least, what Elsie had done.

"Now I will ask again, why are you in Brilend, child?"

"I've come to look after my family."

"After all this time."

Elsie paced in front of him, snapping her fingers as she pointed at his boots. "You can stop the holy act, High Father. I know your kind. That is fine leather you're wearing. And your accent, isn't it a bit refined for a town as small as this one?"

"My origins are not a secret." He chuckled, laughter that didn't reach his glacial eyes. "For decades I served in a court of criminals. I saw unspeakable lust and greed. Warmongering monsters that would send children to battlefields over petty disputes."

"Aye, I've met those monsters. I've seen the scars they leave on the skin of their own daughters." She narrowed her eyes. "Am I to believe you aren't one of them? A pious, holy man embedded in a corrupt court?"

"I was the very worst of them. I called for violence. I raised my cup at the call for war." He bared yellowing teeth at her. "Then the Gods sent a message from the heavens and rained dragon fire down on all of us and I saw the error of my ways." He tugged the sleeve of his robe up, revealing the marbled, pink burn scar.

So, he was there when Gannon scorched the king. Elsie almost laughed at the idea that Gannon was Gods sent to punish the Dunhill court.

Then again, *drakonmein* were believed to be favored by the Gods. Descended from a man that did their bidding and earned a glorious gift: the ability to shapeshift and carry dragon fire within them. More than once she'd heard Eoin and Gannon insist that what they were was not a gift but a curse. They were bound to a life of secrecy, violence, and, without their intended mate, loneliness.

A loneliness that drove some to slip into centuries-long slumber, and sent others scouring the countryside, devouring livestock, and burning anything that kept them from the woman fated for them.

"The Beast of the Blackwood made you seek forgiveness?" Gannon would get a chuckle out of that. "Now you've given up your wicked ways to become a High Father. Very noble of you. Now, if you'll excuse me, High Father, I have amends to make with my sister."

An icy silence answered her. Elsie shrugged away his judgmental gaze and stepped toward the door, only to be blocked by the men standing before it.

"This country is cursed."

She turned with an arched brow. "Yes, it's very terrible. There are men all over the place that believe they can and should be telling me what to do and how to do it."

His lips twitched into a reptilian smile, sending goosebumps up her arms. "Brilend is only the beginning. Dunhill is filled to the brim with depravity. It is my duty to the Gods to cull the weeds from this beautiful garden they've given us."

Ice pooled in her legs. *Culling* was never a good word when it came from religious powers. Elsie wasn't well educated—she never took to the studies Eoin arranged for her—but she knew what happened the last time there were High Fathers babbling about culling wickedness.

Women burned. *Witches*, as they were accused of being. Not only women but whole families, towns, half of Svalta. It was a dark time, one that took centuries for the continent to come back from. There were some regions in Dunhill that didn't have a single woman left to bear children. Blood lines vanished from history, entire generations withered away without families to care for them in their old age.

"Speak plainly, High Father. What is it you want from me?"

The door flew open, smacking one of the brothers standing sentinel. He turned with well-trained swiftness, hand on the hilt of his sword only to stay that hand as he recognized the intruder.

Irene stood pale and breathless in the doorway, clutching her belly, and leaning heavily on the wood frame. "High Father," she gasped. "An audience with you. Please."

Elsie hurried around the overstuffed furniture, elbowing both brothers out of the way and taking her sister under the arms. Irene accepted the help without protest, allowing Elsie to guide her to the nearest lounge and lower her gently.

"How long before the baby comes?" Elsie asked with urgency.

"Not for..." Irene paused to catch her breath. "Not for another month, at least." She stared up at Elsie, obviously conflicted. "I'm only winded."

Elsie palmed her sister's round belly. She'd never delivered a child, nor seen one born, but she'd helped Edgar when the mares were laboring and she knew the signs. There was no tightening in her belly, and the baby seemed to be sitting beneath her ribs rather than low in her hips.

A tiny foot rocketed into Elsie's hand and she froze. The first kick was followed by a series of them, gentle little thumps that bounced against the taught skin on Irene's belly.

The prickling in her eyes worsened.

"He likes you," Irene whispered sadly.

"Irene," the High Father interrupted sharply. "What is the meaning of this? You are not meant to be about town by yourself."

His concern for Irene was obvious, and Elsie was momentarily surprised. Then she saw the lines around her sister's mouth, the way her eyes rounded, her body tensing with his presence, and Elsie felt ill.

How long had this High Father been in Brilend, and just how much damage had he already done?

"Forgive me, High Father." Irene ducked her eyes, distancing herself from Elsie. "My husband cannot close the bakery and I had to speak with you urgently."

Suspicion soured his already tart expression. "What could be so urgent—"

"Send her away!" Irene interrupted. "Send my sister back to where she came from."

Elsie sputtered a wordless objection. She'd only arrived this morning. Whether Mother wanted her here or not, she wasn't leaving without Irene. Eventually her sister would see the lies she was fed for what they were and forgive Elsie. She had to.

Elsie had nowhere else to go. She couldn't return to the Black Estate alone, without family, without anyone that truly loved her.

"Your sister is—"

"A killer!" Irene blurted, again interrupting the High Father, and risking his ire. "I am fatherless because of her."

"You are not fatherless," the High Father argued. "I am your father."

Irene visibly shuddered. "I am wed now. My husband provides for me. But when I was a girl, I needed him, and it is because of my sister that he is gone."

"I know, my child," he crouched, prying her hand from her belly to squeeze it. Irene went so still that Elsie wasn't sure she was breathing. "That is why the Gods want to see her punished."

The Gods wanted to see her punished. Of course, it was their desire and not his.

"The midwife said that I am too weary. The babe could come early."

Elsie bit her tongue hard enough to draw blood, willing her errant words to stay in her throat. She needed to understand this, to know what danger her sister was in that she hadn't seen before.

The High Father studied Irene for too long, his eyes tracing the lines of her face in a manner that was lacking fatherly intent. "I cannot defy the Gods."

Irene righted herself, taking both the High Father's hands in hers and bearing down on him with her gaze. "The threads that bind her life to this world are fraying. Do not let her dark soul linger here and taint the birth of this child."

"That is exactly why she must be cleansed. The Gods bid me to redeem the darkest of us."

"I beg your favor this once, High Father, and I will never beg for more," Irene was on the brink of tears. "My sister does not deserve redemption. Banish her from this place."

Mother chose that moment to reappear, rearing her head back and demanding, "get away from my daughter, you snake!"

Bodies shuffled about the room, Irene awkwardly rising to meet Mother in the entryway. The two brothers at the door filled the gap between Irene and the High Father, looming over Elsie where she was still perched on the lounge. The High Father stood on rickety knees, glaring down at Elsie with obvious disappointment.

"Very well," he finally said. "You have until sundown to be gone from this place. I do not defy the Gods lightly. You will not be shown mercy a second time."

Mother spluttered a slew of questions. Elsie didn't hear them.

"Father, you can't just—" one of the brothers began.

"That's High Father to you, Bastard!" Mother interrupted with a snarl.

Stay away from the bastards. Elsie understood the farm boy's warning far too late.

These brothers were the High Father's bastards, which would explain why they held high esteem in town but were treated no different from the help in this home.

"The Gods bid women be silent pillars of their home, Sara," the High Father chided calmly. "Your temper is a sign that your time in the temple has come."

Mother bowed her head solemnly. "Gods forgive me."

The High Father drew his attention back to Elsie. "Seek redemption, beg mercy of the Gods, or suffer the same fate as the one you forced onto your father a thousand times over. I will see no more harm done to my family because of you."

Mother accented his preaching with a terse command of her own. "Go! Be gone, and do not return here."

For once, Elsie did as she was told, whirling from the sitting room, elbowing the Bastards in her haste to escape. She didn't dare glance over her shoulder at Irene and Mother, didn't dare allow a single tear to fall as the High Father and his sons keenly watched her retreat.

They would follow her, no doubt. Already Elsie could feel the prickle of eyes on her, the hushed voices of townsfolk wondering over her. It wouldn't be hard for them to find her so long as she was in Brilend.

What would they do to her when they caught her?

The High Father's threats weren't obvious, or even clear. He was raising an army but for what purpose? To return women to being silent servants in their homes? To make all of Dunhill adopt grey as the most fashionable color?

It wasn't Elsie's concern. Irene and Mother would not offer her forgiveness in this lifetime. They would not let her make amends. Why should Elsie care about what troubles befell them?

Elsie should leave. Immediately, while her horse still had a chance of outrunning anyone that might pursue. She knew that was the wisest choice and yet, her feet carried her in the opposite direction of the barn where she'd stashed her belongings, following the road east until the new, crisp buildings gave way to trees and overgrown fields.

Soon the neatly cobbled road broke away, leaving her to walk over bumpy, hardened dirt. Dirt collected at the hem of her dress, dulling the lovely color. Elsie was breathing too rapidly, her legs breaking into a run.

Trees blurred around her, dancing green shapes in the corners of her vision. The scuff and scrape of her feet was loud, and she focused on it desperately, trying to drown out the sound of her roiling thoughts. She stopped abruptly when she saw the first quivering remains of a home.

It belonged to a neighbor once, a widower with only one daughter and little else to his name. The renewal efforts in the town hadn't reached this far, and families like his were forgotten.

Vines crept over decaying wood, climbing in and out of broken windows. Charred earth and bits of charcoal were the sole indicator that there had ever been homes on some plots.

What happened here?

Anguish climbed up her belly to snatch at her chest, making her lungs feel tight. Her family home was at the end of the road, the last home in the village, hidden away so no one had to see the shame Father brought on all of them.

Hidden away so the wicked men that associated with him could gamble and drink and commit acts of cruelty without anyone to witness them.

Elsie stumbled forward, hand over her mouth. The house still stood, which was better than the neighboring homes.

Each pane in every window was shattered, scattering splinters of glass across the soft ground. The door was ajar, and Elsie couldn't help imagining the house was screaming. Blood rushed through her ears, blocking out the sweet, peaceful noises of the forest. She took one step forward and stopped. Paralyzed.

What would she find in there?

Her mind was quick to answer, picturing the greying bones of her Father splayed across the floor. Or worse, her father still alive, waiting for her, knife at the ready.

Elsie curled her hands into fists and forced another step. Another and another before she was pushing the door open, wincing as it groaned. She kept her feet light on the decaying floors, worried the wrong move would send her tumbling beneath the house.

Some of the nerves wrapped tightly in her chest began to relax. The furniture was gone. No tables or chairs, not even a bedframe in the corner that had once served as a bedroom for Elsie and her sister.

It was a relief not to look at it and remember huddling under it with Irene in her arms.

No skeletons.

Tension strung her tight as she stepped into the kitchen. Dust and forest detritus littered the floors, but even that couldn't hide the dark circle marring the wood. Bile climbed up her throat and she coughed, determined not to lose her stomach. She'd lost enough because of that man.

But standing here where it happened, the memories were suddenly harder to contain. They leapt at her, wrapping her in their spindly arms and dragging her backwards until she was barely more than a girl, standing in this very spot.

Onions burned her eyes, still coating the knife in her hand. Father was looming over her, his voice booming. Elsie didn't flinch, instead pressing her shoulders back and facing him. Mother might cower to him, might let him defile her, but Elsie refused to do the same.

A hand wrapped around her throat as he demanded, "you will do what needs to be done, ungrateful wretch."

Until that moment, she hadn't realized how impenetrable a man's flesh and bones were. Her knife was dull as she jammed it at his ribs and the force it took to stab through snapped something in her wrist. With a roar the hand on her throat tightened. His face disappeared down a black tunnel as she gasped for air that would never come, sinking further and further into darkness. Even so, she thrust the knife, pushing it as deep as possible, aiming for his heart.

Glass smashed into her face, shattering over her head, and momentarily stealing her consciousness. Blood poured down her cheek, into her eye, trickling into her mouth.

Suddenly Elsie could breathe again. Father hit the floor with a thud, moaning, mumbling, panting.

Then nothing. No sound. *Nothing*.

Standing over his body as the life bled from him, Elsie felt no remorse. She couldn't remember when she stopped loving her father, but she knew the moment he walked into that kitchen, intending to use her as he used Mother, that she hated him. She would always hate him.

Except for that small part of her that couldn't. The little girl that recalled him smiling at her, picking up her tiny body and spinning her until she was too dizzy to plant her feet back on the ground.

"A son for me!" He smiled widely. "Finally, your mother grows a son to carry my legacy."

Even then he was bleary. Happy, but obviously more than a drink in. He drank less during those nine months, only because he didn't want to miss news of the birth of his son.

Then Irene was born a girl, and he was never clear headed again.

Father could blame his behavior on Mother's failed fertility or her inability to give him a son but ultimately, it was his own evil that drove him. Whatever madness made him hunger for power over those lesser than him.

No, not lesser. Elsie was never less than him. *Smaller*. Helpless. Too young to know how to fend for herself.

Elsie replayed her final memory of him over and over, watching from a new angle and wondering if she really was the villain in this story. Was killing Father the wrong choice?

She could have run away. Taken Irene and vanished in the night. But Irene was only twelve and Elsie had no way to provide for them.

And what about Mother? Mother who hated her very being, who wished that she smothered Elsie in the cradle.

It hurt. It hurt so badly that Elsie dropped to the floor, kneeling in her Father's dried blood. Secretly, during the loneliest nights at the Black Estate, she dreamed of returning home. Of holding her sister in her arms, of being embraced by her mother again.

Secretly, she would imagine Eoin coming with her. Introducing him as her husband. Bringing Irene and Mother back to live at the Black Estate.

Yet during all those years she never returned, and this was why.

Not because Elsie feared punishment for Father's death, but because in her heart of hearts, she knew the truth. No matter her motivation for killing Father, it tainted her. Made her untouchable for the likes of Mother and Irene. For a man like Eoin Black. Elsie sacrificed herself for them and they hated her.

Or had she? Was killing father a sacrifice made out of love, or a selfish act of self-preservation?

"You will do what needs to be done, ungrateful wretch—or will your sister have to hold this family up for you?"

Elsie could almost feel the handle of the knife solid in her hands. She was a lot of things. Outspoken, crass, uncultured, but she was not selfish.

She wasn't.

And Irene knew she wasn't too.

Brilend wasn't a quiet farming village anymore, and Dunhill wasn't a stable country with a wealthy king. From the isolation of the Black Estate the chaos in Dunhill seemed distant, inconsequential. For everyone outside the shelter of the Blackwood, the world was suddenly more treacherous.

Her sister was once again in the clutches of evil men. Elsie could smell it on them, could feel it in the air that curled around them. Perhaps Irene couldn't forgive Elsie for what she did to their father, but she didn't rush into the High Father's home because she was so desperate to see Elsie gone.

Elsie was in danger, and Irene protected her, as sisters do.

Now, it was time for Elsie to do the same.

CHAPTER 12

ELSIE

NOISE CAME WITH THE return of her composure. Indistinct, a drone in the distance, easily drowned out by the blood pumping in her ears. Elsie was calm now, relatively so, and curiosity had her stepping off groaning wood planks into overgrown grass.

No one was living in old Brilend, so why did she smell fire? The murmur of sound grew louder as she followed the visible wisps of smoke that danced through the sunbeams breaking the canopy of nearby trees.

There was a thicket between her family land and the neighboring property. Old oaks twisting and reaching around each other for the best light. Elsie used to bring Irene to play here when Mother was *occupied*. In the summer they would collect wild raspberries—a delicious treat for children whose bellies were almost never full.

Irene nearly broke her leg falling from the branch of a leaning snag once. Even at only six years old she had done her best to disguise the limp, not wanting to provoke Father's ire because of her carelessness.

She was protecting Elsie then, too. For all his faults, Father never raised a hand to Irene. It was always Elsie that was to blame.

That reminder fueled her determination, sending her tiptoeing to identify the hum of activity coming from the neighboring pasture. No animals were raised here anymore. Their presence would be obvious. So, who was occupying the old homestead?

The danger in Brilend was not immediately evident, invisible to the naked eye. Perhaps whatever lay on the other side of this thicket would shed light on the secrets the High Father and his mercenaries were keeping.

Elsie swallowed down her breath when she cleared the last line of trees. She quickly retreated into the shadows, crouching beneath a holly bush, and craning her neck to observe.

It was hard to understand the activity at first glance. There were mountains of crates blocking her view, stacked in high towers as if to build a makeshift wall. If she angled herself just so Elsie could see beyond them, to where dozens of tents were erected in the trampled field. Cook fires burned between tents, surrounded by dozens of grey-garbed men.

A startled panic spread through her as her eyes whipped from one detail to the next. Supply crates, tents, weapons, horses.

This was an army encampment, except these were not Dunhill soldiers.

Soldiers of the Gods. The High Father was speaking literally when he told her there were men dedicating themselves to fight for their faith. He truly had an army at his call.

She shifted as far over as she dared, finding the center of camp where the largest tent stood. It was tall and round, opening wide for men to pass in and out. Standing at the entrance, surrounded by three large, imposing men, was one of the Bastards.

Elsie thought finding this camp would be illuminating. On the contrary, it only birthed a thousand more questions. Was the High Father planning a coup? Or was this a war on not only the king, but all of Dunhill?

A war for the Gods.

History had a terrible habit of repeating itself, and if the High Father had as many followers as it appeared, the outcome of his war would be devastating.

The sensation of being watched sent goosebumps crawling up her spine. Elsie expected that the Bastards would follow her, even if she left Brilend. What she hadn't expected was that they had an entire army ready to hunt her down.

Was her presence so disturbing to their peace that they had to pursue her as a fugitive?

Well, if her role in Father's death was common knowledge, then she supposed she was a fugitive. Elsie needed to leave—*now*.

However she planned to get Irene out of Brilend and back to the Black Estate, she couldn't do it if they discovered her. Father's home would be the first place to look. It was foolish to come here.

Elsie backpedaled as quickly and quietly as she dared, keeping her eyes locked on the encampment until it was hidden through the leaves. She was a heartbeat from turning to sprint back the way she'd come when her back rebounded off a hard surface.

Not a tree trunk. The trunk of a man.

A huge man, whose hand came down over her mouth before she could inhale. An arm locked around her middle, dragging her backward through the trees.

Elsie thrashed, gnashing her teeth beneath his palm, sending her elbow behind her. None of her hits impacted his movement, or even drew a pained breath from him.

She was about to reach for her dagger when a deep, familiar voice vibrated at her temple. "Don't fight me."

The arm around her slackened and Elsie saw her chance. She whirled, fists raised, hands pummeling the beast that towered over her.

"What is the meaning of this, Eoin Black!"

"Shhh," Eoin hushed, catching her angry fists, and hauling her backwards. "Not another word."

His eyes were like black steel, deadly serious, and she knew he was right. This was not the time to air her many grievances with him. They made it halfway to Elsie's old home when Eoin suddenly dropped to the ground, yanking her with him. His body settled over hers, hips pressing against the backs of her thighs.

Thunder rattled her veins as her pulse quickened. Breathing was impossible, and Elsie didn't know if she was compressing her own lungs because of fear or thrill. Curse Eoin for his muscled stomach and the way it excited her nerves. There were more important issues at hand than the weight of him atop her and the way she craved it.

But Elsie was struggling to remember what those issues were.

Eoin was a sorcerer, enchanting her with his mere presence. The sound of his breath at her ear could bring her to ecstasy. His fingertips burrowing into her side were the greatest pleasure she'd ever known.

She wasn't even cognizant enough to chastise herself for being pathetic.

Eventually voices broke through the storm of her heartbeat, echoing from the ruined building she'd huddled in only ten minutes earlier. Feet crunched over leaves as two soldiers followed her path through the thicket. They paused with their backs to Eoin and Elsie, staring out at the encampment just as Elsie had.

One pivot was all it would take for them to be discovered. The forest floor was loamy and free of detritus as last year's leaves decayed into soil. A sparse collection of briar and holly wasn't enough to hide them from keen eyes.

Perhaps the Gods were not on the side of their soldiers, because these men did not have keen eyes. They argued for half a minute, debating whether to report back to the Bastards or continue their search.

Eoin quivered above her, a strange rattling in his chest. When Elsie risked a glance away from her pursuers, she saw droplets collecting across Eoin's forehead, plastering his black curls to the skin. Radiant rays of orange sunset exploded from his irises, and as he met her gaze, Elsie saw the unnatural gleam of reptilian eyes.

Hello, dragon. She didn't dare speak it aloud and still she could almost hear the dragon rumbling response, his movement reverberating through Eoin as if he was trapped in the hollow of Eoin's chest.

The last time Elsie had seen Eoin's dragon was nearly a decade ago. Despite his size, he was a gentle creature, carefully stepping around her as he explored.

The fury radiating from Eoin now did not feel gentle.

Two sets of feet barely disappeared between the trees before Eoin moved, flipping her onto her back. His thick hands shackled her wrists, trapping them over her head. Elsie was stuck beneath his thighs, helpless as he bore down on her with sharp teeth exposed.

"Must you always get into trouble, little birdy?"

Elsie bucked uselessly, whispering, "what do you think you're doing?

"Bringing you home."

The speed with which he lifted her from their sprawled position sent her head spinning. Elsie clung to whatever part of him she could find in the blur of movement, struggling to orient herself. Eoin was carrying her in the opposite direction of the soldiers, rushing deeper into the trees.

"Put me down this instant!"

"No," he growled.

Elsie found the meaty part of his bicep and did the only thing she could think to do. She bit him.

"Gods, woman!" Eoin stopped abruptly, dropping her unceremoniously onto her feet. "You drew blood."

"You ignored me." She poked her finger into his chest to emphasize her words. "You do not get to make choices for me."

Ink bled back into his eyes, and Eoin blinked. He rubbed his bicep, scowling at the wound, then back to Elsie, then at the wound again. "I—" His scowl hardened, and he asked, "why are we still here?"

Elsie cocked her head, studying his face for deceit. "That's a very good question. I'll add to it and ask, why are *you* here, Eoin?"

"I'm not here for you," his answer was sharp and brutal. Eoin quickly amended the blurted remark by adding, "I came to see you home safely on my way north."

Right, so Elsie was a convenient detour.

"You're going back to the training camps?" Amos and Davin told her there were no training camps, that all the supplies had been carted back to a larger encampment near the capitol and what wasn't taken by the royal guard was pilfered by soldiers with nowhere to return to.

Elsie wouldn't be surprised if most of those soldiers wound up here. Some men couldn't give up the trade of war.

"No, I have a responsibility to the clans."

"What responsibility do you have to them?"

Eoin gestured behind her, lowering his voice. "The mountains are crawling with rebels, likely the same men you saw at that camp. They're attacking the clans."

"You're not a captain anymore. You owe them nothing."

He bowed his head. "It's more complicated than that, Elsie. I owe them a great deal."

She tapped her foot, waiting for him to explain. When he didn't, she crossed her arms and asked, "so, you're going to defend them on your own? An army of one?"

A hint of that orange hue flashed across his eyes. "I'm more formidable than you remember."

"Well, that's very good of you. Always protecting the innocent, and whatnot. Now, if you'll excuse me, I was in the middle of—"

"You're not going anywhere," Eoin snarled, taking her upper arm, and holding her in place.

"I'm tired of being trapped between your moods, Eoin," Elsie sighed. "Please, go about your mission to free the world from wrongdoing. Perhaps when you're done up north, you can come back here and give the High Father a good beating."

"I can't," his fingers flexed around her arm, as if he truly couldn't control them. "Not until I escort you to the Black Estate. I don't know what trouble is brewing here, Elsie, but I won't leave you in the middle of it. I do believe Dunhill is on the cusp of an internal war."

"Yes, I think you're right, which is why I'm not leaving." She raised her chin. "Not without my sister."

"Gods dammit—where is your sister?"

"Probably with my mother and her new husband, the High Father that commands this army." Elsie took a moment to explain the situation to Eoin, leaving out the part about the Bastards dragging her to the High Father's home against her will, and any other detail that would deter him from helping her. Getting Irene out of Brilend was going to be a more difficult challenge than she'd originally anticipated, and Eoin's tactical skills would be welcome.

"These are trained soldiers, Elsie. I recognize their training. I may have even been the one to train some of them," he said with regret. "You forgot to explain why they're crawling the countryside in search of *you*." Eoin told of how he'd seen them take her horse, making an example of that poor farm boy as they did.

"A woman travelling alone ruffles feathers in these parts." She shrugged as casually as she could, hoping he didn't recognize her dishonesty anymore. "Now, are you going to help me get my sister out of here, or should we say our farewell?"

Eoin's hand was still on her arm, his thumb slowly circling her flesh. Their gazes clashed, his flinty eyes boring into her with the newfound hardness Eoin carried with him everywhere. She had a sudden urge to touch him, to reach out and draw him as close as he would allow. Even standing beside her, his hand on her, Eoin seemed so far away.

Come back to me, she wanted to beg.

But Elsie was too proud to beg a man for love. She was too proud to beg anyone for anything.

With a sigh, Eoin dropped his eyes, his hand following suit. Their contact was broken, and the distance grew wider, sweeping him away. In his mind's eye, he was already in the mountains, making battle plans. Shielding the innocent with that beautifully muscled stomach of his.

No matter the pain he'd caused her, Eoin was good. He was a good man, perhaps the only one in the world.

Elsie snatched his hand back before she could think better of it, linking her fingers between his. "I know you didn't come here for me. You have no obligation to stay."

"I did come here for you," he assured her, contradicting his earlier statement. "I wanted to see you arrive safely." *From afar,* were the words he hadn't spoken but she chose not to point that out. "Cleary, that isn't possible here. There is no safety for you or your sister, so I will see you both back to the estate."

"And then?" His answer didn't matter. Eoin was giving her what she wanted, more than she could have hoped for, and it should be enough. But Elsie couldn't bear for this moment to end, couldn't let him go yet.

When she left the Black Estate, it was believing she might never see him again. Truthfully, she wasn't sure if she planned to return to Gannon's service or if she would live out her days as happily as she could at her sister's side. Only the distraction of danger had saved her from the agony of that decision.

Leaving Eoin felt like tearing the seams that kept her heart in her chest. He was a pillar in her life. Even when he wasn't there, his return was as inevitable as the sunrise. She need only watch the horizon, breathe the fresh morning air, and wait for those stunning cadmium eyes.

"And then," Eoin exhaled, clenching her fingers as he tugged her further into the shadow of the trees, "I must go north."

There was a finality to those words that made them sound like a death sentence.

CHAPTER 13

EOIN

MOVING THROUGH BRILEND AND back to where Valor waited took hours. Elsie was smart, leading them across pastures and fields of high grass, keeping them mostly out of sight, but she was still a beacon in red. More than once Eoin felt the weight of eyes on them, and he didn't doubt their presence would be reported.

It wouldn't matter if they fled swiftly.

Valor was right there, patiently waiting to be saddled. Eoin could seat Elsie between his thighs the way he had ten years ago, flying down the road to the Black Estate in record time. They could return for her sister later, when Eoin had a chance to brief his brothers and garner their strength.

"She's with child," Elsie argued, her chin high in that superior way. The stubborn crease of her lips stole his gaze, and Eoin tensed himself to resist the temptation. He never wanted to kiss her more than when she was angry. "She can't travel after the baby comes. It's not safe."

It wasn't safe either way. They might as well return with reinforcements.

"Are you here to argue with me, or help me?"

I'm here to say goodbye. Or he should be.

That wasn't even his original intention. Eoin only wanted to see that Elsie wasn't bothered on the road. He hadn't realized Brilend was a breeding ground for an army of rebels to the crown.

He hadn't realized how impossible it was to leave her behind. In the end, Eoin was a selfish monster.

Elsie narrowed her eyes. "Why are you smiling?"

"I've forgotten how bullheaded you are."

Her front teeth clamped down on her bottom lip, hiding her own smile. "How could you forget that? Stubbornness is my most irredeemable personality trait."

"There is nothing irredeemable about you."

Elsie turned away from him, reaching a hand up to stroke Valor's snout. It was clear by the way she avoided his eyes that she was still upset. Why wouldn't she be? Eoin could do nothing but hurt her. Only hours ago, he'd watched the light fade from her face as he lied through his teeth.

"I'm not here for you."

Eoin was going north, that was true, but to claim he wasn't here for her was dishonest.

Everything he did was for her. Every sacrifice he made until the moment Lia ended his life would be for Elsie. It was all Eoin could give her.

He plunked onto the ground with a weary sigh, reclining against the nearest tree and watching Elsie pretend not to look at him. She wasn't going to leave without her sister, and if he dragged her back unwillingly, she would simply escape him and return here. The only way to protect her from her own foolishness was to do this for her.

Very well. Eoin would retrieve Elsie's sister, but they would follow his lead.

"Tell me your plans," he commanded, "and I will improve them."

◆◇◆

Elsie

THERE WAS NEVER SILENCE in a town this enclosed, never a complete absence of activity. Axes swung in the dead of night as firewood was brought in to keep the cold away. Animals shuffled and murmured to each other. Or so, that was what should have occurred.

Even the horses fell quiet as the sun left them, as if they sensed a darkness more insidious than night.

Elsie remained huddled in the undergrowth at the top of the slope, listening. Waiting for her moment to strike. She still wasn't sure if she could make it to the bakery without being noticed, but she was careful not to express those doubts to Eoin. He was unhappy with her plan, that permanent scowl causing wrinkles to form on his lovely pale skin.

Night came slower than it ever had and the longer the minutes passed, the more her confidence wavered. It was one thing to face her father, alone in the kitchen when her own survival was threatened. Walking into a village full of soldiers was a completely different task.

"You can't go alone," Eoin had insisted, standing over her in that way men seemed to think gave them authority.

"I must go alone. Irene won't trust me if I arrive with an imposing stranger at my back."

He rolled his shoulders forward. "I'm not imposing."

"Maybe if you stopped scowling for once," she muttered under her breath. "You can wait for us here. Have your horse ready. If I haven't returned by midnight, you can come searching for me."

"I'll be no help to you if I'm here, unable to see where you are or what's happening to you." Eoin clenched his fists, pacing sideways then whirling back. "You have a tendency toward disruption, and I fear your presence will not go unnoticed."

"A tendency toward disruption? What a nice way to call someone objectionable."

He slipped his fingers through his hair, tugging it violently at the roots. "I am not trying to insult you, Elsie, I'm trying to protect you. You never used to argue with me when it came to your wellbeing."

"Yes, and you never used to believe you could make decisions for me." Elsie clenched her teeth, trying to hold back the flood of words that wanted to come out. "You never used to avoid me for weeks only to stalk me through the woods and make demands of me like I'm one of your soldiers!

"There is much that I never used to do, Eoin, but time has passed. Years have passed and I am not the same woman I used to be. Both of us have changed, and somehow, I seem to be the only one that sees it. You want to see me as this helpless girl that needs you to take care of her. I'm not. I don't need you. I can take care of myself."

As soon as the words left her mouth, Elsie regretted them. For one, they were cruel, and she wasn't in the habit of being cruel to anyone that didn't deserve it. She was also afraid that Eoin would saddle his horse in a fit and finish his journey north without so much as a farewell.

It wouldn't be the first time he left her without a word.

The problem was that Elsie wanted to hurt him. She was pleased with the way he flinched at her remark. Perhaps now he understood a modicum of the pain she felt when the first words from his mouth were, "I'm not here for you."

Of course, he wasn't there for her. Eoin never would be.

She wasted so much energy justifying his behavior, building him up into this honorable hero that felt tortured at the idea that he couldn't love her, and it was pathetic. If Elsie's love made him uncomfortable, then he could tell her so. And if he knew that they would never be more than friends, he should tell her that too.

It was only because of his dubious communication that she continued to entertain the fantasy of a future with him.

If she was such an intolerable pest to him, then why couldn't Eoin leave her alone? What was he doing here, sneaking through the forest on her heel, snatching her away from danger?

A man that didn't care for her wouldn't take a two-day detour to escort her home, even if he was doing it without her knowledge.

"Then you can take care of yourself tomorrow, after we arrive at the Black Estate," Eoin snarled, slamming his fist into a tree, and causing acorns to rain down on them. Valor snorted unhappily, stomping further away from the argument.

"Since we're talking about the ways we've changed..." Elsie cleared her throat. "You never used to have a temper." Eoin was the most patient, calm man she'd ever known. "What are you so angry about? It can't all be my fault."

"I'm not angry." The snap of his voice disproved the sentiment.

"You never used to be dishonest, either."

Eoin's throat bobbed as he slumped onto the ground. "As you said, years have passed, and I have seen the darkest parts of the world in those years. You are my—" he coughed, choking on whatever nearly fell from his lips. "You are my friend, Elsie. Please let me do right by you before I'm gone."

There it was again, that note of finality. As if Eoin was making amends at the end of his life.

"Fine," she murmured, sitting as close beside him as she dared. "But I *will* go into Brilend alone."

"And if you don't return before midnight," he warned, "I will search every corner of this town until I find you."

Their eyes met, his burning brightly with his promise. Elsie's lips parted, her breath heavy, and all she wanted was to be taken into his arms.

She hated him.

She loved him.

She was completely at war with herself, and every moment with him was agony. Every moment without him was turmoil. How could a man bring her world peace and break her world into pieces all at once?

How could Elsie ever continue her life after this, knowing that someday he would be in the arms of another?

What once used to be a quiet fantasy had become a persistent ache, an obsession that drove her to the brink of insanity. Distance was supposed to be her saving grace but how did she gain distance from a man that couldn't seem to leave her be?

Elsie shifted closer, her fingertips brushing his in the grass. Eoin inhaled, tearing his gaze from hers to stare at their hands. Evening had fallen, the gloaming light reflecting dimly through the trees, and when Eoin glanced back up, it was a perfect match for his irises. The dragon was restless, peering out at her from the place where he waited, incorporeal until magic allowed him freedom from within Eoin's body.

What did it mean when he looked at her like that?

Eoin took her hand, drawing it to his lips. He watched her as he brushed the skin of her palm with the finest kiss. She sucked in a shaky breath and suddenly Eoin snatched a fistful of her hair, angling her head up, dipping his nose to skim along her throat. Elsie could feel the heat coming off him, the fire in his blood. She shifted her face as much as his hold allowed, brushing her lips at the pulse point on his wrist and tasting that heat.

A bell tolled into the coming darkness, echoing through the valley below.

Elsie and Eoin jerked away from each other, staring into the melting dusk, and trying to see what the commotion was from their vantage point.

"Worship, at this time?" he asked, clearing his throat.

Elsie was grateful for the poor light, feeling the blush burn bright across her cheeks as she replied, "this High Father makes his own rules."

"I suppose he speaks for the Gods, too."

"They have tasked him with culling the wicked."

Eoin stiffened. "How do you know?"

"I spoke with him," Elsie answered lightly, standing to brush off her dress. "This might be the distraction I need. Fetch my clothes, please."

"You didn't tell me you spoke with the High Father."

"It doesn't matter." Eoin didn't move to hand her the grey garments he'd stolen from a soldier, so she retrieved them herself. He was growling about danger and deception, but Elsie wasn't listening. Her fingers made quick work of the laces on the side of her dress, sliding it off her shoulder and down her legs.

Eoin cursed, followed by a thump that sounded suspiciously like him hitting the tree in his haste to turn around. It was a shame he was so honorable. Elsie wasn't the most beautiful or well spoken, but at least she had a figure to be proud of.

A figure Eoin was carefully avoiding, hand over his eyes and back turned to her.

"Does your sister *want* to leave Brilend?"

Elsie paused halfway through the buttons on her grey shirt. "What?"

"You said she's with child. What of her husband? Will you take her from him?"

"He'll come too."

"Our party is growing," Eoin mumbled unkindly.

"I'll do whatever I must to get her out of here," Elsie snapped, stuffing the extra long hem of the shirt into the waist of her pants. These clothes were comically small on Eoin, but they were uncomfortably large on her. It would be an effort to keep her pants from slipping off while she walked.

"Why?"

"How can you ask that, when you would move mountains for your brothers?"

"In ten years, I've only heard you speak of your sister twice."

She turned, bracing a hand over her heart to protect it from the weight of guilt that threatened to crush her. "Remembering was too painful. I left her behind. I did what I did to protect her, and then in my cowardice I left her to face misery alone."

Elsie wiped tears from beneath her eyes before they had a chance to touch her cheeks. She wouldn't shed anymore tears in this wretched place. "I will not leave without my sister a second time. I owe her this."

Eoin's fingers brushed across the top of her hand. "You were barely more than a child. Elsie. Your sister was not your responsibility."

"My sister will *always* be my responsibility." She straightened, swallowing down the fear that had been trying to choke her all evening. "And I'm going to fetch her now."

Eoin's uncertain fingers became a shackle around her wrist, holding her in place as she headed for the slope. "You will return by midnight."

"I will try."

Eoin's voice was crushing stone, his promise threaded with fire. "*You will return by midnight, or I will come for you.*"

With a final nod, Elsie left him standing in the shadows at the top of the valley.

I hope that you do, she whispered to the dragon.

CHAPTER 14

ELSIE

ELSIE WAS FAMILIAR WITH magic. She'd felt the tingle of it in the air as man shifted to dragon. Whatever magic hovered over Brilend and the countryside now, it was sinister. The sort of magic born of forked tongues. Charisma twisted into a weapon, beguiling sheep into slaughter.

Or, rather, beguiling the sheep into behaving like wolves and slaughtering their own flock.

Living with dragons had given her a false sense of invincibility, and Elsie needed to tap into that idiotic courage if she was going to make it down the hill. She would use the element of surprise unless it didn't serve her. If she had to, Elsie planned to be vicious.

The first looming buildings came into view. A door opened in a nearby home. The slam of another door closing followed. Voices murmured quietly down the road, joined by the shuffling of feet. Elsie shifted closer, crouching behind shrubs as she watched people gather in the square. They filed into the temple, its stained glass windows glowing wanly as candlelight shimmered within.

Why were they worshipping in the middle of the night?

It didn't matter. Why did this madman that called himself High Father do anything? Finding out wasn't her business here. The Soldiers of the Gods would be a threat for another day, a distant fear when she had her sister safely inside the stone walls of the Black Estate.

Except, that was her sister, wobbling on her feet as she carried her round belly over the stones. Her husband was behind her, his hand resting gently on her shoulder for support as she passed through the temple doorway.

Well, that complicated matters.

Elsie crept through the shadows, slipping into a narrow gap between two brick buildings across from the temple. Two soldiers stood to attention in the double doorway of the temple. They waited until the last man hobbled inside before following behind him and closing the doors firmly.

The bell stilled, leaving an unnatural silence in its absence. Elsie watched for late arrivals and when she found the road to be empty, she sprinted across it, ducking below one of the windows and raising her head to peer inside.

The glass was opaque and impossible to see through. She scuttled along to the next one, checking again and finding it impenetrable to the eye. A journey around the entire side of the temple proved to be fruitless. The only way to spy what was happening behind those walls was to enter.

That would be stupid though, and Elsie wasn't stupid. Even if Irene was among the worshippers, Elsie could slip into her home and wait for her there without anyone being the wiser.

Right, no reason to stay here.

Curiosity was a vicious little critter, nipping at her until she took notice. Why did this High Father have such a grip on Brilend? What was he doing that inspired such loyalty among even the least devout?

Voices rose in unison, an undulating song with indiscernible words. When it ended there was another long stretch of silence, followed by a singular confident declaration. The High Father shouted his words of worship the way she imagined a king might speak to his soldiers preparing for battle. It wasn't an inaccurate comparison.

His speech was followed swiftly by a loud crack and a feminine shriek. Every instinct that should have sent her fleeing back to the shadows went dead, and Elsie hurried to the heavy wooden doors in thoughtless fury. The hinges were smooth and silent as she heaved one open and slipped through the crack.

Nothing could have prepared her for what she would witness inside.

Pews lined either side of the far walls, as was common for temples. Beyond that was a platform which ought to hold no more than a stand for a holy book to be placed upon. There was no holy book in sight. At the center of the platform stood a massive wooden rack, angled, so that whoever was bound to it lay prostrate before their tormentor.

Lying slanted atop the rack, pale skin cinched in leather straps, was a naked woman. Her head was bowed, shoulders arched with pain as a whip came down upon her bare flesh, but Elsie would recognize that form anywhere.

Mother.

Her first instinct was to run to her mother, to throttle the High Father standing before her with a thin leather whip in his hand. But when Mother opened her mouth to speak, it was not to beg for mercy.

"Please," she whimpered, "cleanse me of my wickedness."

"The burden of wickedness is heavy!" The High Father bellowed. Murmurs of agreement rippled across the crowd. There were some who were huddled in their seats, complexion watery, fear and shame curving their necks. Others sat upright, eagerly watching as colored stripes painted Mother's skin. "The Gods will take this burden from you, if only you will surrender your soul to them."

The next words out of his mouth were not words at all. Not many could read the old tongue and even fewer could speak it. Elsie wasn't even sure that's what it was. To her, he sounded like a serpent, hissing and sputtering guttural sounds as his eyes rolled into his skull. Rapture brightened his face, a grotesque mockery of this cruelty.

The whip swung unexpectedly, and Elsie jumped. Mother wailed as it connected with her skin, snapping against her until flecks of blood flew from the end of it and sprayed across the High Father's grey robes. When he finally ceased, he was panting, licking droplets of blood from his lips, and smiling viciously.

Elsie didn't stay to witness what happened next. Bile crawled up her throat, and she stifled a gag, rushing from the temple and hurrying around the side of the building to vomit. What was this madness?

She wiped her mouth with the back of her hand, rolling her shoulders back and exhaling a shaky breath.

"Gods, what monsters have you created?" she whispered to the night.

They had to leave this place. *Now.*

Elsie stood on quivering legs, trying, and failing to drown out the sound of the whip as the High Father began again. It was a man crying out his pain to the deafened Gods this time, and Elsie wondered how many people of Brilend the High Father would "free" from their wickedness this night.

Irene was in there, witnessing that horror and Elsie had so little time left to convince her to leave.

Staying here to risk getting discovered wasn't going to help. Steadying her feet, she raced for the bakery, glancing back every few strides to make sure the road was still empty behind her.

There were two exterior doors to the bakery, one for customers to enter, and one for the baker and his family to come and go. It wasn't common for buildings in towns as small as Brilend to have complex locks. Why bother with the expense when there was nothing of value to steal? At night, most doors would have a simple wooden bar placed across them.

Unfortunately, the bakery turned out to be the uncommon sort. There was a shiny brass lock beneath an ornate door handle on the back door. Elsie hadn't noticed it upon arrival, but a matching lock held the front door securely closed.

She eyed the offending metal on the back door, rattling the handle and finding it was in use. This was suspiciously expensive for a baker. A High Father with a disturbing affection for her younger sister, on the other hand...

Elsie cursed the High Father. She cursed his disgusting, twisted smile, and the toothy dolts he called sons. Of all the villages in all of Dunhill, why did he pick this one to build his army?

The first stars blinked wanly above her, and Elsie glanced up, trying to judge the time. Midnight was hours away, but she had a sudden fear that Eoin would grow impatient. He had somewhere to be, after all, and he hadn't been too keen on helping her.

Elsie remembered the brush of his lips on her skin. He seemed keen enough before they were interrupted. That confounding man and his beautiful black curls. She was going to tug on them until he screamed.

That thought spiraled quickly, sending her images of fingernails scraping his scalp as his mouth traveled over more of her exposed skin. Earlier, before the tolling of bells, that was where her mind wandered. Shedding her expectations was too easy around him, forgetting herself and every ounce of heartbreak he filled her with. Elsie would have forgiven him for every wrongdoing if that moment continued, if only he would let her explore the planes of his stomach with her tongue.

Gods damn Eoin Black too.

Snapping herself back into focus, Elsie searched the back door of the bakery in a futile attempt to find cover. There was a small pile of empty wooden crates stacked beneath a high window. They would hide her enough, but only if no one came down the alley behind the neighboring businesses from the other direction. It would have to do.

Hours seemed to pass, and a cramp formed in her leg as she huddled behind those crates. Elsie hated being a coward, shivering in her hideout like a scared mouse. Fear was a useful companion, though. Eoin taught her that. Fear taught a man when to tread carefully, when to protect himself.

Perhaps Eoin harbored his own fears because he protected himself from her as if she had a plague.

Elsie was on the verge of returning up the hill to beg Eoin for a second chance at reaching her sister when the temple bell began to toll. After three mournful rings the drone of hushed voices filled the night. She could almost feel the excitement, as if they'd spent their evening watching entertainment and not men and women being brutalized by their High Father.

Blood pooled in Elsie's fingers as she clenched her hands into fists. This could not be allowed to continue. She would not see the barbaric end of innocent people because a man like the High Father believed he knew what the Gods wanted.

If only she had a well-trained soldier with preternatural strength willing to aid the people of Brilend...

But Eoin was too distracted by *obligation* to the clans.

Dark shapes came around the corner of the bakery and Elsie had to snatch back her attention for a second time. The stars were bright overhead now, but the shadow of buildings made it difficult to discern features. It was Irene's gait that gave her away, the sway of her belly obvious even in her loose fitting dress.

Elsie inhaled, praying her sister's husband was not one of the manipulated devout.

"Irene." She stood, legs tensed for flight. Elsie didn't intend to leave Irene behind again, but she also didn't intend to get caught by those Bastards.

There was a soft gasp, then Irene was rushing ahead of her husband, arms outstretched. She gripped Elsie by the forearms and drew her out from her hiding place. "Elsie, what are you still doing here? Are you mad?"

"I think that I'm the only person in Brilend who hasn't gone mad." She glared over her sister's shoulder, studying the baker as he watched their interaction with rigid posture. "Do you trust him?"

Irene glanced back at her husband, smiling weakly. "Hamish is the only one I trust."

Elsie nodded. "Then he can come with us. We're leaving Brilend. Right now."

"I can't. You don't understand." Irene dropped her hands, running a nervous hand over her belly as if comforting the unborn child. "Leaving is impossible. It's not safe."

"I have help. My friend is a soldier. He's waiting for us up the hill. His brother will give you refuge but we must leave immediately."

Hamish put an arm around Irene and looked to Elsie as he asked, "do you trust this friend? Many of the men occupying Brilend are soldiers too. They've recently changed alliances."

"I trust him with my life. He won't let harm come to you."

"Then we will leave with you."

"I'm sorry," Irene whispered, "for what I said when you arrived. Mother never told me about the letters or the coin."

"It doesn't matter." Elsie gestured to the lock on the door. "We can make amends when we're safe. Gather your things. We'll leave as soon as the streets are clear."

"But—" Irene hesitated; eyes downcast. "We have to take Mother with us."

"You want to take that—" Elsie nearly bit through her tongue. She didn't have time to upset Irene and draw this out any longer. "Mother is perfectly content with that monster she calls a husband. Let her stay."

"He is a monster." Irene's lip trembled. "And Mother has been fooled by him. The things he's done to her…"

Elsie clawed through her hair. "Mother is out of our reach. We can find our way safely to the Black Estate and then we will arrange to rescue her." Maybe. If Elsie was feeling especially generous.

Irene's chin jutted out in an expression that Elsie knew well. Her own stubbornness looked the same. "I'm not leaving without her."

"Gods damn it all!" Elsie snarled.

Hamish shushed them both. "Irene, your mother—"

"I'm *not* leaving without her," she repeated. "She was all I had once. I will not leave her to the wolves."

She would have left you to the wolves if it got her what she wanted.

"You don't owe Mother for taking care of you. That is a mother's responsibility."

Irene's next words were a swift blow that left Elsie breathless. "I know that we are kin, but you do not know me anymore, Elsie. Don't presume to understand why I want to do this."

She waited until her voice was strong to respond. "How do you propose we get Mother to come with us? She is the wife of the High Father. I don't imagine he'll take kindly to us knocking on his door and requesting a private audience."

"He won't take kindly to *us*, no. But he will let *me* speak to her."

CHAPTER 15

ELSIE KNEW SHE WOULDN'T make it out of Brilend tonight. The moment she stepped from the shadow of the bakery, silently following her sister across the temple courtyard and to the High Father's home, Elsie knew. Yet, in her desperation to save Irene from whatever horrible fate was coming for this town, Elsie disregarded that intuition. She ignored the Gods, warning her of the true wickedness hiding amongst their people.

Irene wouldn't leave without Mother. Elsie wouldn't leave without Irene. It was that simple.

And even when vicious hands ripped her from behind the shrubs and into the dim lantern light above the door, Elsie didn't believe it was over. She returned to Brilend to right her wrongs, and she wouldn't leave without her sister again.

Not unless she was leaving this world.

By the look of victory on the High Father's face as his Bastards forced Elsie to her knees in his sitting room, she would be.

"I told you to be gone from this place," he purred, stroking a strand of hair from Elsie's face.

Elsie swatted his hand away, looking not at him but to Irene. She stood behind mother, tears streaking her cheeks, and it was clear what had happened.

"I see you for what you are now, Mother," Elsie said calmly.

"And we all see you for what you are, *snake*."

If Elsie was a snake, it was only because she was born of one. Mother's smile was reptilian, her eyes empty and cold as her viper poison finally made its way to Elsie's heart.

"It is my duty to uphold the laws of the Gods," the High Father said, "and I was remiss in my duty because of my weak, mortal heart. I heard the call for mercy, and I offered it, not realizing what danger would befall my family."

"She isn't—" Irene started.

"She is!" The High Father interrupted sharply. "Think clearly, foolish girl. Her hands are coated in the blood of her own father." He sneered at Elsie like a dirty animal. "Imagine what she would do with my only true heir. Don't you see? She doesn't want *you*, Irene. She wants the child."

Elsie's head whipped up so quickly her neck burned. Frantically she searched Irene's features, trying to understand what she was hearing.

Only true heir.

Irene wasn't related to him by blood. The child would gain no more from the High Father than his unloved bastards. Unless...

"Heir?" Elsie whispered, turning her gaze up to her mother as if the woman would politely deny the implication. "What does he mean *heir?*"

Peripherally she saw the word crack Irene's already crippled composure, sending a fresh stream of tears to glisten at her chin.

Mother must have heard the lethal edge to Elsie's words, or perhaps seen the viciousness on her face. She raised her hands in placation, sputtering a flurry of half-formed sentences before landing on, "I'm barren! What was I meant to do? I'm barren and my husband must have an heir to carry on his mission."

"What were you meant to do?" Elsie carefully pronounced each word. "Irene is carrying the High Father's child." It wasn't a question. The defensive jut of Mother's chin was confession enough.

"Come now, Sara. You mustn't justify yourself to the wicked. We've discussed this, the three of us. The Gods ordained this pairing. It was done under the blessing of the holy words." The High Father waved away the horror he'd just admitted to as if this was a petty disagreement.

Irene's husband was cornered in the back of the room, his complexion green around his hollow eyes.

"Irene?" Elsie was gentle with her sister's name, afraid even the sound of it might hurt her. Irene didn't speak, only nodded stiffly before hiding her face in her hands. "I see," Elsie murmured. "I understand now."

"Understand what?" Mother's voice shook because she knew. She alone knew what Elsie was truly capable of, and she saw it coming for her.

"Why I'm here," she answered softly, the discarded daughter accepting her fate.

Perhaps the Gods played a role in her life after all.

Elsie was not destined for happiness. There would be no mercy for her now or beyond this world.

That was not her role. Mercy was for the weary. The battered and wounded.

Mercy was for the innocent.

Elsie wasn't innocent but Irene was. And how many other women in this town were? In all of Dunhill? Innocent women at the mercy of a man like the High Father, a man who would take what he wants from anyone, even his wife's daughter.

Her hand rested gently on her belt, feeling the comforting coolness of the leather sheath. The dagger was light as she palmed the hilt, ready to slide it silently from its hidden resting place.

"I came to make amends," Elsie reminded her mother. "There is a man that I love…I wanted to be worthy of him. I wanted to be worthy enough to return here and be welcome. I understand now that I won't be."

"The wicked always seek the Gods in the end," the High Father added to her speech with such charisma. He was a spellcaster, weaving enchantments around every person in the room. Convincing them to sacrifice their own children in the name of his *mission*. "No mortal man can make you worthy. Only the Gods decide if you will be welcomed into their eternal service. First, we must cleanse your soul."

"No!" Irene shrieked, jerking from her grief.

"Don't worry, sister." Elsie smiled at her, a wistful farewell. "Everything will be alright."

There was only one chance. One chance to right what she'd done wrong ten years ago. To save her sister and perhaps save many more too.

This had to end.

"It seems I killed the wrong parent." That final utterance sucked all the breath from the room, leaving pale faces gaping in horror. Such false outrage from people who moments earlier were whipping each other to rid themselves of wickedness.

Elsie utilized their shock to her advantage. At her back she could feel the Bastards, watching like hungry animals from the doorway. They were close, but not close enough to react in time to stop her hand as it flew upward, dagger at the ready.

Mother screamed as the dagger sank hilt-deep into flesh. Quick as a whip Elsie withdrew her weapon from the High Father's side, hearing the telltale squelch of blood that told her this wasn't a wound he would recover from. She propelled herself upward, using the momentum to slice the dagger across any part of her mother she could reach.

The last sight Elsie witnessed as a blow came down on her head was the blood welling beneath Mother's left eye, leaving a nearly identical mark to the one her eldest daughter bore.

⊷◇⊶

ELSIE WAS SURPRISED TO wake up. Despite the endless dark around her, a quick assessment told her she *was* alive. Unless death was fleshlier than the temple described it.

Pain drummed constantly at the top of her head, distracting her from assessing anything beyond her body. It was dark. She was obviously injured. The surface beneath her was hard.

The High Father was dead.

Suddenly, memory rushed back to her. Elsie jerked upright, regretting the movement as the world tilted sideways. Or, at least, she thought it was tilting. Her hand was stationary on the ground, propping herself up, and it felt as if the ground was sliding from beneath her.

On instinct she reached for her dagger even though she knew it wouldn't be there. The last time she saw it, she was trying to bury it in her mother's throat.

Is it any wonder the Gods have forsaken me?

Elsie was a killer twice over now. Had she succeeded tonight, she would have murdered both her parents.

Yet, was it not the Gods will, as the temple taught? Wasn't every action of mortal man, good or bad, the will of the Gods? That was the conundrum that drove Elsie from worship hours with fury in her belly. What reason did the Gods have to torture her and Irene as they did? To put innocent children in the path of cruel men?

If it was their will for her to suffer, then she would forsake them too.

Perhaps they hadn't abandoned her. Perhaps they knew she had a different sort of purpose. Not to be a wife and build a family, not to grow old and wizened managing the dusty Black Estate, but to bring order to a world crumbling into chaos. Just as the High Father believed Gannon put revolution in motion, maybe Elsie was meant to halt it.

This is not the way. She knew it down to her bones. Violence would only beget more violence.

Unless it was one singular violent act to end all others.

To protect Irene, and all the women and children of Brilend and beyond.

If only it were that simple. Elsie saw her foolishness in the dim light of a lantern as a familiar figure swept through a newly visible doorway. One of the Bastards—they were remarkably similar—was looming over her with predatory eyes.

"You killed my father tonight, wretch."

"Don't take it too personally," Elsie groaned, trying not to grasp her head as if that might hold the pain in. "I killed mine too."

The Bastard surprised her by smiling. "You think you're terribly clever, don't you?" He knelt beside her, raising the lantern high to cast shadows on his narrow face. "My father was an old man. He wasn't going to raise an heir and build a legacy; he was going to leave another bastard in the care of a baker.

"My brother and I were born on the wrong side of the blanket because our mother was an unmarriageable whore," he spit. "If she hadn't died pushing my brother out, we would have been raised among whores and beggars. My father took liberties with the holy words, and we all knew it. That child is nothing more than another illegitimate whelp."

Panic clutched at Elsie's throat, holding in her breath as she waited for some implicit threat to be made against Irene, making her sacrifice wholly useless and stupid.

His smile returned, sharper now. "But you've changed everything, now haven't you, little snake? *I* am my father's legacy now. My family name is of no consequence because I am a Soldier of the Gods. A vessel for their word. A revolutionary king on the eve of battle, and it is a battle I will win."

"You can't believe that." Elsie tried to scoff, but it came out weak and throaty. "The King of Dunhill has an army at his beck and call."

"The King is dead, and I own his army now!" He pointed wildly into the dark. "A thousand men sit in Brilend, and more join each day. They are hungry for transformation, and they are eager to serve the Gods."

"What would you know of Gods, *Bastard?*"

A palm connected with her cheek, stinging the skin with the impact. "From this moment forward, *I am* a God. My power grows exponentially. There is no limit to what I can do."

"Does your brother share your delusions of grandeur?"

The Bastard spit again. "My brother is a brainless oaf. We might share a face, but it's me who was born clever and swift."

And so, there will be no end to this treachery after all.

It was a pain to ask her next question, but Elsie could already feel his inevitable answer encroaching on her, burdening her heart and sending it racing through her chest. "What will you do with me, then?"

"You are a disgrace under the eyes of the Gods. A wickedness of the very worst kind. There is no redemption for you in this life, but you can serve as an example for the others that think to betray their creators as you have." He turned his attention to the lantern, watching the candle flicker back and forth as his hand swayed. "Fear not, you will give the people hope in the end. You will show them that the Gods are not without mercy. Even the filthiest of us can be cleansed."

They moved before she could process those final words, shapes descending from the shadows to grasp her every limb. Elsie kicked and writhed, furiously fighting this fate she had only hours earlier chosen for herself.

There's no escape, a quiet voice warned her. *For once, give in. Stop fighting.*

It was a tempting request. Elsie was born with her teeth bared, fighting the world every day. Fighting cruelty and violence, fighting hunger, fighting frailty. Then later, fighting expectations, fighting unfairness as a woman among men. Fighting her own heart for wanting what she could never have.

Eoin! It struck her and she realized her mistake. Eoin was waiting for her, counting down the minutes until midnight. Elsie was simultaneously relieved and horrified.

Eoin would come after her. She believed him. She knew to the marrow in her bones that he would come for her.

And he would be too late.

Or worse, he wouldn't be, and Elsie's rash and violent behavior would put him in an impossible position. She had no doubt he could fight a hundred men with his sword. But a thousand? How many would try to stop him?

How many of these men did he serve with, only to strike them down with his sword because of her?

Eoin was a good soldier, not only because of *what* he was but because of *who* he was. He never gave up, never stopped fighting for the people he was responsible for.

And Elsie was one of his responsibilities.

Gods, even at the end of her miserable life, that word still hurt more than the wound on her scalp. It pierced her, sickened her with want for a different future.

If only she was *the one*. Elsie would never have returned to Brilend. She could be happy, tucked away in a wing of the Black Estate as she filled the household with a new generation of untamable *drakonmein*.

Elsie never would have returned, and Irene would be left in the hands of a poisonous Mother and a predatory stepfather.

She cursed herself for not expecting this. She should have told Eoin not to come for her. When midnight came, she should have begged him instead to seek out Irene. However frightening a figure Eoin was in the dead of night, he was good. Good to his core, and Irene would see it, eventually.

In her mind she willed Eoin to hear her, to feel her final plea projecting into the endless night sky.

Don't come for me. Forget me. Save my sister.

The sound of fabric ripping drew her back to the room and her fight increased tenfold. She would not suffer this fate.

She would die first.

Elsie must have spoken the words aloud because the Bastard watching from the corner of the room chuckled. "We are not tempted by your wicked flesh. We delight only in serving our High Gods."

Then what were they—

The last scraps of Elsie's stolen shirt were cut from her body, and she kicked out, catching one of four men in the jaw and sending him backward. Another took his place, taking her ankle in a bruising grip and twisting until she froze. Any more pressure and the joint would snap.

A sudden shift in light burned her eyes. There were torches everywhere, their orange glow so bright the stars were dim shapes overhead. Every inch of the town square was illuminated, including the grim faces of the crowd that stood around the temple.

That was where she was, Elsie realized as her captors dragged her naked body onto the street. The temple doors closed ominously behind them, and the murmur of the crowd grew louder, buzzing with an eagerness she didn't understand.

Mother's face stood out to her at the edge of the temple. Firelight flickered across her bandaged face, only one eye visible beneath the tightly wrapped linens. When she saw Elsie staring at her, she smiled. Her smile tilted from Elsie to the center of the square, where she noticed the strange markings on the stone.

Scorch marks.

They were covered by a wooden platform and enough dry wood to burn half the town. Jutting from the middle of the platform was a young tree, cleaned of bark and branches.

A stake.

Elsie's insides crystallized and for a moment too long, she ceased fighting. The shock of what they planned to do made every muscle go limp. Even her heart seemed to stutter and falter, flopping uselessly within her ribs.

"People of Brilend!" The ambitious Bastard boomed across the square. "The High Father is dead, struck down by this wicked woman." He accentuated the word wicked with a kick to her gut. Elsie's head drooped, her body suspended only by the many arms of her captors.

The crowd echoed the Bastard's fury with howls and curses. A stone flicked across the square and hit Elsie on the shoulder.

"But the Gods are good. They are not without mercy." His speech was well practiced and bold. "Tonight, we pray to the Gods for reprieve for this tortured soul," he shouted above the buzz of agitation. "Merciful All Father on High, we cleanse this lost child as you have instructed, and send her into your hands for judgement."

A hush so thorough fell over the crowd that they seemed to have ceased breathing. Their stillness was haunting, the eerie calm before a raging storm.

The Bastard broke the spell of silence with a bellowed command to his men. "Cleanse her!"

His words rippled across the village, man, woman, and child taking it up in a chant. The hands shackled around her arms became bruising in their grip, yanking her forward. Elsie could have gone limp, made herself heavy enough to drop. But even if she broke free of them, it would be a momentary relief. There were too many of them, flocking around her, watching with morbid delight as she was led to the square.

The fear curdling in her gut was animalistic and wild, and she was failing to tame it. Torches waved tauntingly around her, the heat of them reaching her from lengths away.

Fire. They were going to cleanse her with *fire.*

The fight she gave increased, body thrashing until she felt her muscles tearing away from her bones. She didn't care if she dislodged all of them if it meant escape from this most dreadful fate.

Forget pride. Forget dignity. Elsie screamed out a sob. A plea. A prayer to the Gods above to smite this misguided evil.

Her prayer went unanswered.

Had she not done the same? Invoked the Gods as she killed the High Father in cold blood, as if that justified her wrongdoing? As if *she* was the righteous one?

All mortal men were doomed, and Elsie's personal doom was mere minutes away now.

Her desperation seemed to make the crowd wilder. A pack of baying hounds about to close in on a fox and tear it to shreds.

"Irene!" she shrieked. "Forgive me, sister! Forgive me!"

Amidst the crowd Elsie spied a handful of sorrowful faces, heads bowed with pity as her eyes beseeched them.

"Fuck your pity!" she snarled, resignation rooting bitterly in her heart. "Fuck your cowardice!"

They'd stopped, her feet inches from the platform where she would be bound and burned.

Burned.

Gods, have mercy.

By now her limbs had gone numb, both from the harsh grip and her unending battle to be free. Even as they lifted her to the platform, pressing against her to bind her hands around the pole behind her, she kicked and thrashed. One man arched around her to tighten the rope and she sank her teeth into his pectoral. He reared back with a howl, dislodging her with a swift smack to her cheek.

Blood pumped in Elsie's ears, sound echoing hollowly through the haze of pain. Her eyes focused and unfocused, the crowd blurring as blood pooled on her lip. Curses were hurled at her, names so foul she wouldn't even think them.

So, this was her fate. After everything, it would end in fire.

Very well.

"If I burn, you will burn too!" she promised, shouting over the cheers as torches flew.

It wasn't an empty threat. In the darkest recesses of her chest, Elsie felt a presence. She didn't have to speak his name to know he heard her. He *felt* her need, and he was coming.

Eoin.

No, not Eoin.

A midnight inferno.

Darkness absolute.

An angel of death.

Fire came alive beneath her, a beast devouring the wood, reaching hungry orange teeth for her exposed skin.

"You will burn for this! All of you!"

Already heat climbed up her feet. Searing. Agonizing. Her legs shook with the useless need to escape the burn.

With her final breath, Elsie screamed. A battle cry. A promise of death.

Deep in the shadows of the starless night, a monstrous roar echoed her.

CHAPTER 16

EOIN

THE MOON HUNG WEAK and pale over the hill as midnight crept closer. Elsie had not returned, and every moment she was hidden amidst the shadows, out of sight, was another moment his will slipped.

Elsie had not returned, and the dragon was furious.

Furious to have lost his plaything, Eoin reminded himself. The creature was like an untamed cat, looking for something to shred before carelessly moving on.

A roar of protest visibly shook his chest.

Scales covered his forearms, burning as he resisted them. Eoin felt as if he'd swallowed the dragon and it was alive in his belly, writhing, searching for a route to escape. He clamped his mouth shut, counting, inhaling slowly, waiting.

Waiting for the midnight hour that would never come.

There was an odd stillness in the air that would have sent goosebumps up his back had he not been too preoccupied with the dragon. The expanding well of fear and despair in his middle should have alerted him too.

Eoin was so accustomed to fear, it hadn't occurred to him that it was not his own.

Fear was a constant companion, drawing ice into his lungs every time the dragon made itself known. Why shouldn't he be afraid? He was days—maybe hours—away from permanently losing the fight with his dragon.

His dragon that wanted to maim every innocent villager that passed him on the road as he stalked Brilend. His dragon that wanted to burn an entire camp of soldiers before they became a true threat. His dragon that wanted to rend the flesh of his own mate simply because he could.

Simply because she's mine, the dragon amended.

He was becoming too clever for Eoin, learning the tongue of mortal men so he could whisper dark suggestions at all hours of the night. So, he could override Eoin's control without ever changing forms, fighting his way to the surface and pretending to be a man and not a monster.

Soon enough, Eoin's strength would fail, and if he wanted to, the dragon would become him.

Both he and the dragon jolted from their clashing desires as the strange stillness was broken by a flurry of activity. A hum began in the center of town, the murmur of many voices. The ominous clanging of a worship bell came next, cutting sharply through the blackness and sending Eoin to stand at the top of the slope, watching as clusters of firelight gathered in the distant square.

Fear, unlike he'd ever experienced clawed at his bones, and he shuddered.

Elsie.

Eoin needed to get to Elsie.

Already the voices had risen into belligerent shouting. His feet carried him down the hill before he realized what he was doing, flying over cobblestone. Bodies blurred past him, congesting his movement as an earnest presence lit up in his chest.

The bond that shouldn't exist was alive once more, whispering to him—no, screaming to him. To Eoin it was barely audible, a distinct buzz in the roar of noise. To the dragon, it was clear as still water.

Come to me. Burn for me.

Images of fire danced in his vision. Burning buildings, burning bodies. Elsie at the center of an inferno, hands outstretched, smiling down at him.

No, that was wrong. That wasn't what she wanted. Elsie would never—

This couldn't be happening now. *Not now,* he begged the Gods. *Please, give me strength. Once more, give me the strength to do what must be done. To save her.*

There were so many people in the square—the whole town plus hundreds of armed men—and they moved like animals gone rabid. Arms flailed, torches waved back and forth. All of them had their backs to Eoin, pushing and wrestling to make their way to the front of the crowd that spilled between the buildings.

Ahead of them was the square, overflowing with onlookers to whatever chaos was ensuing. A man's booming words rang out above the others. He had that steady, serious cadence that High Fathers used to convict their audience. Eoin couldn't understand what he was saying.

He couldn't understand anything except the stake jutting from dry wood stacked taller than his shoulders. Four men were struggling to bind a thrashing woman to the stake.

The woman's hair streamed around her in dark waves, her naked skin pale and bloodied. It wasn't the blood or even her nakedness that sent Eoin over the edge.

It was the scream.

Flames exploded around Elsie, and she tilted her head to the heavens to scream. His body convulsed, the colors around him dimming until he saw only red.

Red fire.

Red rivers of blood flowing through the streets of Brilend.

They thought *she* would burn.

They were mistaken.

Every person standing in this square would be ash by sunrise.

CHAPTER 17

ELSIE'S LEGS HAD GONE numb. Not the tingling, cool sensation from too much time in the winter air but a clammy, feverish numbness. She was too terrified to look down and make sure they were still intact.

Unfortunately, the rest of her flesh had not lost its sense. Heat coiled around her, pressing into her, devouring her all the way down to her bones. Soon her insides would be molten, her mouth unable to continue screaming as the heat liquified her. She would be nothing but unrecognizable char.

Elsie screamed for a second time, and through the rush of flames, heard her voice echo in a fierce roar. It had to be a trick of the ears, sound resounding against the barrier of heat and bouncing back to her in the voice of a—

Dragon.

There, melting from between buildings, wearing scales like black diamonds, stood a dragon. Wings outstretched, neck raised, maw opened to trumpet his fury. He was nearly as wide as the road, the hooked ends of his wings catching nearby structures and ripping chunks of wood from them.

Firelight reflected in his eyes, a brilliant orange like the most beautiful dawn. This too had to be a trick, her mind desperate to believe she would be saved. But the numbness in her legs was spreading, her skin drying and crackling under the all-consuming heat.

Still, her smoke battered voice rose in a wild cry. "Eoin!"

The dragon answered, smashing through the crowd, and scattering them with one swipe of a powerful clawed hand. Jeers turned into twisted screams. A stream of fire shot straight down the middle of the road, catching those that fled too slowly. Thatch and wood snapped as the flames dashed up the sides of buildings.

For once the Gods had answered her prayers. She was burning and Brilend would burn with her.

Elsie blinked and suddenly the dragon was before her, reptilian eyes fixated on her. The same clawed hand that moments ago was rending flesh wrapped around her waist and yanked. The stake came free from the ground and Elsie came with it, dangling off the wood by the ropes that bound her.

Eoin didn't bother to remove the binds, only grasped her with his other hand to hold her steady. Her stomach lurched as he propelled himself from the ground, taking to the sky too quickly for her to process.

Stars whirled above her, flames danced below. Elsie's already battered body was limp, whipping this way and that as the dragon flew in an uncoordinated pattern.

Eoin should have been the image of grace as a dragon. Carefully crafted muscles bending and shifting to carry them weightless and gentle out of chaos. Instead, he careened left and right, tumbling through the canopy of the forest.

The long stake still bound to Elsie's body snagged on a treetop, breaking in two with a frightening *snap*. If not for the second hand gripping her roughly, her body would have snapped right with it.

"Eoin! Please!" Elsie could barely squeeze the words out of her parched throat. If they kept up like this, he would impale her on a spruce limb or crush her between his scaly palms.

Her plea hit its mark. They whizzed through the trees, branches whipping at leathery wings and scratching them both violently. His hind feet landed on the earth with a thud, debris raining down from the branches as the impact rattled nearby trees. The front of him skidded forward and Elsie rolled two feet away from him in a bruised heap.

For a dangerous heartbeat there was nothing but those sunset eyes. Pin prick pupils swelled into black wells, scaled nostrils flared and puffed. The heat of his breath was agonizing against her sensitive skin. A fresh flicker of fear danced along her ribs, jabbing at her lungs, and quickening her already labored breathing. He was here to rescue her, wasn't he?

Massive claws pierced the soft soil on either side of her head, caging her beneath his monstrous body. A long, strange tongue emerged from his parted lips to taste from her shoulder to her forehead. It was scratchy and cat-like, doing nothing to quell the pulsing discomfort from the fire.

Eoin lifted one of his clawed hands and pinned her. As if she could escape him with her own hands knotted and trapped. The noise he made as he watched her struggle was one she'd never heard from a dragon. Chirping. Elsie couldn't help but picture him as an overgrown rooster.

She might smile if she wasn't so shaken and breathless.

Then another scream was ripped from her hoarse throat as suddenly his teeth were buried in the flesh of her forearm.

Light danced in her vision. Shock made her body vibrate violently. Elsie tried to make sense of her surroundings but even the ground under her back seemed to be shifting.

Because it *was* shifting. The ropes were untwined from her wrists and ankles, and tender hands were lifting her gently from the forest floor.

Eoin's hushed tone as he murmured her name was too soft in the sudden stillness of the night. It frightened Elsie, making her worry that she was so mortally wounded that she couldn't feel the life seeping out of her, too numb with horror to comprehend her own end.

He was speaking again, carefully, as if even his delicate words might shatter the last of her life force and send the crumbling pieces heavenward. Elsie blinked, trying to quiet the throbbing in her ears long enough to comprehend him.

Sensation was returning to her legs in a dull but constant burn. The skin around her ankles and calves felt too hot. Her heartbeat was a skittering, rabid thing inside of her and a shadow lingered over her left eye. Blood dripped steadily from the fresh wound on her arm.

"Eoin?" Her voice was too loud to her cotton filled ears.

He was crouched on the ground, cradling her to his chest. It occurred to Elsie in her pained delirium that they were both naked. Finally, she found herself bare in his embrace. If only it wasn't because she was dying.

"You aren't dying!" He snarled, hoisting her up and tracing her skin with one hand.

The sear of his hand was so different from the heat from those devilish flames. If ice could burn, that was what Eoin's touch would feel like. A cooling balm to her battered muscles.

"I feel as if I'm dying."

His eyes fell closed, stoic mask fracturing. With a deep inhale he drew her closer, clutching her to him. "I'm so sorry, Elsie, for that demon. I couldn't—No, there's no excuse for what I've done."

With two fingers in his mouth, he whistled. Consciousness swam in and out, leaving her thoughts sluggish and confused. She wasn't sure if seconds or hours passed before Eoin's fierce steed trotted up to them, unperturbed by the obvious signs of dragon all around them. The horse shook his mane haughtily before dipping his head to acknowledge Eoin.

Eoin spoke softly to the animal, running a hand down his neck and reaching for a bag strapped to the saddle on its back. He withdrew clothing first, arranging it over her as best he could before kneeling to wrap a bandage over her arm.

"You bit me," she said.

"My dragon bit you."

"You speak as if you and he are not the same."

"We're not," Eoin said, ripping the excess fabric with undue force.

"But you are," Elsie insisted, trying to sit up only to regret moving. "Why did you do it?"

His eyes fell shut, accentuating the deep lines around them. "Please, Elsie. Not yet."

"Fine," she coughed.

The question slipped from her grasp and Elsie found herself standing, trembling, as Eoin slid oversized clothing over her small frame. She watched him cover himself, wondering if that would be the first and only glance she would get of his sculpted beauty, then wondering how she could still think such thoughts after what occurred moments ago.

For once, Elsie was silent. Utterly, unnaturally silent. The words were crushed in her lungs, burned to ashes along with her heart. She'd fled the Black Estate and returned home to recover from the ache of unrequited love, only to meet abuse and betrayal at the hands of her own mother.

Elsie never believed she was the kind of woman that could be broken, but as Eoin urged his horse on through the night, she swore she heard an ominous crack deep in her soul.

Chapter 18

Eoin

Elsie was ghostly quiet as they fled Brilend. Huddled beneath his oversized cloak, she reminded Eoin of the girl he'd found on this same stretch of road ten years earlier. Bruised, wordless, broken.

Her stillness was almost as unsettling as her silence, and if he couldn't feel her pulse where his forearms wrapped around her to hold the reins, he would be worried that her wounds were mortal after all.

The wounds *he* gave her.

"Why did you do it?" Eoin couldn't answer her because the truth was, he didn't know.

The dragon alone understood his motivations, sharing nothing coherent with Eoin unless he wanted to. When he saw Elsie bound and burning, his only purpose in the world was to save her. Even as the men responsible ran underfoot, fleeing his fire, he didn't give them a second thought.

Rescuing his mate mattered. Getting her far from that place was his sole focus.

Trying to tear her arm off was in complete contrast to that mission. Then again, Eoin was trying to make sense of a war-mad monster. Perhaps there was no *reason* for it. Elsie was easy prey, and the dragon decided he had an appetite for blood.

The dragon made his disagreement known with a hot chuff that left Eoin's mouth unbidden. For a creature that was hungry for the flesh of his own mate, he was unusually silent now that she was resting softly against him.

Watching for the perfect moment to strike, Eoin warned himself.

When Eoin directed Valor onto the western road, urging him to move as fast as he could with two riders, he didn't know where he was going. Home seemed a reasonable destination until he remembered that it would take two days under good conditions, which these were not. Elsie was in no state to ride for endless hours, or to sleep on the ground when night fell.

The trouble was that he didn't know if the High Father and his army would pursue. Only madmen would chase a dragon.

Only madmen would watch as an innocent woman burned to death.

There was no telling what the Soldiers of the Gods would do. History suggested that these men would stop at nothing to achieve their goals. More capable men dying to fulfill the greedy, irrational ambitions of wealthy Dunhill lords, tricked into believing they served some higher power.

Eoin had no doubt this new High Father had roots in the Dunhill court. All treachery came from that place. Perhaps when he was done making ash of Brilend, he would turn there next.

No, he would do no harm to anyone except those that meant harm to Elsie. Not until he finally made his journey north, where Lia claimed more Soldiers of the Gods were secretly building their forces.

An hour slipped away as Eoin urged his horse forward. They had no direction, but he needed more time to plan. The longer the distance between them and Brilend, the better. The night air was cool though, and he needed somewhere safe to fully assess Elsie's wounds.

As if answering a prayer, the road forked. With it came a worn wooden sign pointing them right to a nearby inn. The scent of smoke and meat carried on the wind. Not long after, the glowing windows of a three-story structure came into view.

It was simply built, as most inns were. Logs stacked high atop one another to create sturdy walls. The roof was made to match, thick pillars of wood greying after years of exposure to the elements. Still, it was a welcome sight and Eoin was quick to dismount. He slipped Elsie down after him, placing her gingerly on the ground.

Setting her on the stone pathway to the inn, he realized that her feet were bare. Blackened with soot, he could barely make out the shapes of her toes on the dark stone. Eoin had a strange clashing of emotions. Rage and disgust at the people that had done this to her, left her wounded and tented in his clothing with nothing left of her own. At the same time, he felt a rush of affection toward her, at the thought of something as simple as seeing her uncovered feet.

Yes, he was a man starved if the sight of her feet made wings flutter in his chest.

Eoin made quick work of rearranging her cloak, covering as much of her as he could before yanking the hood up over her head. Tangles of mahogany curls dipped from beneath the shadows, drawing the eye. Careful of brushing her skin, he swept the hair behind her neck. Elsie let out a soft gasp, and he hurried to mutter an apology, his palms sweating with the need to assess every inch of her skin.

How badly was she burned?

Three patrons lounged before a wide stone hearth when they entered the inn. Plain wooden chairs supported their weight, softened by threadbare cushions. It was a traveler's inn, not a place of luxury. Eoin inhaled, preparing himself for the state of the room they might receive and making note of each stranger surrounding them.

He took Elsie's hand, tucking her tightly against his side as they approached an old woman in an apron. She was hunched over a wooden table in the back of the room, scrubbing mercilessly at a greasy stain. Behind him, Eoin could feel the three men at the hearth watching them. He barely stifled the irritated hiss from his dragon.

"My wife and I have traveled a long way. We want quiet and privacy." Eoin didn't bother with frivolous introduction. He needed to see to Elsie, and he needed to do it now. From his pocket he withdrew a bag of coin, holding it eye level with the woman. Inside was thrice what a room would cost, maybe more based on what he'd seen so far.

"I-I, yes! Of course, sire. Our very best room for you and your lovely wife." The old woman stammered, rising from her work at the table and nearly knocking it over in her haste. She disappeared through a small door cut into the wood panel beneath the stairs, returning minutes later with a brass key and a pitcher of water.

Eoin accepted both quickly, wordlessly ushering Elsie up the stairs and eyeing the strangers by the fire as he followed. They wore regular travel clothes, not the telltale grey sported by the soldiers in Brilend. That didn't exempt them from suspicion.

Now that the heavy weight of pre-dawn morning was settling over them, and the immediate danger had passed, Eoin's emotion returned to him. Fear and horror cinched his throat until each breath was an effort. Rage burned it away just as rapidly, filling his lungs with hot cinders, fire waiting to consume every man, woman, and child that stood in that square tonight and watched his mate burn.

Suddenly it felt as if there were enemies everywhere, and Eoin itched for action. To feel the weight of his sword in his hand. To feel the stretch of leathery wings as he took to the sky and doled out punishment across Dunhill.

He was startled from his violent spiral when Elsie stumbled on the steps. In seconds he had her in his arms, lifting her and his heavy saddlebag to the top floor, where a lone doorway waited for them.

Not now, he pleaded with the dragon. *She needs me.*

Elsie

Elsie didn't speak when Eoin carried her up three flights of stairs, nor when he opened the door. The room within was unexpectedly neat. A plain, clean rug covered the floor beside a small hearth. Two chairs were arranged beside the lone window, their green cushions a match for the hand sewn blanket on the bed.

The *only* bed.

Perhaps Eoin planned to sleep on the floor.

Or make her. She was only his housekeeper, after all.

"We'll only stay until sunrise. Then I'm taking you home," he told her gruffly, tossing his saddlebag onto the nearest chair. It clanked loudly, and Elsie wondered just how many weapons he traveled with.

"I don't want to go home."

"Where else would you go, Elsie? Clearly returning to your family home was a mistake."

"What made that clear? Was it the burning stake I was bound to? Or my own mother throwing stones as I was dragged *naked* through the square?" A frightening noise ripped from his throat. She ignored it.

Elsie was strong. She had always been strong. That strength pulled her out from beneath her violent father. It dragged her from poverty and into the home of a baron. For years Elsie held Nigel and Edgar together. She kept Gannon steady. When Baron Black passed, followed swiftly by their mother, Elsie shouldered the grief of all four black brothers. She cradled their pain, withstood the destruction that was born of their anguish.

Elsie was a deeply rooted tree. She weathered every storm that shook her. But time had hollowed her out. Loneliness rotted away her insides.

I don't have the luxury to crumble, she told herself. *Not while Irene is still trapped in that wretched place.*

But what more could she do for Irene? What more could she do for anyone? Elsie made reckless choices for her own benefit. She wasn't selflessly defending her sister or doing the bidding of some made up Gods. The High Father was dead because Elsie hoped it would rid her of the guilt she felt, knowing she left Irene behind to be mistreated by Mother and abused by men no different from her father.

Without that guilt, Elsie had nothing to hide behind. She saw herself for what she truly was. Her constant need to serve others was a desperate attempt to make herself worthy. To give Eoin, Gannon—all of them—a reason to keep her around.

Did she even want to rescue Irene for Irene's sake, or was it to satisfy her own need for the love she could never seem to earn?

A sharp tug on the tie of her cloak sent it down her shoulders to pool on the floor. Elsie stepped over it and settled on the edge of the mattress. Ruining it, probably. She was sooty and dusty from their ride.

What did it matter? Sleeping in a filthy bed was the least of her problems.

"I have nowhere to go." No more strength to hold in the torrent of tears. Elsie held them at bay for far, far too long. "I am nothing to anyone."

Swirls of sunset orange shimmered through her tears, and despite what he'd done to her, Elsie wasn't frightened to see the dragon in Eoin's eyes. The hands that gripped her face were rough as leather yet the way they touched her was so very gentle.

"No, Elsie, you are *everything*." Eoin hadn't spoken so softly to her since before the war. "You will always have a safe place to return to so long as you have me."

She shoved his hand away. He didn't mean any of that. "I don't want your pity."

"I have never pitied you, little sparrow. Never."

Eoin lifted himself from the floor to pour the pitcher of water into a wash basin beside the bed. He returned to her with a wet cloth, thoughtfully running it over her face. It was black by the time he was finished. With his thumb, he traced the side of her cheek. Elsie winced and he let out another growl, quieter his time.

"I would like to look at your injuries but..."

But they were under her clothes, and she had no undergarments.

Elsie stood, shoving his oversized shirt over her head. The pants dropped from her hips with an angry flick. Let him see her. It wasn't as if Eoin wanted what she had to offer.

His sharp intake of breath claimed otherwise. Orange burned in his gaze when he met her eyes. "Elsie, I don't know if this is a good idea."

"There's a mirror over there. I'll look for myself."

"No." He caught her arm. "I need to see that you're unharmed." She wasn't, though, and with every bruise and bloody cut that Eoin cleaned the heat in his eyes became rage and not lust. "I'm going to burn Brilend to the ground. I will raze every home, turn every field to ash."

Would he really do that on her behalf? Or was it simply because his sense of justice demanded it?

"You can't," she begged, thinking of Irene again. "The people of Brilend are innocent. It's only the Bastards and their father's soldiers that are responsible for this."

His voice was an otherworldly horror when he promised, "then I shall make them suffer."

"Don't go. Please." If he left her here, Elsie truly would crumble.

He grew silent, cleaning her as circumspectly as he could. Her legs were pink, the skin taut and itchy, but there were no blisters. Eoin promised her that was a good sign, and the burns would heal without scarring.

The same could not be said for her arm. Blood caked the jagged teeth marks in her skin, plastering to the fine hairs and pulling at the wound. It was the worst of her injuries, but Eoin was reluctant to give it his attention, focusing on every tiny scrape before finally taking her wrist to examine the damage he'd done.

"You bit me."

"My dragon bit you."

She still didn't understand what happened, and Eoin wasn't keen on enlightening her. Elsie stared at the wound as he cleaned it, noticing the measured spacing between each tooth mark. The bite looked like an intricate band, almost decorative.

Eoin wrapped a fresh bandage around her arm, failing to tie it twice as his fingers shook. He pushed off the mattress, staring anywhere but her.

"I'm sorry," he murmured, handing her the same shirt she'd worn before. "I would have packed more if I'd known you would need it."

Elsie took the shirt, making no move to put it back on. Eoin did it for her, lifting her arms and sliding the sleeves over them.

"So, you are capable of tenderness," she whispered.

He cupped her face again, kneeling to meet her eyes. "It was never *me* that wasn't capable of it."

"What's wrong with your dragon?"

He recoiled at the question, rising to pace the room. "War."

She chewed her lip, holding back the desperate urge to beg for more. *Never again.* She would never beg Eoin for anything again. If he wouldn't give it to her freely, then she would find someone that would.

Liar.

"My dragon has gone mad." It was spoken like a diagnosis of a fatal illness. "All that death...it changed him. It changed us both."

"You don't seem mad to me."

"Because you only want to see the man I *was*, Elsie," he snarled. "You want to see a better man than the one that stands before you, and I cannot fulfill those expectations any longer."

"No." She stood too, jabbing her finger at him. "I see you for what you are, Eoin, and you *are* a good man. Whatever you've done, however you've changed, your heart is the same. I love you exactly as you are, despite the flaws you see in yourself."

"I wish you would stop!" he boomed, startling her back onto the bed. "I wish you would stop loving me. It would be easier if you hated me."

"Yes, it would be easier," she agreed coolly. "For the both of us."

Eoin dropped his chin to his chest. "Forgive me. I have been so cold to you."

"You cannot help the way you feel. Or don't feel."

"But I do feel." His pupils were thin lines, his irises shades of orange and yellow when they snapped to her face. "If your love for me is like a poison, then my love for you is a fatal dose of the same kind, and I am a dead man on my feet. I do feel, Elsie, and it's killing us both."

Elsie had the urge to slap him, to shove him until the branding heat of his hands was no longer burning into her. "*Why*?" she hissed. "Why are you saying this to me?"

"You nearly died! You nearly died because *I* drove you away." He scrubbed his face. "I knew about the suitors. All of them. Gannon told me in his letters. When you turned them down I...I felt no fear of losing you. I knew that I could always come home and find you waiting."

Ice pooled in her belly, contrasting with the throbbing pain of her burns. "*Waiting*, Eoin. Waiting for you. Watching you leave with barely a goodbye, never knowing if you would return. Believing my love was unrequited! *That I was an obligation to you!*" The tears that came this time were hateful. "Am I her?"

"Yes, *I know*. A cruel fate for you, Elsie. To leave you waiting was cruel, and I saw that. When I came home, I saw how I've made you suffer. That was why I was letting you go. I thought you would be happier if you returned to your family. I only wanted—" He exhaled, as if he couldn't bring himself to say it. "I only wanted a chance to see you safely home before I was gone."

Gone had a finality to it, an emptiness that set her on edge. Still, Elsie could not ignore the way he avoided her most important question.

"Gone where?" She knelt on the bed, not wanting to feel dwarfed by him. "Answer me, Eoin. *Am I her?*"

Your mate. The other half of your soul.

"Yes."

Eoin could have removed the dagger from his belt and stabbed her and still, she would hurt less than she did now. "You—you abandoned me. Made me feel so unworthy of you. I thought you hated me. That you had grown tired of my girlish affection and you—" She couldn't form words. Was she furious? Shattered? Relieved? There wasn't room for all the reactions clambering for attention.

"I'm sorry, Elsie. I never meant for it to be this way."

"You're *sorry?*" As if that one word could give her back *years of her life.* Her voice was rising, too loud to be confined by the walls of their room. "*Why Eoin?*"

"I was trying to protect you!" he shouted, pacing across the room.

"Protect me from what?"

"The monster that tried to take your arm off tonight!" Eoin shoved his bag from the chair and slumped into it. "You were so young when I found you. I wanted to give you time to grow into your womanhood, to wash away the memories of your old life. I had two more years of my enlistment. When they were finished, I planned to come back home and take you as my bride. I only wanted to give you time.

"Then the king declared war, and I was ripped away from you. And war...Elsie, war destroyed me. It warped me. Twisted me until I couldn't recognize myself any longer. I've done unspeakable things." Eoin stared down at his hands. They trembled as he said, "how could I touch you with hands coated in innocent blood?"

"You were innocent too, Eoin."

"No, I was a monster and I'm still a monster! I knew my control over the dragon would slip, eventually. I couldn't live with myself if I hurt you, Elsie." His fingers curled into fists. "And I *did* hurt you."

"Yes, you did," *but not with teeth and claws.* "Now what will you do? How will you live with yourself?"

"I won't," he answered with too much calm. "You don't have to be afraid. I'll bring you home, then I'll make sure I can't hurt you ever again."

Elsie stared at his strong frame, seeing the hidden fissures in the sturdy foundation she'd always believed him to be. She knew he had changed, yet even she hadn't seen his pain for what it was. The tight lines on his face were not born of hatred but misery.

She was desperate to hate him for how he'd betrayed her. For the dozens of times he'd broken her heart as he vanished into the distance without a backward glance. She wanted him to feel the same world-shattering shock that she felt.

And all at once she wanted to soothe him, to save him from the torment he was inflicting upon himself.

Because ultimately, she loved him. No matter what terrible acts of war he committed, what violence he inflicted upon anyone, innocent or otherwise, she loved him. In a hundred years she would still love him. When her bones were dust and her spirit was a mere glimmer in the night sky, she would still love Eoin Black.

Elsie inhaled deeply, searching for the right choice. For a way out of this maze they'd wandered into together, but separately. "Why are you really going north?"

"What I told you was the truth."

"I deserve the full truth. I have always deserved the full truth from you." He winced, ducking his gaze.

"I agreed to help the clans in exchange for my life," he admitted softly.

Elsie bit down on her immediate reaction, quelling the near constant anger she felt around him. She lifted from the bed with a grace she didn't know she had, taking a step in his direction. "You planned to die?"

He rose from the chair as if compelled to close the distance between them, stilling himself before he could prowl across the room. "There was no other choice."

She took another step. "There were many other choices."

"No, Elsie, there were *none*." He put a hand up, urging her to stay away from him.

Elsie was opening her mouth to disagree when a burst of sound jerked her attention downward. Through the floorboards they heard a sudden rise in voices.

Eoin hurried to the window, flinging back the drapes, and snarling at whatever he saw. Elsie stood beside him, and her stomach dropped.

Torchlight painted the early morning in shades of orange, casting haunting shadows across the faces of the soldiers gathering outside the inn. There were three times the men she'd seen in Brilend, at least. Some rode on horseback, others clutched the hilts of swords.

The Soldiers of the Gods truly were an army. How had the High Father grown such a force without word spreading? He wasn't merely playing puppet master in a remote town to satisfy his own ego. This was a revolution. A civil war in the making, falsely proclaimed to be the will of the Gods.

"They're here for me," she whispered.

"They can't have you." Eoin spoke in that stone deep voice, his body hunched as he held back the supposed madness of his dragon.

Elsie saw the struggle play across his face, resolution settling in as his pupils shrank and the black of his eyes bled orange. Patches of black scales marred his pale, smooth skin. A snarl revealed too sharp teeth, and she knew without asking him what he planned to do.

"You can't, Eoin." If she let him give in now, she would lose him. There would be no coming back from the guilt of losing control twice.

"I can," he disagreed, "and I will enjoy hearing them scream."

Desperation scrambled to take hold of her, but she fought it, steadying her breath and saying, "I will surrender myself to them before I let you paint yourself in more blood."

Eoin gripped her arms, walking her back until she was pinned against the nearest wall. "You will do no such thing."

"Then take me away from here." She caressed his face. "Vengeance is not the answer. Not here, not now." There was a part of her that wanted vengeance, would revel at the sight of them burning the way they intended to burn her. But Elsie was more concerned about what would happen to Eoin if he was forced to take more lives. How far could a *drakonmein* be pushed before they truly did go mad?

He refused to agree, body building with tension until he was harder than stone. Finally, Elsie used the weapon she knew would strike its mark. "If you leave to destroy them, you are abandoning me to my fate. I will be unguarded, helpless as they storm this building."

"None shall live to storm this building."

"They're already within it. What's to keep them from throwing a torch to the building while I am still inside?"

Eoin roared from deep within his chest, an ancient, monstrous beast bellowing his fury at being thwarted.

"Dress yourself!" he commanded, sounding every bit the skilled captain.

While Elsie stuffed her feet into her discarded pants, Eoin made quick work of gathering his belongings. He poured the wash basin over the fire, darkening the room so only the glow of torches from the window made it possible for Elsie to see.

The glass panes of the window opened soundlessly. A hand took her wrist, Eoin dragging her to the narrow window. Surely, he wasn't planning—

"Wrap your arms around my neck."

"Have you gone mad?"

"Madder with every moment that you are not safe, Elsie." Danger still lurked in the strange iridescence of his eyes. Lifting up on the very tips of her toes, she looped her arms around the front of his neck.

Eoin gripped her calves, aggravating the burn and forcing her to bite her tongue lest she scream. He hoisted her onto his back easily, his bag clanging where the strap was wrapped around his forearm.

With unbelievable speed he squeezed them through the window, tearing the fabric of his shirt on the wood frame. Elsie pressed her eyes shut, clinging desperately to Eoin, and praying to the Gods she wasn't sure she believed in anymore that he wouldn't slip. Somehow, she was more terrified of falling now than she had been when flying in the clutches of a dragon. Then, at least, Eoin had wings and could catch her if she dropped.

Below them the hammer of angry voices was louder. Elsie didn't dare breathe until she felt Eoin's feet thump against the ground. She couldn't fathom how he managed to carry them both down the wall of a building and she wasn't interested in learning.

Eoin carefully lowered her from his back, taking her hand and leading her around the side of the inn. It was luck more than anything that kept them from being spotted. The party of soldiers was swelling and spreading out as they moved to search the barn.

"We'll never get Valor free and ride away unnoticed," Eoin said, eyeing the barn with regret. He loved that stallion, she knew, and if they left on foot, they may never find the horse again.

"And flying is out of the question?" Elsie asked hopefully. She wasn't keen on repeating the experience from earlier tonight, but it would be much faster than walking. They were days away from the Black Estate on foot and the night was brisk.

"If I let the dragon loose, he will kill everything in sight. There will be no stopping it." He spoke of the violence so matter-of-factly, yet Elsie could hear how it haunted him. She couldn't imagine being two halves fractured as he was. Never being free to relax, always on guard against the creature that was meant to be his ally.

"Getting home on foot will be an impossible task. I haven't even got shoes!"

Eoin stared down at her bare feet and cursed.

A shout rang from within the inn, this time from a window overhead. It was followed by the sound of cracking wood. The soldiers had breached the rooms, whether the innkeeper allowed it or not. Their presence would soon be discovered, and Eoin would be faced with an impossible choice, one Elsie didn't want him to have to make.

Suddenly Eoin scooped her up, cradling her in his arms and running faster than any mortal man could. Elsie held her breath as they bolted across an open field toward the foothills, where the shadows of mountains were just visible beneath the stars.

No one yelled after them. No arrows or stones flew at their backs. Even as he grew breathless, Eoin didn't stop running until they were tucked safely into the tree line.

The inn was a grey pillar in the distance, illuminated only by the ring of torches surrounding it. Elsie clapped a hand over her mouth, gasping as the pillar suddenly brightened and crackled. Flames licked up the side of the inn, burning suddenly and wildly as the wind whipped off the mountains and fed the fire.

The distant murmur of shouts took on a hungry buzz, like a nest of angry wasps announcing their intent to attack.

Gods, she prayed, *please let those poor innkeepers make it out of there alive.*

But she knew they wouldn't.

The High Father had infected the people of Dunhill. His words were a plague, spreading from mouth to mouth until every one of them was withering and sick in their soul. This was not the work of the Gods. This was the devilry of man, and Elsie feared what kind of hell it would rain down on them all.

CHAPTER 19

EOIN

LIGHT FADED BEHIND THEM, giving way to thicker and thicker darkness. Eoin was in a daze, disoriented by the swallowing black of the forest and the rushing of wind in his ears. He couldn't think clearly with the dragon clambering for release. By now his vision should have adjusted to the darkness but the dragon was punishing him, denying Eoin the gifts that made him more powerful than ordinary men. Until now, he wasn't aware the dragon could do that.

There were many clever tricks the dragon had learned to evade confinement.

The pace Eoin kept as he ran full out through the foothills was exhausting. Endless minutes passed as he carried Elsie further into the forest, breathlessly climbing the rising slopes. He felt it when they reached the base of the mountains. The air thinned, becoming foggy and cool in his throat. Elsie shifted in his hold, shivering, and his arms tightened reflexively.

She smelled smoky and sweet, and he wanted to drop to his knees and drown in that scent.

Dawn was a distant hope when Eoin finally collapsed with his back to the trunk of a tree. His skin was drenched with sweat, so hot he felt like a piece of damp coal from a freshly doused fire. Starlight crept in through the broader openings in the canopy above them, giving him a faint view of Elsie's features.

She perched on her knees, watching as he rested, waiting for his breathing to steady. It didn't, instead growing wilder and more erratic until he finally removed himself from her reach, leaping back to his feet and pacing away. He vanished into the shadows, hoping the cold mountain air would untangle his warped mind.

A trembling word brought him back in an instant. Elsie waited with her knees tucked to her chest, curling around herself, and visibly shivering. He braced himself against another tree, too afraid to offer his warmth. Touching her was fraying his last stitch of self-control. Years passed since Eoin had this much uninterrupted time with her, and there was a reason for that.

Sweat beaded on his brow and when his agonized eyes cut to her, he knew they were monster's eyes. He could see the light of his irises glowing across her face as the dragon reared up, trying to force Eoin's hand.

He distracted himself by asking, "what's really going on, Elsie? Why were they trying to kill you?" His hands flexed into fists with the last two words, and he pounded them against the tree so hard it groaned.

Elsie shuffled away, rising to her feet, and wrapping her arms around herself. "My sister refused to leave Brilend without my mother."

Eoin remembered what Elsie said about her own mother throwing stones at her. He'd assumed she was being metaphorical. What mother could watch as their child was burned alive?

"When I fled ten years ago, I left my sister in my mother's hands believing she would be safe. Looked after with the support of the money I sent home." Her gaze grew distant, staring far into the past. "It turns out I was wrong to believe my mother would look after anyone but herself."

"What happened?" His teeth were bared defensively, as if the story itself could wound him.

"My mother gave Irene to the High Father to birth him an heir so, I killed the High Father, and tried to take my mother's head off."

Eoin shook his head, wondering if his hearing was distorted or if Elsie actually admitted to killing the most significant man in a rebel army in the two hours she was away from him. "You *killed* the High Father?"

"Irene wasn't the only woman in Brilend who would suffer in this *new world* the High Father was creating. I thought killing him would be like cutting off the head of the serpent."

Pride had his lips stretching into a grin before he realized it was the wrong reaction to her gruesome confession. Fangs protruded from his gums, and he was sure he looked every bit the monster he was. Elsie didn't flinch away. She studied his upturned lips, her eyes crinkling around the corners.

"I haven't seen your smile in ages."

Eoin turned his back on her, unable to bear the hopeful way she looked at him. Admitting that they were mates didn't change any-thing. It couldn't. "I should never have let you return to Brilend alone."

"It wasn't your choice, it was mine."

"I'm supposed to protect you."

"You still haven't learned, Eoin." She tsked, coming around to face him, refusing to let him hide.

"Learned what?"

"That you can't always protect someone from their own foolish-ness." Elsie shook her head, matted curls moving to cover her face. "It doesn't matter now. The High Father is dead, and his bastards won't sleep until they find me."

"They don't want you," he said. "They're looking for the dragon."

"How do you know?"

Instinct. History. "They're always looking for the dragon. My kind is the power that could tip the scale, if only greedy kings could find a way to catch us. To use us. Why do you think the Blacks have lived isolated in the Blackwood for so many generations? Why do you think the clans keep to themselves in the depths of the mountains?"

She fixed him with a cold glare. "What do the clans have to do with this? Don't tell me *Lia* knows about *drakonmein.*"

Eoin heard the bite of jealousy in her words and remembered the look on Elsie's face when he told her, *"I'm not here for you."*

"It's only an old legend. No one knows if it's true."

"Tell me," she insisted.

"Another time. The sun will rise soon, and we will lose the advantage of darkness."

"Right." Elsie brushed invisible dirt from her hands. "Let's get to it then. Fly me home so I can enlist your brothers to return with me and rescue Irene."

Eoin nearly laughed at the suggestion. "You will not be returning to Brilend." *If I have it my way, you'll never leave the Black Estate again.*

"I'm not leaving my sister behind."

"Do you even know if your sister is—" He shuttered the words too late, cursing his own bluntness. "Safe. Do you know she's safe?"

"I know that I will gut every man in that army if she's not."

The dragon purred his approval, happily proposing they do that first.

"We can discuss your sister when we're home. I know you're weary but we need to start moving. It's a long journey back, and we will surely have company if we take the road."

Elsie stared blankly at him. "Why would we take the road when you have wings?"

He doubled over, holding his middle as if that might hold the dragon in. "No!" he snarled.

Cool hands brushed the sides of his neck and instantly the pain vanished. The sudden stillness was so jarring that Eoin felt as if he was in Edgar's chains again, magic wrestling the dragon back.

"You have to stop fighting him," Elsie murmured, rubbing circles across his shoulder blades with her palms.

"I can't." He jerked away from her touch. She brought his walls down quicker than a whole battalion could, and there was no telling what would happen when they were no longer there to impede the dragon. He could feel the creature watching Elsie through his eyes, plotting, biding his time.

"Fine, torment yourself." She whipped around, holding up a finger to measure the stars above. "I can't protect you from your own foolishness either."

Eoin knew her well enough to hear the hurt layered beneath her impatience.

"You never told me," she whispered suddenly.

"Told you what?"

"What I was...what we are."

"Yes, because I knew what you would do. You believe everything that is broken can be mended."

"It can!" She looked to him, almost pleading, and he wanted to blind himself.

"No Elsie, it can't. I am broken beyond repair. The damage has been done."

She swallowed whatever else she wanted to say, holding up her other hand, squinting at the fading lights as the first blue hues of dawn colored the sky. Then, nodding assuredly to herself, she took one long step and began to march away from him. He glared at the patches of snow still clinging to the base of trees like long white skirts. Spring had come in the valley, but it would be weeks before it made the journey north to melt the ice and call for the flowers.

The air was cold and thin, the ground was frozen, and Elsie was walking barefoot into the woods. What did she think she was doing?

"I'm going home to request Gannon's help," she explained, reading his thoughts. "Write when you reach your beloved clans, assuming you still have a head."

"Petulant woman," he muttered, heaving his bag over his shoulder, and catching up to her in two strides. "You're not going anywhere without me."

"You decided that several years too late." Her words were a series of knives tossed over her shoulder, hitting Eoin exactly where she intended.

He didn't dare respond as he followed silently behind her into the wilderness.

CHAPTER 20

*H*OME.

The word was warm with longing and with each painful step, Elsie wanted it more than she'd ever wanted anything. To be back within those old walls, the cold stone, bleak colors, and even the dust and decay. How wrong she was when she claimed she had nowhere to go.

The Black Estate would always welcome her back. The manor itself was an old, tired creature, and it needed her to keep it alive.

Elsie had been a fool to leave but she would never admit that to Eoin now. Selfish as it was, she needed him to suffer. To feel the hurt that he'd caused her.

Hours had passed, or so it seemed, and Elsie decided she'd waited long enough to broach her request again.

"Are you sure you won't simply fly us home?" Eoin had offered to carry her half a dozen times, and she adamantly refused. Even he couldn't carry a grown woman for two days without tiring. Not to mention, her pride was feeling pummeled, and Elsie had to preserve what little life it had left. She would carry herself.

"No!" His patience had little life left in it too. "Rid yourself of any fantasies about my dragon. He is a blood-hungry monster, and I will not allow him freedom to ravage you or anyone else."

"Oh, please!" she scoffed. "This is ridiculous, Eoin. *You aren't a monster.* You've believed yourself *terrible* for so long that you've tricked yourself." It wasn't the kindest response to his vulnerability, but she was fresh out of kindness at the moment.

"What do you know about monsters, Elsie?"

She lifted her chin. "Quite a bit, actually."

Eoin cursed. "I didn't mean—"

"Yes, you never mean it! You never mean to be hurtful or absent or cruel. And yet..."

They stared in furious intensity, the rising sun painting them a violent shade of red through the sparse evergreens. Wispy, cold mist whirled between them, and Elsie wasn't sure if it came from the rocky soil or her bitter soul.

She hated herself for the way she spoke to him almost as much as she hated him for what he'd done.

Ten years. Ten years of her life wasted.

None of this would have happened if only he'd been honest with her. If only he'd stayed. Gannon would never have believed himself mad, Mara would never have run away if Eoin had been there to strategize. Gannon wouldn't have killed the king and all would be right in the world.

No. It wasn't fair to blame this on him. Whatever choices he made, she could not extrapolate them to these circumstances.

"Very well," she said. "On foot it is." Then she continued walking, trying to hide her wince as her heel scraped yet another rock.

Eoin hastily offered his boots again, and she silently refused. They were too big and would cause just as many blisters as being barefooted. Besides, she was further wounding herself to spite him, and she was too committed to the petty act to back down now.

Elsie didn't know the foothills well—surrounded by ornate maps in the Black Estate and she'd never improved her geography skills—but she knew which way was west and that was where she would find the Black Estate. Whether they made it there on foot or by flight didn't matter. Eventually the Bastards' soldiers would be on their doorstep. Through the Blackwood was the most direct route to the capitol, and clearly a dragon wasn't deterrent enough.

Elsie shivered to think what kind of world they would live in if these madmen got their way. If there wasn't a war amongst the people of Dunhill, there would be war between countries. The new King and Queen of Calos would not stand for mistreatment of innocents. Brula, their neighbor to the northeast, did not have a significant army but Eoin had told her the royal family of Brula would sacrifice every subject in their kingdom to safeguard their wealth.

"Elsie, wait!"

She didn't wait, instead increasing her pace to the point of agony in her tender feet. Peripherally she realized how impossible a two-day journey would be without any shoes. Or proper winter attire, or bedding, or adequate food. Perhaps she would find a horse to steal. She could return the animal and repay the inconvenience with coin once she made it safely home.

"Elsie!" Eoin growled right behind her, gripping her shoulder, and whirling her to face him. His fingers twitched, and she glanced up at him, noting how the muscles in his face were doing the same. How much was he struggling to control himself? She didn't know what it felt like to be *drakonmein,* but she had known the Black brothers long enough to understand their anguish.

A blessing and a curse, Eoin once told her. For they had the strength of a hundred men and a lifetime as long as the Gods, should they remain unmated, but they were also at the mercy of their nature.

Always tempted to act out their most base instincts. Their minds infiltrated with violent thoughts, their bodies fighting to maintain supremacy over a creature that was larger than life and powerful beyond definition.

Her bitterness left her in a whooshing breath and she covered his hand on her arm.

His eyes softened, and she wanted to hate him for that too. For years she wanted only this. Not wealth or power, simply to see her love mirrored in his gaze. Now he was giving it freely, and it felt too late. They wouldn't survive the day, and her last hours on this earth would be spent on the cusp of fulfilment before it was ripped away forever.

Then softness was replaced with his usual stern glower and Eoin was ripping her from where she stood, arms tight around her middle, hand clamped over her mouth. She had half a mind to bite him but decided against it as she heard the click of hooves and the flurry of distant voices.

They hid frozen behind a tree for several long minutes, listening for the last soldier to disappear. They were further north than Elsie had believed the soldiers would go, which showed how far out of her depths she was. She'd never been pursued by anyone, much less an army with unknown motivations.

Why *did* they want the dragon? Surely, they weren't foolish enough to think they could catch him. And then what? Put him on a leash? That didn't end well for the King of Dunhill.

Killing the dragon didn't make sense either, not after the High Father referred to Gannon as Gods-sent. Perhaps they intended to bow down and worship Eoin as a deity.

Eoin finally released her from his stranglehold, and she shoved away, slapping the offending hand that covered her mouth. "Was that necessary? You couldn't warn me to be silent?"

"No, Elsie." He readjusted the strap of his bag, "I couldn't warn you to be silent. I suspected you would do the opposite and give away our position just to spite me."

Elsie opened her mouth for a retort but found there wasn't one. His assessment was unnervingly accurate. "I never do anything out of spite."

One side of his mouth curved, and she could almost see the dimple beneath the fresh dusting of black hair on his cheek. "You do everything out of spite, little sparrow."

Another uneventful hour of trudging up a hill, and Elsie was exhausted. The burns on her legs felt puffy and hot, and her feet ached so badly she wanted to sob. At this rate, it would take six weeks to get anywhere. Eoin walked at her back, scanning their surroundings constantly, head tilted. More than once she glanced back at him to see his irises were a burnished orange, catlike and inhuman.

He grinned at her with sharp, reptilian teeth, and she whipped her head back around. Maybe his dragon really was mad. How was it that he seemed to be present even when Eoin hadn't shifted forms? Not only present but in control, stealing Eoin's features and figure.

As far as she knew, the dragon couldn't do that. Or at least, he couldn't do that before.

She would unravel that mystery another time. For now, her most important focus was breathing as Eoin crushed her body with his, pinning her to a tree. His fingertip pressed to her lips, urging silence, and she decided staying alive to rescue her sister was more valuable than her anger.

Those wildfire eyes bore into hers from above. Eoin loomed like the surrounding mountains, stony and rough. Black scales gleamed on his neck, not unlike the black stone jutting up from the earth. With a finger still on her lips, he drew a small line, tracing her bottom lip and pulling it down.

That same finger dipped lower, touching her chin, feeling the veins in her neck, moving dangerously close to her breast. She could taste his breath, that strange charcoal scent of him. There was a mere inch between his lips and hers, and she forgot that they were here because they were hiding.

Eoin was hot, and she was freezing. His lips were a warm hearth, promising her comfort. Relief.

Kissing him would be a relief for him too, perceived as forgiveness, and he didn't deserve that.

A blaring voice told her she was being ungrateful. Eoin came for her. Eoin *saved* her, more than once.

But that was always the balance of their relationship. He had the power. He was the wealthy baron's son, and she had to ingratiate herself to earn any meager attention. At the mercy of his moods, always trying to fix what she'd done wrong.

Always trying to fix herself for him.

Except, Elsie wasn't broken. She *wasn't* nothing. It didn't take Eoin to tell her. She knew it, once, before she let the words of others trample her.

All this time she let herself believe she was unworthy of his love. That she had to earn it.

Not just from Eoin but from her cold, detached mother. From her sister who saw only what their mother allowed her to see. Love was a currency that Elsie was poor of, and only sacrifice and hard work would gain her any.

Lies. Her view of the world was built on blood-sucking lies that had bled her of her strength.

Fury licked up her body as her overflow of emotions finally combusted, and she flicked his hand away. Even as her chin rose to the heavens to meet his eyes, his shoulders towering over her, Eoin flinched. The mighty, immortal *drakonmein* recoiled away from a starved and battered housekeeper.

It was then that Elsie realized how truly powerful she was. All along, she'd been the one in control. Pride was her downfall, blinding her from recognizing what was happening. If Elsie had demanded his presence, Eoin would have provided it. Had she demanded his honesty, he would be obliged to confess his secrets.

And if he wanted to hide himself from her because of his own past, to destroy himself? Well, he would be met with a new battle to fight, with a foe the likes of which he'd never seen.

A woman on the war path was a woman who would win.

Eoin loomed, rigid as steel, eyes flashing oddly as orange and black fought for dominance in his irises. The growing tension between them was a flurry of sparks on dry grass, but now was not the time for more fire.

If Elsie wasn't careful, they would burn everything to the ground.

When long minutes passed without soldiers stampeding through the trees, she shifted her weight from beneath him. Eoin watched her peripherally, his gaze still fixed in the distance.

"We're too close to the road," he murmured.

"Are we?" she yawned.

Eoin's head snapped in her direction, lines tight around his mouth. "This isn't going to work."

"What's not?" she yawned again, feeling that newfound power drain out of her as the last two days caught up with her weary body.

They weren't going to make it to the Black Estate. Elsie wasn't being pessimistic. Realistically, walking that far in her condition was going to be impossible. There had to be another way.

Eoin didn't give her a chance to broach the subject for a third time. His hand was on her lower back, steering her in the opposite direction they'd been walking.

"We can't go back!"

"We can't stay here, either."

She blinked to clear her vision, searching for more arguments, and finding none. After a few more hurried steps they hit an obstacle. Rough volcanic rock jutted out from the slope, creating a narrow cliff with no obvious way around.

"Need I remind you that only one of us can grow wings?" she asked as he craned his neck to see the top.

"Get on my back."

"I will not be repeating those acrobatics in this lifetime."

"You can get on my back," he cornered her, teeth bared in a dragon grin, "or I'll toss you over my shoulder. The latter will be much more jarring."

"Don't make a habit of threatening me, *dragon*."

His grin widened into a terrifying display of dagger-sharp teeth. "You can pretend you don't like it, little birdy, but I can hear how your heart flutters."

"You—" the breath required to finish that sentence was forced from her lungs as Eoin followed through on his promise, heaving her over his free shoulder like she was another bag of travel gear and not a full-grown woman.

It was useful that she was too breathless to speak because otherwise, Elsie would be screaming. Eoin scaled the rock wall with ease, clawed fingers digging into handholds that were invisible to her eye. His body swayed back and forth as he shifted his weight, and she swayed with him. The movement felt violent and unsteady, and she clutched the fabric of his shirt for dear life.

She wanted to look away, Gods she wanted to look away, but not seeing the drop below them seemed worse than knowing it was there, waiting for her to fall from her precariously balanced position on Eoin's shoulder.

Then suddenly she was on her feet, stumbling backward as she acclimated to her own center of gravity. Eoin kept one hand on her upper arm, guiding her clumsy steps away from the cliff's edge.

Her back hit stone too hard, and she whimpered pitifully.

"Bastard," she spit, rubbing her bruised muscle. At this point, it would be double bruised. There didn't seem to be a single inch of her that wasn't bearing some injury or another.

"You love me," he purred, dropping his bag, and prowling her way with an easy smile.

"You're not Eoin."

"I am," he said teasingly, "and I'm not."

"How is it you can speak?"

"Poor fool put himself in chains believing that he was binding me too," the dragon explained, his voice deeper and rougher, but still very much Eoin's. "While he was shackling himself, I was setting myself free. *Adapting*."

"Where's Eoin now?"

His response was simple and smug. "Fighting fictitious monsters."

Elsie wasn't afraid of the dragon, necessarily, but she didn't trust him either. When it came to Eoin, she had the power. When it came to the dragon? Elsie didn't know where his loyalty or desire fell. Dragons were supposed to be creatures of pure instinct. They weren't known to speak eloquent sentences or use any kind of cleverness that wasn't innate to all predatory beasts.

"Don't worry, little birdy," the dragon swept his arm beneath her knees, knocking her back off her feet and into his embrace in one swift motion, "I promise I won't bite. This time."

Elsie wanted to fight him as he settled cross-legged on the unforgiving stone. She wanted to ask after Eoin, to beg the dragon for mercy on Eoin's behalf. But perhaps the dragon's anger was as justified as her own. Perhaps being deemed mad and unfit for love was as harsh a sentence as what Elsie was given by Eoin and his misguided honor.

"If you bite my hand again, dragon," Elsie snuggled into his warmth, burying her frosty feet in the crook of his leg, "I will never feed you."

CHAPTER 21

ELSIE WOKE STIFF AND cold, but for the warm chest beneath her. The sun was higher than when she'd fallen asleep, though she couldn't say how high because a thick blanket of clouds had moved in to block out the only other source of warmth. Tiny, wet flakes of snow pelted them sideways as the constant wind caught them in their freefall.

She shivered in Eoin's arms, feeling the weight of hopelessness crushing her.

Eoin shifted beneath her, trying to offer more of his body heat. When she looked to his face, she saw familiar black eyes, red rimmed and weary.

"So, you defeated your monsters?"

He frowned. "I know only one monster and I also know I can't defeat him."

"So dramatic," she tsked, stretching her arms above her head and *accidentally* whacking him in the face with both hands. "Did you know he can talk?"

"He can do many things a dragon shouldn't be able to do."

"You sound so disappointed." She stood, hugging herself as the wind found a better angle to pummel her. "Shouldn't you be proud that your dragon has adapted to his circumstances?"

"Pride is never a feeling associated with what I am."

Now Elsie was the one frowning. "Plenty of men would give any-thing to have your strength and power, you know." She attempted to tame her tangled hair, braiding it out of her face. "I would be pleased to have the strength and prowess of a dragon."

"You have no idea what you're talking about, Elsie." Eoin stood abruptly, rifling through his bag and pulling out a package of salted meat. "There is no rest for *drakonmein*. The moment I let my guard down, the dragon will strike. Even when I believe I have the upper hand, he is there, swallowing me as if I too am mere prey to him."

"Have you considered what it feels like to be constantly ignored, insulted, and denied your freedom?"

Eoin gaped at her, stunned by the question. "You're taking his side?" He stomped over to her, shoving up the sleeve of her shirt. "You're defending the monster that did this—" he ripped the bandage from her forearm, expecting to reveal a gory wound.

They both sucked in air as the fabric fell away, exposing a series of fine white lines. They rose and fell in a perfect pattern, reminding Elsie of the design carved into the silver band Gannon gave Mara as a wedding gift. It belonged to the late Baroness Black, a family heirloom passed down to the women in the Black family for generations.

Her skin prickled with goosebumps, and it had nothing to do with the weather.

"That's impossible," Eoin murmured. "You shouldn't be able to heal that fast unless we—" he clutched at his chest, grabbing for some invisible thread that wasn't there.

Unless we bond.

Those were the words he was too scared to speak aloud. One of the perks of mating a *drakonmein* was receiving a small taste of their power. For some, the effects were subtle; more stamina in their daily lives. But Eoin had told her stories from their family history where women recovered from lethal wounds.

Rare, but not impossible.

Except, Eoin was right. They hadn't bonded. And yet...

There was a moment in Brilend as the torches were thrown where she felt him in a way that went beyond fickle mortal feelings. It was corporeal, a presence inside of her that was not her.

"Perhaps we have," she suggested cautiously. "Perhaps when you find yourself lying headless at the feet of your beloved clans people, I will meet a similar fate without ever knowing what killed me."

Another *perk* of mating a dragon. Their lives were bonded literally, meaning if Eoin died, Elsie would too.

Eoin was on her too fast to react, one hand firmly beneath her jaw, the other covering the fresh scar on her arm. "Stop it! Do not speak of your death again."

Elsie shoved away from him, snarling, "do not touch me without permission again."

Bright hues of orange bled into his eyes, pinprick pupils sizing her up, and Elsie gulped down her fear.

He was afraid his dragon would kill her. That was why he stayed away. Was he right? Elsie focused on her forearm, noting the only source of pain was Eoin's tight grip. The wound on her arm was painless.

Did the dragon know what he was doing?

One fatal strike was all it would have taken. Why rescue her from the flames only to destroy her?

Elsie backpedaled, testing.

Eoin mirrored her, stalking her like the predator he was. "I will touch you whenever I please." The next words that came from deep in his throat were a rockslide, or the guttural sound of mountains erupting with fire. "You cannot deny me. *You belong to me.*"

Elsie felt the rush of wind behind her. She felt the rough stone under her feet, and the way it slanted downward. Two more steps and she would be at the edge, staring at the earth from hundreds of feet above it. The tips of spruce trees fluttered past her shoulders in the wind.

This push and pull between Eoin and his dragon had to end. For his sake, and for hers. It was the only way they would make it off this mountain alive. It was the only way home.

She risked one terrified glance over her shoulder. There was a possibility that forcing his hand wouldn't work. Eoin clearly didn't have the hold over his dragon that he wanted to, but there was no telling if now was one of those times he was restraining it with an iron fist.

Only one way to find out. Only one way to finally end this.

"Prove it," she said, feigning courage.

Then Elsie took two steps backward, watching as Eoin moved at an incredible speed and missed her by an inch. She was falling as rapidly as the snowflakes, destined to become yet another wet mark on the ground if Eoin didn't react *now*.

Please Eoin, she pleaded silently. *Please let him free.*

His movement happened faster than her vision could track. Where once stood a man was a snakelike beast, scales of obsidian painted across his sleek form. A thick reptilian tail whipped through the air, constricting around her, and immobilizing her limbs. Massive leathery wings beat wildly against the wind, pushing them away from the unforgiving ground.

It was much closer than Elsie ever cared to know.

Trees quivered as Eoin's claws slammed into stone and soil, barely bracing their impact. Immediately he whirled on her, bending his body in half to snarl at her from where she was held captive by his tail.

The first hint of fear returned to Elsie in a cold stream of sweat. She believed she understood his motivations. What if she was wrong?

The fresh scar on her forearm tingled, reminding her that it wasn't always painless. She wriggled against the thick muscle of his tail, scales scraping her soft skin. The very tip of that tail made a loop around her throat, tightening enough to show her the power he held over her.

I am the one with power over him.

Despite the reassurance, Elsie struggled to keep calm as deadly teeth snapped inches from her face. The dragon coiled in on himself, bringing her with him as he settled to the ground. With careful precision he removed her unscarred arm from the binds of his tail and gripped it in his maw. A warning or a declaration of his intention?

"You're trying to mark me," she said, knowing her assumption was correct.

The points of his canines pressed into her skin, and she winced, forcing herself to keep talking and ignore the painful pressure. "I already have scars left by men that claimed they were hurting me because they loved me. Yours isn't special."

He pressed harder and a bead of blood welled to the surface of her forearm. Elsie doubled down, repeating, "your mark isn't special. It means nothing to me."

The dragon froze, hot breath hissing in and out as he processed her words.

Still, Elsie continued. "If you want me to wear your mark, you must give it to me the proper way."

Sparks brightened the forest when Eoin reappeared, eyes still burning sunset orange as he tore the pants from her waist. Tree bark scraped her back, and the air left her in a noiseless gasp as their bodies collided.

Elsie clutched at his shoulders. She was suspended above the ground, her hips pinned by his, every muscle tense as he speared through her maidenhead. It wasn't a gentle introduction to love making, and though she'd entertained many fantasies about Eoin Black doing far worse to her, it wasn't as pleasurable as she hoped.

"Eoin," she rasped. Her throat was dry. Sweat trickled between her shoulder blades, her insides too hot even as her skin pebbled with an icy chill.

Elsie was on fire all over again, only this time it was inside her, burning hot at her core and spiraling outward to the tips of her ears and the ends of her toes. She needed—she needed, and it wasn't in a way she understood.

A confusing medley of sensation hit her at once. The discomfort as his length stretched her beyond her limits, the instinct demanding that she thrust her hips, harder, faster. An edge of ecstasy overwhelmed the pain, only to vanish as Eoin stumbled backward.

The black void of his eyes returned only momentarily before it was swallowed by white. Clumsy arms clutched her against Eoin's heaving chest. Elsie cinched her legs tighter around his middle, clinging to him and panting as only the pulsing length still buried between her legs kept her from sliding to the ground.

With stunned slowness Eoin bent his knees, lowering himself to a seat with Elsie astraddle his hips.

Eoin blinked to where their bodies connected, then back up to her face. He touched her thighs, then hips, finding the torn sleeve of her shirt and cupping her arms though it. His hands followed that path a second time, barely daring to touch her even as his cock flexed impatiently against the walls of her core.

"What have I done?" He whispered, holding her so carefully she ached at his softness. Eoin fisted the fabric of her shirt, snarling, "what have *you* done?"

Elsie made a show of sliding the tattered fabric over her head, letting her breasts fall heavy onto his chest. The cool air teased at her nipples, sending Eoin's gaze down to stare at their peaks. His tongue traced his bottom lip, even as his brow wrinkled angrily.

"What have I done?" She shifted her hips experimentally, rising off him and slowly, slowly lowering herself down again. Eoin was not a small man—anywhere. He was like a sword piercing through her. She was afraid to glance down and find the moisture seeping between her thighs was blood.

Well, it wouldn't be the first time Eoin made her bleed.

"I have protected you, Eoin Black, just as you have protected me."

"Elsie." He grit his teeth, unable to resist cupping her breasts. "You have no idea what you're doing."

The fire inside her burned brighter, but it was sweeter somehow, more pleasure and less pain. With it came more confusing sensations—shame, desire, failure—and that was when Elsie realized what she was experiencing.

The bond.

Mara had told her more details about her bond with Gannon than was considered polite. Elsie always reasoned that if men were allowed to brag about their exploits, women ought to be as well. So, Mara would cover her blushing face, whispering secretly about the way she experienced every ounce of Gannon's pleasure, making their mutual pleasure tenfold.

Elsie had no doubt that Eoin was experiencing pleasure now, if only he could notice it amidst his constant self-flagellations.

"I know exactly what I'm doing." This time she rose higher, giving him the opportunity to escape from beneath her if he chose. Palms pressed to his chest, she met his midnight eyes and asked, "do you want me to stop?"

It was a little late to ask, but he hadn't exactly given her a chance to introduce the conversation before he sliced through her maidenhead like a savage.

Eoin didn't answer, and Elsie swallowed the familiar sense of heartbreak threatening to creep up her throat.

"Do you truly not desire me?"

"I could walk a thousand miles in the Gazari desert and still I would desire you more than water."

He looped his arms around her, drawing her so close that their lips brushed. This time he followed through, capturing her in a soft, questing kiss. Now Elsie felt as if *she* had walked a thousand miles in the Gazari desert and Eoin was cool, crisp water.

Yet, there wasn't anything cool about him. His body was molten stone beneath her, hot and unyielding. He shifted experimentally, rocking his hips where her movement faltered, and Elsie winced.

"I'm hurting you—" His retreat was instantaneous. All warmth bled from his eyes, and it was clear he was a heartbeat from lifting her off him and fleeing.

Elsie cut him off with another kiss, harsher and more demanding than the last one. "Nothing hurt more than longing for you every day and believing my love was unrequited."

"I was *protecting* you."

"And I'm protecting you," she repeated, holding him closer when he tried to create distance. "If you bleed, I will bleed too. If you forfeit your life, my life will also be forfeit."

Eoin stared at her, taking in every line of her face. His palm came around the side of her neck, brushing beneath her chin. The constant wrinkle in his brow softened, and he drew her mouth down to his.

That one kiss changed everything. Within that kiss was a decade of unfulfilled longing. There was passion and anger, regret, and hope. The entirety of Eoin's heart was poured into his kiss, and it healed Elsie's deepest wounds.

She hadn't provoked the dragon to complete the bond because she forgave Eoin. In fact, until that very moment, she believed she would never truly forgive him. But cocooned in the sweetness of his lips, those ten years melted away.

It didn't matter if it was ten years or fifty. It didn't matter if this was their last day. This was fated to be, and it happened as it needed to. It happened as they both allowed it to.

Perhaps they were both a little broken, and both a little mad.

But what was broken could always be mended, as far as Elsie was concerned.

And what fun would life be without a little madness and mayhem?

One sweet kiss turned into a dozen, then lips roving over her collar bone as she tangled her fingers in his coiled black hair. There was no more than a distant thrum of pain now, contrasting deliciously with the louder buzz of pleasure.

Elsie's back collided with the cold earth, and she gasped. Eoin was over her, moving faster, pale cheeks flushed. She traced the muscles of his hips, admiring the way they flexed and softened. Fire burned her from the inside out, not biting, and vicious as the fire the night before, but crackling and bright. It drew something from inside her, the hot edges of it unfurling in her middle.

Again, Elsie needed, but she couldn't grasp *what*.

It was right there, building. Waiting.

Eoin rose to his knees, gripping her thighs, widening her to take more of him, and she muffled a scream behind her hand. His eyes were twin suns, burning her alive. They gleamed at her, twinkling smugly with his victory.

"Beautiful little birdy," he purred, circling his thumbs across the inside of her thigh. "I like the way you sing for me."

Elsie tilted her body forward, urging him to move faster. Harder. To give her that *something* she needed. "Don't celebrate your victory yet," she panted. "You still have to—"

"Like this?" Those roving thumbs moved inward, brushing through the slick skin where they were joined. Elsie sucked in a breath, her body stiffening unexpectedly. Eoin saw her tension for what it was, like a bowstring pulled taut, ready to be released. With one hand he explored between her legs, stroking, and pressing until he found the spot that drew a strange warble from her throat.

The other hand cupped beneath her hip, lifting her off the ground and using his strength to hammer into her. Despite his speed and vigor, it felt as if Eoin was struggling to move inside her. As if she was squeezing him, cinching her muscles around him to feel the drag of every ribbed vein on his length.

His pumping hips combined with the purposeful stroke of his finger proved too much, and that *something* finally happened. It was utter ecstasy, blinding her with intensity. White fire danced across her vision, blurring Eoin until she saw nothing but those eyes. One was sunset orange, the other midnight black. Two halves of the same whole.

Both watching her fall to pieces in his arms with bold satisfaction.

Eoin's own ecstasy came like a rockslide, crashing into her. His muscled body pinned her into the frozen earth, crushing the breath from her. He flexed and bucked, his knife-sharp teeth scraping along her collarbone.

It was more primal than she ever imagined love making to be, and not because they were naked in the middle of the forest. She always thought there was some logic to it, as if men maintained a level of thoughtfulness beyond what beasts were capable.

But minutes passed with Eoin still throbbing inside her and she still hadn't gathered her wits. Her mind spoke single syllable words.

Fuck. Yes. More.

She was no better than any beast in heat.

"I want to do that again," she mumbled, still bearing more of Eoin's weight than she could without suffocating.

Eoin laughed, so deeply and heartily, that he tumbled over onto his back. Elsie closed tearful eyes, memorizing every note of that sound, and the way it echoed in her chest as carefree joy.

He rolled to her, grabbing her head, and nearly yanking it off her neck to smash his mouth to hers. If they weren't bare beneath the trees with nothing to drink and barely a scrap of clothing to wear, she would have thought him drunk.

"You brute, what do you think you're doing?" She feigned indignity when he lifted her easily off the ground, planting her on his belly.

"You said you wanted to do it again, didn't you?"

"Is this how all dragons treat their mates? Fucked mercilessly into the ground, and not even offered a drink before he takes more?"

Eoin grinned, looking more like himself than he had in years. "I'd almost forgotten how vulgar you are."

"I prefer to call it *imaginative.*"

"Then tell me every *imaginative* thing you've dreamt of, and I will give it to you." He dipped his head to kiss her, freezing halfway there, his eyes wide. "Your face..."

She resisted covering her cheeks in embarrassment. Elsie's wasn't exactly well groomed but surely, she didn't look that horrifying. "What's wrong with my face?"

"I don't know if you're going to hate me." Eoin traced across her left cheek with one finger, following the path of the scar under her eye. The pattern was wrong though, swirling instead of striking down.

Then she understood. When *drakonmein* took a mate, they left a mark on her skin. Mara's was simple, a black dragon coiling against her pale skin.

"The mark is on my face?"

"It's covering your scar." When she didn't say anything, he asked, "are you upset?"

Elsie beamed, pecking his lips. "How could I be upset? Now no one will ever dare lay a finger on me. They need only glance at my face and know that I have a dragon at my beck and call."

"And you do," he said seriously. "No matter where you are in this world, Elsie, I will come for you when you call."

Chapter 22

Eoin

Eoin was weightless. For so long he and his dragon were opposing forces. The effort of always keeping him at bay left Eoin exhausted, joints aching, head pounding, heart heavy.

Now suddenly that fight was over, and it was like being untethered from solid ground.

Elsie rested atop him, smiling sleepily, and he couldn't think straight. He knew there were things he was supposed to care about, a problem he was supposed to solve, but he couldn't for the life of him recall what it was.

All thoughts were Elsie. The smoky scent of her hair, the cinnamon heat of her kiss, the way she panted and gasped and begged him—*him*, the monster—for more.

More of everything

His body, his heart.

He was only a handful of shattered pieces, midnight in ruin, and she wanted all of it.

"Will you fly me home now?" Elsie murmured, her naked skin so unbearably soft against his.

Eoin had carried her back up the cliff—with a furious warning about going near the edge—and spent another hour warming her in the most satisfying way. She was tired and sore, and he knew she needed rest, but he physically couldn't keep himself from her.

Elsie had to be infused with the scent of him. He wanted to brand her with his essence from the inside out, making her irrevocably his. The bond pulsed like a living thing each time he touched her, reminding him that she already was his.

That didn't stop him from proving it again and again until she was too tired to even lift herself from his chest.

He twirled a springy curl around his finger, watching it bounce back against her breast. His voice sounded distant and drunk when he asked, "why go home at all?"

An emotion pelted him internally—irritation—and he momentarily felt a ripple of shame. There was a good deal of shame and guilt, still buried deep under the beautiful glow of the newly formed bond, but every time it began to surface, Elsie managed to shove it back down.

"Firstly, I imagine making love would be even more pleasurable in the comfort of your own bed. Clean, surrounded by blankets, *warm.*" She said the final word with a shiver, and he reached for the last remains of her shirt, pulling it over her head with a disappointed scowl.

"There's also the issue of starvation. I am absolutely famished, and I'd like to have a hot meal." More shame. How could he be so selfish? Eoin put one hand on her backside to steady her on his lap, using the other to rifle through his bag and pull out the last of his dried meat.

Elsie's eyes crinkled around the corners, accepting the bite he offered her and covering her mouth as she chewed. "Finally, I need to go home and fetch your brothers so we can return here and rescue my sister."

Her final point was delivered sweetly, uncharacteristically so, and he wondered if that was the reason she'd completed the bond. It didn't matter one way or another. She was free to manipulate him, to use him for her own gain, because in doing so, she still gave herself to him.

Elsie could run from him if she wanted, flee to Calos, or even across the sea to a faraway island, and he would be able to find her.

Elsie must have believed bonding would tame the dragon. Based on the unusual stillness and silence, she was right.

That didn't mean Eoin trusted the beast. He was quiet now, a cat with his cream, but that didn't erase the horrible memories burned into Eoin's mind. For years he was haunted by gory images dreamed up by his counterpart.

Elsie pinned beneath his claws, her naked skin streaming with blood as he buried his teeth in her flesh.

Blood running through her dark hair.

Blood running down her fingertips as it dripped from her shoulder.

Jagged wounds decorating her arms.

Eoin froze, taking Elsie's wrist and staring at the healed bite on her forearm. All her wounds were healed, now that he was looking. The pink burns on her legs were gone, her skin returned to that beautiful caramel color. No cuts and bruises were visible.

It was a remarkable recovery.

And that scar on her arm...

He forced himself to replay the worst of his nightmares, viewing them from a fresh perspective. There was always blood, his teeth buried in her flesh, but he never killed Elsie. Not once in his fantasies did the dragon depict her dead. It was never the idea of her wounds that excited the dragon either.

It was the mark that wound would leave on her skin.

His eyes snapped to the mark on Elsie's cheek, a black serpentine dragon spiraling in on itself.

When the shame found him this time, there was no stopping it. Was it really that simple? Had he misinterpreted years of restless, wild behavior from his dragon as violence, when in truth it was longing? A desperate need to fulfill his greatest purpose.

Marking his mate.

Eoin wouldn't do it himself, and so the dragon found another way. The dragon couldn't claim Elsie in flesh, but he could make his claim known by marking *her* flesh. He could find a way to manipulate Eoin's body, slip in where he didn't belong and control aspects of Eoin's life that he shouldn't have been able to control.

All because Eoin refused to claim Elsie.

Years wasted on a misunderstanding.

Or so he thought until exhaustion finally claimed him too.

Eoin didn't recall falling asleep. He didn't recall anything except the screaming. Even the bravest men screamed in the end, calling out to their Gods, their mothers, anyone that would show them mercy.

Eoin never showed mercy. How could he, when mercy would only lead to the deaths of his own men? His sword felt light in his hands, swinging easily through bodies. Heads flopped from shoulders, stomachs came open like a pillow with ripped stitching.

The ground squelched under his feet, soaked through with blood and sweat and piss. The coppery tang of it mixed with the disgusting stink of fear, and the dragon reared up.

Eoin had no stomach for such violence. The dragon did. He was a predator of unnatural kind, born not with the drive to survive but to destroy. Violence was his nature. He yearned for it, thrilling with every crimson drop that sprayed across Eoin's face.

His sword was gone, replaced with long, black claws. They tore through flesh quickly but chaotically, leaving jagged holes and tattered wounds. Somewhere, distantly, Eoin heard a voice begging him to stop, to please put an end to this.

There would never be an end. War was a thousand-legged demon, crawling after him, sometimes trampling him, and there was no escaping it.

No escape.

No end.

Only blood. Blood and death and blood.

Eoin!

He roared, slicing out with clawed hands, startling when he felt the pain of the blow as if it was his own.

"Eoin!"

Eoin blinked, vision blurring as he tried to understand what he was seeing. Elsie gaped at him, the whites of her eyes flashing. She was crouched cautiously behind his bag, clutching her stomach.

Her bleeding stomach.

Reality crashed back to him, and he rose so fast his head spun. He was tearing through his bag, searching for bandages and finding none.

None because he'd already used them all on the previous wounds he left on her.

What have I done?

What have I done?

Elsie was speaking, her voice gentle, but he couldn't understand her. He couldn't understand anything except she was bleeding, *again*, because of him. She was bleeding and there were no bandages, and he could have *killed her*.

Gods, he could have killed her.

He was always going to be a risk to her. It didn't matter if the dragon was momentarily quelled by carnal touch. He was mad with war. Both of them were, and that was never to change.

"What have I done?" he cried, pulling the fabric of her shirt away and staring at the blood seeping from four red lines across her belly.

Her perfect, soft belly. That beautiful skin marred by his hand. He did this. Eoin did this.

"It doesn't hurt, Eoin," Elsie said carefully, reaching out for him.

She was lying. He felt the sting of it through their bond, those jagged lines pulsing as the skin split.

"What have I done?" He couldn't seem to form any other words, couldn't explain to her the agony he was experiencing.

And how selfish he still was, thinking only of his own pain when it was her that was *bleeding*.

"It isn't deep," she promised. "It's already healing."

Her reaching hand finally connected with him, taking his arm, and bringing him as close as he dared. Elsie lifted her shirt, using her palm to wipe away the blood. Eoin barked at her to stop. He knew how quickly infection could spread to a wound like that. But when she drew her hand away, it was to reveal fresh scabs.

The scabbing was already brown and dry, as if the wound was days old and not minutes.

His momentary stillness brought the bond back into awareness. Eoin felt a tugging sensation through it, as if it was leeching some of his energy to feed to her. He closed his eyes, finding that sensation and focusing on it with everything he had. He pushed that energy, overwhelming Elsie with the strength of his abilities.

Streaks of blood dried on her skin, looking out of place on her now smooth stomach.

"You see?" She smiled softly, coaxing him to her. "I'm fine."

"Fine?" he shouted. "I gutted you!"

"It was only a scratch."

"With dragon claws! I could have—" Eoin couldn't say it. He couldn't think it. For nearly a decade, those fears haunted his every waking moment. Even the worst of his nightmares were not of the battlefield, but of her, lying still as he begged her to return to him.

For once, the dragon didn't fight him. He shifted in a breath, scales coming over him like rivulets of warm water. The gentleness of the change should have been a relief, but Eoin couldn't celebrate it now.

He didn't deserve gentleness. He deserved to be punished by the pain of transformation, to feel the agony of every joint breaking and reforming.

What have I done?

Elsie was screaming at him as he lifted her with two reptilian hands. She wanted to go home, didn't she? She was going to get what she wanted now.

Eoin would take her home and then he would—

What would he do then?

"If you forfeit your life, my life will also be forfeit."

It wasn't as if he could go to Lia and ask her to end him anymore. The bond twined their lives together. If Eoin died, Elsie would die too.

What was the purpose in destroying himself if it also destroyed her?

That was the problem. No matter what choice he made, he always hurt her in the end.

Gods, what was he to do?

Eoin couldn't think that far—couldn't think at all. The only focus he had was returning Elsie to the Black Estate. At least there she would be warm and fed. Perhaps Edgar would put Eoin in the chains again.

Perhaps he would wear them permanently, if that was the way to keep Elsie safe from him.

She was wild in his hands, flailing and kicking. It didn't matter to her that his wing beats brought them high over the foothills, where trees looked as small as dandelions below them. The sun was a glimmering coin on the horizon, dipping low behind the distant Black-wood.

Eoin could almost see the estate, like a black hand clawing out of the stony steps of the mountains.

It wasn't home that caught his attention as they moved gracefully with the wind, but the odd movement and color on the road leading to home.

Torches.

Torches burned on the road to the Blackwood, hundreds and hundreds of orange lights brightening the evening.

Soldiers were marching on the Black Estate.

Eoin wasn't sure if he was awake anymore, or if this was a new dimension of his dark dreams. Each of his greatest fears was coming to fruition, and he couldn't decide the right course of action.

The Soldiers of the Gods were marching on the Black Estate, their grey uniforms out of place among the greenery. Did Eoin return home to warn his brothers? Did he bring Elsie there and risk her once again getting caught up in their madness? Did he return Elsie to that cliff to wait for him as he dispatched every last man who dared to threaten his mate?

Two things happened at once, and the decision was made for him.

Six riders came down the road to meet the soldiers. They were cloaked in black, their swords gleaming in the reflection of torches. Eoin couldn't hear the shouts chanted by the soldiers, but he recognized the cadence of his older brother as he snarled a warning.

His brothers had come to fight for their home.

Eoin wanted to fight too.

For the first time since he went to war, he *wanted* to fight, to protect something meaningful. Not the wealth of the king, or the exploits he sought in a foreign land, but his own land. His own wealth, which was not the gold, finery, and furniture in the Black Estate.

He was wealthy in love, for he had three brothers he would die for, a mate that risked herself to bring him peace, and loyal friends that sat fearlessly atop their horses as death awaited them at the hands of a rebel army.

At the same time, Elsie took advantage of Eoin's distraction, prying his claw from her middle and wriggling in just the right way. She was falling before he could react, once again barreling for the ground with nothing to stop her from smashing into the unforgiving earth below.

He trumpeted his panic into the sky, and all eyes were on him. Fear and thrill rang out from the gathered army below, men pointing stupidly at the black silhouette contrasted against the purple velvet sky.

Eoin wasn't paying any attention to them. Not to the call of his brothers, the threats murmured amidst the chaos. He heard nothing but the frantic beat of Elsie's heart as she fell.

And fell and fell.

He was too near to the ground when he snatched her from the air. This close to the Blackwood the foliage was thick, leaving no room for a tidy landing. Eoin curled in on himself, wings tucked, front legs wrapped protectively around Elsie.

The ground shook as he crashed into it. Trees were felled by the force of him.

Eoin shifted, pain lancing through his spine and up his left leg. A human leg, he realized. The impact of landing forced the dragon to recede, leaving Eoin naked and crippled in the shadow of trees only a few hundred feet from nearly a thousand soldiers.

He twisted, wincing but capable of enough movement that he knew within a handful of hours, he would be fine. Nothing was permanently broken, except for the dozens of tree branches scattered around him.

Eoin twisted again, looking behind him, and still didn't find what he was looking for. The pain he felt was his own. Elsie was uninjured.

Or so he hoped because he couldn't be sure until he located her.

Eoin jerked himself up, standing stiffly on his right leg and peering through the dark foliage.

No. It wasn't possible. He hobbled in a circle, searching the dragon sized crater he left, and finding nothing.

Elsie was gone.

Reaching inside himself, he gripped the bond as if it were an invisible rope, feeling the pull of it. Healthy and vibrant, taut as Elsie moved away from him.

Had they—No, that wasn't possible either. Even now he heard soldiers calling out, cautiously making their way up the hill as Gannon bellowed more threats at them. No one had taken her from him in the mere seconds he was down.

Eoin took another hobbling step, then he spotted her. Legs bare, tattered shirt billowing around her, barely covering anything. She had her chin raised in that signature stubborn way, and Eoin knew before he heard her voice ring clearly above the rest, what she intended to do.

When he glanced past her at the first line of soldiers, where twin Bastards stood grinning at her disheveled state, Eoin understood *why* she intended to do it.

Perched precariously on a horse, hands bound, was a heavily pregnant woman. Her hair was spun gold, eyes light, but the similarities in their faces was unmistakable.

Elsie was going to sacrifice herself for her sister.

CHAPTER 23

ELSIE

"**A**M I REALLY SO impressive that you need an entire army to capture me?" Elsie shouted into the coming night, shoulders back as she approached the High Father's bastards.

She *was* impressive. Any other woman facing off with an army of soldiers that tried to burn her alive would have delivered those words with a quiver in her voice.

Elsie was doing a remarkable job at hiding hers.

Strangely, she wasn't afraid for herself. Not anymore. There was nothing these men could do to her that would frighten her. Eoin was here, and with him at her back, she was invincible.

Even if he was worse for wear after their less than graceful landing.

He was a dragon, Elsie assured herself. He would be fine.

If he hadn't carried her off like a maiden stolen from a dragon of lore, she wouldn't have had to take such extreme measures. Elsie could feel his panic rising with each beat of his wings, saw the indecision as they came upon this display at the edge of the Black Estate, and knew he wouldn't let her go freely.

But Elsie had to.

She had to because even before she saw Irene mounted unsafely on a horse, face pale and painted with the dried tracks of many, many tears, Elsie knew they had her. How else did the Bastards know to come to the Black Estate? She'd been careful not to give herself away. Even in her letters to Mother, she mentioned being employed by a baron but never which one.

It wasn't until she'd been huddled behind Irene's home, trying to convince her to flee, that she mentioned the Black family name.

Elsie couldn't blame her sister for giving it to them.

There was no one to blame but the twin demons standing smugly on either side of her horse.

The ambitious Bastard made a show of eyeing her bedraggled state, scoffing. "Not impressive at all. That dragon on the other hand...now that was a show to remember."

"Dragon?" she tapped her chin, taking as many more steps as she dared. "I don't recall seeing a dragon."

Peripherally she saw Gannon and the others shifting anxiously on horseback. They were all there, armed and furious. Even Nigel sat plump and scowling on a short mare, a massive hammer in his hand. A young woman rode beside them, vaguely familiar, but Elsie didn't have time to remember where she knew her from.

Based on the emerald glint in Gannon's eyes, he was moments away from dispatching everyone.

Elsie didn't intend to stop him. Let the lot of them die by dragon fire.

After she saved her sister.

"Baron Black, my soldiers mean no harm by entering your estate. We don't seek to harm anyone who is faithful and good in the eyes of the Gods." The ambitious Bastard addressed Gannon while his brother continued to leer at Elsie. "But you should know, you have been housing wickedness under your roof."

"Who lives under my roof is no business of yours. I have warned you once already, and I am not generous in my warnings. Remove yourself from the Blackwood or suffer the consequences."

Soldiers audibly laughed at the threat. To them, they were a thousand men against five. They had no idea how many of their rivals were dragons.

"We aren't here for your wealth or your women," the ambitious Bastard promised. "We want only what was promised to us by the Gods. Judgement from the sky. Fire to cleanse the land of wickedness." He turned to face Elsie, pulling the reins of the horse with him and jolting Irene from her ill-balanced position in the saddle. "Where is the dragon?"

Elsie traced the mark on her cheek instinctively, wondering the same question. There was pain in the bond as she brought it back into her awareness. She hadn't thought to see if Eoin was okay. He always was.

What if he wasn't?

Her heart was torn down the middle, drawn between Eoin and Irene.

The ambitious Bastard was feeling impatient, his tone sharp as he repeated, "where is the dragon?"

Elsie took a step closer. A thousand swords pointed in her direction. "What do you think you're going to do with a dragon?"

"You truly know nothing of the holy words, you snake," he spat. "This is the age of the dragon, promised to us by the High Gods. It is a time of redemption. The end of mortal man, unless we cleanse ourselves of the wickedness we have sown into this precious paradise."

"Never heard of it," Elsie shrugged. "Now release my sister or die burning."

The ambitious Bastard withdrew his own sword, pointing it directly at Irene's gravid belly. "I think not. Remove whatever spell you've cast over that sacred beast. I do believe you have good reason to comply, *witch.*"

Elsie wanted to laugh at how little they truly knew of the world outside their holy books, but her throat was closed at the sight of Irene only an inch from being run through. She forced in a breath, steadying herself as she admitted, "I can't undo the magic that binds us, but I will return with you. Take me in Irene's stead and the dragon will follow."

She didn't know what she planned to do if they accepted. She didn't know anything except that she wouldn't let any more harm come to her sister.

Those sweet blue eyes sprouted fresh tears, her face crumpling as Irene stared helplessly at Elsie.

The ambitious Bastard attempted to speak but only a strangled scream escaped him. That was probably because he was suddenly short an arm, his sword and the hand that gripped it lying limp and bloody on the ground. Elsie hadn't heard the blade that whipped through the air, cutting muscle and bone as if it were butter. It was thrown with such precision she'd scarcely seen it.

Eoin stood shirtless between his brothers' horses, wearing a pair of pants much too small for him, his eyes blazing like the distant sunset. "She's not going anywhere with you."

Chaos erupted with Eoin's declaration. A battle cry shook the trees, the second Bastard charging into action against an unarmed Eoin. The reins on Irene's horse were dropped, and Elsie saw her chance.

But the animal was scared, sensing the true danger that lurked beneath Eoin's skin, and the horse reared back.

Elsie was running before she registered what was happening. Her legs pumped, throwing herself directly into a sea of swinging swords. Horses knickered, running wildly into the Blackwood. Gannon was on the ground, calling out to his brothers. She spotted Eoin in the corner of her vision, sporting a new sword and cutting men down like they were made of paper.

Madness twisted his features, a real madness unlike what she'd seen before completing their bond. He would kill every man here to protect her.

What would that do to him?

She couldn't think of the guilt yet, couldn't think of anything but getting to Irene.

Irene who was lost amidst moving bodies, a flash of gold in an endless wave of grey. Elsie watched the shimmer of her hair, clinging to the tiny hope that she was fine, miraculously unharmed after toppling from the horse.

A sword swung at her head, and she barely managed to duck in time. It was only Eoin's defense lessons returning to her in muscle memory that kept her from losing her upper half.

Over the noise of steel clashing with steel she heard him roaring her name. Soon he would be a dragon again, if he wasn't already.

The Black brothers guarded their secret to the grave. They told no one of what they were, and for good reason. Gannon found himself at the mercy of a greedy king last year. What would a man like that do if he discovered the dragon could shift into a form that could be reasoned with? Threatened?

If one of them shifted now, in plain sight of a thousand or more men, someone would live to tell the tale. The brothers could be deadly when they wanted to be, and she didn't doubt they would kill a thousand men to keep their secret safe.

But they didn't want to. Above all else, the Black brothers were good. They shared Eoin's heart, steely on the outside but secretly soft. Gentle to those that needed it. Honorable and kind.

They understood these men were not here on their own volition. They were downtrodden, hungry, and weak, tired of serving greedy men that didn't care if they lived or died. The High Father sold them the dream of a new world and they bet their lives on that dream, believing it was possible.

Believing you could carve a new world from the flesh and blood of the old one.

Now the Black brothers were facing an impossible choice. They had to fight to protect their home. They would fight to protect her and Irene, too. But whichever way this battle went, they would be left exposed.

Their secret exposed, or their safe haven.

It was because of Elsie that they would have to choose. Because of her that they would be haunted by the face of every man they dispatched.

No, she reminded herself. *It's because of **him**.* She pictured the High Father in his final moments. The way his eyes rolled as Elsie's dagger found his spleen.

This army would have marched through the Blackwood one way or another.

Suddenly Elsie found herself crushed, two soldiers colliding with her in the middle. She tumbled forward, following a frightened cry. Irene was there, huddled protectively over her belly, bleeding from head.

"Eoin!" she screamed his name, knowing he would find her. He would get them out.

A man flew straight over their heads, landing mangled and limp. More toppled backwards, crashing into each other as Eoin pummeled his way through the crowd. His second sword was gone, fists bloody as they extended again and again, too fast for Elsie to follow. The pale coloring of his face was gone, replaced with a sheen of black scales.

Somehow, Eoin had become both man and dragon. His skin was armored and hard, his eyes blazing like molten rock, yet he stood on two legs. She watched, horrified and fascinated, as Eoin gripped the collar of a soldier's uniform and dragged him close enough to *bite through his neck*. The soldier swung wide with his sword, sending sparks spraying as it was deflected by scales.

A circle opened around them, widening quickly when Amos and Davin joined the fray. Elsie hefted Irene onto her feet, barely moving her in time to avoid being trampled. Her sister was shaking violently, her legs too weak to keep her upright.

"Eoin! I need you!" Elsie screamed a second time, drawing him from battle right to her side.

He took her by the arm, prepared to carry her off like some savage once again. "Don't you dare, Eoin Black. Irene first."

"I don't—" he shuttered the words with a growl, smart enough to realize the repercussions if he finished that sentence.

"Get her out of here. I'll be at your back."

Eoin stared her down, pupils shifting in the glow of discarded torches. Chaos continued around them, the sound of steel on steel making her ears ring. His indecisiveness was going to get Irene killed.

"Take her *now!*"

He obeyed with a vicious snap of teeth, carefully lifting Irene into his arms. Orders were barked over his shoulder as he ran from the battle, and his brothers closed ranks around Elsie like well-trained soldiers. They took two steps back at a time, leading her with them.

Elsie's bare feet squelched, and she didn't have the stomach to look down. Blood soaked everything. Moans of pain filled the air, and at least one body was burning somewhere, the scent of it sickening.

Was it any wonder Eoin was haunted?

The Black brothers had put a dent in the Bastard's army, but it seemed to make little difference to them. It was clear which men were soldiers in their previous life, forming battle positions and easily closing in on the brothers in their attempted retreat.

Couldn't they see how fruitless this was? They would be slaughtered. All of them.

The name of every High God was a prayer on the wind, wordless murmurs and chants calling to them for strength. For judgment.

It occurred to her then that these men truly would die for the Gods.

"Go, Elsie." Gannon appeared at her side, the hilt of a dagger extended to her. "Take this and follow Eoin up the road. Find Mara." He was panting, sweat dripping from his hair.

Elsie accepted the dagger, hurrying into the shadows as Gannon blocked her from view. "They're not going to stop, Gannon," she said with a meaningful glance at his brothers. "One of you has to end this."

Or maybe all of them.

Elsie only made it a few steps down the road before she slipped. Her feet were wet, her legs were shaking, and her body was warning her that she had very little energy left to spare.

Three miles. She only had to make it three miles up the road, maybe less if she encountered Eoin on his way back for her. She could feel him out there, a wall of rage. Every second she was away from him, in the middle of this madness, was a second he grew closer to losing his control.

Elsie put one foot in front of the other, thinking of the dragon. He wasn't a monster at all. He was a protector. He kept Eoin safe from the worst of war. He protected everyone he loved by enlisting.

They needed him to protect them again now. They needed his single-minded focus.

The Soldiers of the Gods wouldn't stop. Their numbers would grow, and the innocent lives they took would be many. If Eoin could stop this now, he wouldn't just be protecting her, or his brothers or the Black Estate.

He would be saving all of Dunhill.

A huge figure stepped onto the road, coming directly for her. It was too dark for her to see anything but those glowing eyes, but she knew it was him.

Elsie nearly collapsed with relief. If Eoin was here, then Irene would be safe. Her sister was safe.

Eoin waved his arms wildly, shouting for her. His pace quickened tenfold, moving so fast he was a blur of color and shadow.

It didn't matter how quickly he moved. Eoin didn't reach her in time.

The blade came silently from the darkness, slicing across Elsie's front and knocking her back. She was too surprised to catch herself, her head smacking against the hard earth and sending her vision trailing sideways. She couldn't see the man towering over her, only the blurry image of his sword as it came down into her stomach, pinning her in place.

Sound exploded around her, the battle pushing toward the Black Estate. The Black brothers falling back.

Why were they falling back?

End this, she begged silently. *Don't let them spread this poison any further.*

No one heard her, though. Elsie opened her mouth, trying to speak. Her throat burbled, her lungs seizing.

She tried to move but the feeling of her legs was gone, as if someone had removed them wholly from her body. Someone was screaming at her, his familiar voice distorted and incoherent.

"Eoin," she moaned, wanting desperately to feel him one final time. Then she choked, her throat wet and thick. "I love you," she tried to whisper, not sure any sound came out.

After everything, it was *her* that would kill *him*.

If you forfeit your life, my life will also be forfeit.

Elsie blinked her eyes closed, and they didn't open again.

CHAPTER 24

Eoin

Elsie was dying.

Eoin could feel her life seeping from the bond like color vanishing from the world when night set in. His brothers were around him, fighting to defend him, and it was utterly pointless.

Because Elsie was going to die.

The sword he removed from her middle lay dull on the ground beside the crumpled body of her attacker. Eoin should have killed him, should have thrown that sword right through his evil head. The armless bastard had survived a mortal wound long enough to return the favor.

He took Elsie.

Claws extended from his fingers, wanting something to shred, someone to kill. There were a thousand bodies here for him to destroy, a thousand men he could snuff out with a few swipes of his dragon claws.

That wouldn't stop his mate from bleeding out on the road. It wouldn't make her sluggish heartbeat faster.

Death begot death. That was why Eoin was kneeling in the mud, cradling Elsie as she left him.

This was his punishment. In the end, he lost her, whether it was by his own hands or not. It did not hurt any less to see her die by other means.

Eoin suddenly remembered being a new soldier, old enough not to need his father but young enough to want to need him. He was returning home from the training camps for the first time, wishing he would be returning to see pride in his father's eyes.

Instead, he was returning home to burn his body.

Mother had passed two weeks earlier, her heart stopping as she slept, and Father had followed her.

It was by choice. *Drakonmein* died when their mates did not because the bond had that much hold over them, but because when the bond ceased to exist, they saw no reason to continue existing either.

Eoin resented his father for that choice once. He thought it selfish to leave this world and his entire legacy behind because of grief.

Now, he understood.

He understood that the absence of this bond would be like the absence of air. How could he go on when he could no longer breathe? Couldn't smell the scent of flowers or taste springtime in his lungs.

For long minutes he grasped that bond, forcing every ounce of energy into it. If he could, Eoin would pour his entire life force through the bond, trading himself for her.

Giving all of himself the way that Elsie always did. For her family, for her friends, for him.

"Elsie," he pleaded, shaking her as her breaths grew shallower. "Take from me! Heal! Why won't you heal?" She didn't respond, her eyelids solidly shut.

"Please! You cannot leave me when you've only just made me promise to stay," he said in a broken voice. "If you forfeit your life, I will forfeit my life too."

"It's too grave, Captain Black." Eoin whipped his head around, startled by the gentle voice. Lia stood over them, her eyes soft with sympathy. He'd barely registered her presence earlier, having forgotten that she was fighting beside his brothers. Perhaps she got tired of waiting for him and had sought Gannon out for support instead.

"It can't be." He stroked the side of Elsie's face. It was so cold. She was growing so cold. "I cannot lose her. *I will not.*"

"You love her."

"More than anything in this world."

"What would you sacrifice to keep her?"

Eoin glared at her, shoving off the ground, and supporting Elsie against his chest with one hand as the other snatched the front of Lia's shirt. "I don't have time for these riddles! Tell me what you know!"

"Your blood," Lia sputtered. "You must let her drink from your vein."

Edgar was there in a heartbeat. His pale hair was pink with blood, one eye swollen shut. Gannon shouldn't have let him come. He was fragile, like Elsie, no matter what kind of power his mother passed down to him.

"*It's forbidden for a reason.*" Edgar swiped his hands wildly through the air.

Eoin was already accepting one of Lia's daggers, digging it into his wrist until his blood was trickling down his arm. "I don't care."

"*There is no telling*—" Eoin wasn't watching to see what else Edgar had to say.

Soldiers were falling on them left and right. Lia whirled, flicking a dagger through the air, and catching a man as he advanced on her. His brothers would lose this battle without their dragons. It wasn't a matter of strength, it was a matter of numbers.

He pinched the sides of Elsie's jaw, forcing it open and letting the stream of blood pool in her mouth. She didn't swallow.

She wasn't breathing.

Eoin snarled, shaking her forcefully, closing her mouth and breathing through her nose until she gagged and swallowed. The breath she finally took was rasping, a death rattle.

The air didn't leave his lungs until it left hers too. This one wasn't any stronger than the last, but at least it came. Then there was another and another. Steady, and smooth.

"She will live," Lia promised, glancing over her shoulder for only a heartbeat before tossing another dagger. "I have never seen it with my own eyes, but I know the history of my people. *Our* people."

Edgar crouched beside him, stroking damp hair from Elsie's face. *"There will be a price. Magic always has a price."*

Eoin wrapped his arms tighter around Elsie, desperate to see her open her eyes. To groan. Anything to prove Lia was right, and he was not wasting his last moments with her. "Any price is worth her life."

"Not everyone takes well to immortality. I have seen men go mad with years. I pray to my mother's Gods to show mercy on her," Edgar signed.

Eoin opened his mouth to argue when a burst of heat cut him off. Sparks sprayed in an aura around Elsie.

Then she was burning, her body bathed in golden flames. It was hot against his skin, uncomfortably so, yet it did not burn him.

The same must not have been true for Edgar. He jumped back, hissing and shaking the hand that had been at Elsie's scalp.

"What's happening?" Eoin asked Lia frantically.

Lia narrowly dodged an attack, distracted by the growing fire behind her. "I don't know."

Eoin lifted Elsie, not sure what he should do. What if this was the sacrifice for what he'd done? What if he'd angered the Gods, and they chose to take her from him, anyway?

The fire crackled loudly, engulfing the both of them in a hazy, golden steam. Eoin roared, begging it to stop. Begging her to return to him.

"Please, Elsie, come back to me." The flames overcame him. "Come back to me."

With a gasp, Elsie jolted in his arms. Her hands flew to her stomach, where blood soaked her. The blood mingled with ash, the remnants of her clothes burning away to reveal immaculate skin. There was no wound. There was not a single mark on Elsie's body. Each and every callous and scar was gone, leaving her glittering as if she was a Goddess stepping down from above.

Her gaze found his, and he blinked, trying to make sense of what he was seeing.

It was Elsie's face that stared back at him, but instead of her lovely brown eyes, Eoin met the gilded irises of a dragon.

She leapt from his arms, a burning figure at the center of battle. The sound of fighting ceased all at once, soldiers collectively holding their breath as they took in the impossible sight before them.

"Age of the dragon," he heard one man murmur. Another repeated it, then another, until they were chanting it mindlessly, dropping their swords at Elsie's feet.

Elsie watched them with reptilian eyes, tracking their movement with predatory precision.

"Gannon," she said, "take your brothers home."

Gannon was dragging Nigel and Edgar with him before Elsie even finished speaking. There was an ominous lilt in her voice, an inhuman note that reminded him of the beast caged inside him.

Eoin stepped into her fire, touching her skin, assuring himself that this was real. That she was living.

But those eyes...this *was* Elsie, wasn't it?

"This ends now," she told him.

Then another vision from Eoin's nightmares came to life. An inferno exploded above Elsie, fire reaching all the way to the heavens. It arced and twisted, growing wider and wilder with stunning speed.

Chants shifted to screams as flames engulfed the road. Trees burned on either side of them, lighting the night and revealing the gory horror of what had happened here. In an instant men dropped, their bodies singed, clothing ash.

There was no escape for any of them. Elsie opened her mouth to roar, the sound like none he'd heard before. From the depth of his chest his dragon answered her, trumpeting his approval of her destruction.

End them all, he urged. *Boil their blood.*

Elsie did. Her fire stretched for miles, devouring everything in sight. Eoin was blinded by it, swallowed whole along with everything else.

As quickly as it began, the fire flickered out. Bits of it remained in the treetops, sparkling as it ate at dry leaf and dead bark.

There were bodies everywhere. A thousand corpses scorched beyond recognition. The men that were closest to Elsie had no flesh remaining, only crumpled black skeletons to prove they had ever lived at all.

It was devastation like he'd never seen before.

Somehow, he couldn't bring himself to feel remorse. Nor regret or guilt, or any emotion really, except relief

"Elsie?"

She collapsed into his arms, her eyes softening to that liquid brown he loved so much. Tears carved lines through the soot on her cheeks, and he knew she would not be untouched by this.

Eoin could live with death. He was a monster, after all.

But Elsie wasn't. Elsie was a reflection of the best parts of this world, and she would suffer the burden of her actions for a lifetime.

"Not everyone takes well to immortality."

And how long would that lifetime be, exactly?

Eoin had more questions than answers, and he wasn't equipped to ask any of them now. Miles up the road he heard his brothers calling for him. He hobbled in their direction, feeling as if he lived a hundred years over the last two days. His body was weak and broken, and Elsie's was too.

But as they neared the Black Estate, Davin and Amos rushing to meet them with clothing and blankets, a series of sparks danced across Elsie's arms.

"What's happening to me?"

"I don't know," he answered honestly. "I don't know what I've done to you."

She curled her arms around his neck, clinging to him with such force he nearly toppled. "I don't care what you've done to me, Eoin Black. I will love you even if we're both monsters."

CHAPTER 25

ELSIE HAD STARTED ANOTHER fire. It was a small one this time, burning only a thin black ring into the wooden table in the corner of the kitchen, but even a small fire was too big, given the circumstances.

With a sigh she returned the wooden serving tray to the table, careful not to slosh the soup stacked on top. There were also cookies, a handful of early blackberries, bread, and fresh goats milk too—drinking milk helped a mother make milk, or so Edgar claimed.

Unsurprisingly, Edgar knew a lot about caring for new mothers. Amos was the reader in the family and so she sometimes forgot that Edgar was a scholar as well. Not in any traditional way, but it didn't matter here at the Black Estate. He was a well of knowledge and they utilized him whenever he was willing to share.

There were plenty of subjects Edgar was versed in that weren't written in any book she'd heard of.

Like a woman that randomly catches fire after drinking the blood of a *drakonmein*.

"Do you mind?" Elsie asked Nigel, staring sadly at the steaming bowl of soup.

"Don't mind a bit." Nigel bumbled over, tapping her forehead quickly before dropping a kiss there. "Can't be too careful these days." He chuckled, his rotund belly bouncing merrily. The frothy white beard that covered his neck seemed thinner since she left home, and she wondered if he laughed like that when she was gone. "I always did say you were a hot head."

"I'm glad that someone is benefitting from my predicament." Elsie wrinkled her nose, swatting him as he reached for the flask he kept in the pocket of his apron. "Not until after you've fed my sister."

She did so want to see the baby but after Irene gave birth eight days ago, she swore she wouldn't step foot into that room unless she knew she wasn't a risk to the child or her mother. Elsie had seen her sweet niece only twice.

It was a miracle she'd made it through the birth without burning the entire Black Estate to the ground. Irene began laboring only hours after Eoin and Elsie returned home. There wasn't anything left for Elsie to give, but she forced herself to give it, anyway.

Emotion appeared to be the trigger for whatever this bizarre condition was that Eoin's blood put her in, and there was nothing more emotional than holding her sister's hand as her womb contracted. Eoin stood at Elsie's shoulder the whole time, pouring water over her, and keeping her damp.

That was the only way to prevent her from igniting, Elsie reasoned, and it seemed to work.

It wasn't practical to carry a bucket of water around and douse herself at any moment, so Elsie was trying to find a better solution.

Unfortunately, she wasn't exactly known for her stoicism. Overcoming this would take time.

She didn't intend to wallow about her circumstances. It saddened her to leave Irene isolated during a time of combined grief and joy, but she knew her sister was in good hands. Mara was at her side all hours of the day, holding the baby whenever Irene needed rest, calling to Nigel to make whatever meal Irene craved.

Besides, her suffering was trivial in comparison to what Irene faced.

Hamish was dead. So was Mother. The world she'd known taken from her in one night.

The baby, at least, was fine. Edgar had warned them that falling off a horse could end poorly for the baby. They held their breath until little Katherine took her first breath, squalling angrily into the cold night air.

Irene sobbed as Elsie helped the baby into her arms. "I lied," she whispered. "She's Hamish's."

"You lied to the High Father?"

"Yes." she trailed a finger across the baby's face, eyes round with awe. "I was already two months pregnant when…"

"Water, Eoin," Elsie begged, feeling the heat come on again.

Eoin splashed her, leaving a dripping mess on the floor. Elsie was soaked as she hugged her sister, trying to absorb some of her pain.

"She will be the safest child in all of Svalta," Elsie promised quietly. It was all she could promise.

There was no returning her husband to her, no true comfort for her grief. Only time could manage that for her.

It took days before Elsie processed Irene's confession. Days before any of it fully registered. Perhaps in some ways, it hadn't registered at all. Life resumed as normal not long after her return, and it was hard to feel as if anything had changed.

Until she looked in the mirror, saw the black mark on her cheek, and remembered that everything had changed.

A wave of tears threatened to drown her as Nigel disappeared up the back stairwell with the tray in his hand, and with those tears came fresh sparks. Elsie raced out of the kitchen, hurrying to the other staircase and praying no stray spark caught the dreaded drapes in the dining room. She hit the main staircase at a run, flying up steps two at a time.

Three stories and six turns later, she found the hall she was looking for and charged down it. Usually, her instinct was to leave the manor when this happened. A walk through the hedge maze momentarily eased her sorrow, and the hedges weren't nearly as flammable as the numerous Black family heirlooms. But what she needed wasn't in the maze now, and Elsie would be better off here, if she could just get there on time.

Eoin must have sensed her urgency, bursting through the closed door of their shared rooms and hurrying to meet her. He saw the tears spilling down her cheeks, the sparks dancing off her skin like a catching fire, and dragged her behind closed doors.

A hiss sounded as he kissed her, and Elsie tried to pull away. She couldn't hurt him with her fire anymore than he could hurt her—an interesting perk to being a dragon's mate—but it wasn't always pleasant for him when it first began.

Eoin gripped the back of her head, forcing her mouth open and running his tongue along her upper lip. There was a noise like thick drapes whipping open and Elsie snapped her eyes wide to see magnificent black wings spreading out from Eoin's shoulders. It was a new talent he'd learned during their battle with the Soldiers of the Gods, and Elsie was still thrilled by it.

In trying to deny the dragon, Eoin had done the opposite, melding them together so thoroughly that he could now hold any number of forms in between. Sometimes it was wings, other times a layer of scales formed across his skin. He wasn't able to control when it happened, or even what part of him changed, and Elsie suspected it was because the dragon was solely responsible for those changes.

He seemed to know precisely what she needed, walking backward with her still in his arms. They pushed through the double doors to the wrought-iron balcony, bumping into the railing so hard Elsie lost her footing. Eoin took advantage, lifting her into his arms and grinning that toothy reptilian grin. His eyes lit orange with mischief seconds before he leaned over the side of the balcony and dropped toward the garden below.

Elsie screamed in fear and delight, watching as his wings pumped air beneath them to cushion their landing. They were on the west side of the estate, where the immaculate flower gardens gave way to vegetables and the greenhouse Nigel tended to all winter. Back here, there were no windows to occupied rooms where prying eyes might spot them.

Here, they were utterly alone so Elsie could fall apart in peace.

Or, if Eoin had his way, fall into pieces.

Her dress was up around her waist before she could say a word, back pressed into a stonewall that divided seasonal garden plots. It was fortunate that she'd chosen to wear one of her least loved dresses today because it would be little more than ash when she was done.

The moment Eoin thrust inside her, Elsie burst into flames. Golden fire danced around them, engulfing them both, licking hungrily at their skin. The fire frightened her, if she was being honest, but only because she couldn't control it.

It was so bad that most nights she'd taken to sleeping outside, making a pallet out of random bedding and using Eoin to keep her warm.

That didn't mean she didn't like it.

Having Eoin's blood course through her veins did strange things to the bond. It was more open, fluid, and she loved the way his pleasure flowed into her. The crackle of fire heightened that pleasure for both of them, making it nearly impossible for her to make it two minutes before she was screaming in ecstasy.

Tears followed ecstasy this time, and Elsie bowed her head as her skin dimmed and cooled. Eoin wrapped himself around her, his black wings cocooning her in safety and warmth.

"I don't know why I'm crying," she admitted.

"You've collected plenty of reasons to cry."

"I don't want to cry anymore."

He tucked a stray curl behind her ear, pausing to caress her earlobe. "I don't think we get to choose how long it takes for these wounds to heal."

Elsie heard the words he didn't want to say. *I don't know if some of them will ever heal.*

They were a mess, the two of them. A war hungry monster who dreamed of death, and a housekeeper who was a fire hazard anytime she set foot indoors.

Elsie expected more tears to follow that thought. She expected the crushing weight of all she'd done to bear down on her. Instead, she felt a raindrop hit her scalp. It was joined by many more, hissing and steaming off their heated bodies.

It was easy to give in to sorrow. Easy to pity herself, to let herself be swallowed by guilt and shame.

But Elsie's life had never been easy, and she didn't intend to make it that way now.

"I think they will," she whispered.

"You think what will?"

"These wounds," she said. "I know they can heal." She smiled against Eoin's lips, kissing him sweetly. "What's broken can always be mended."

Epilogue

Amos

ONE WOULD THINK THAT a manor as big as the Black family home would be a quiet place. An entire wing of the house was abandoned except for his lurking older brother and his mate, and there were a dozen more living quarters than there ever were people. Unless you counted ghosts as people.

Amos didn't.

Frankly, he didn't believe in ghosts, or any other spiritual mumbo jumbo, for that matter. Edgar loved to point out the irony of that refusal. How could a man that turned into a dragon not believe in ghosts and witchcraft?

Simple. He didn't.

Ghosts didn't make sense and witchcraft often had a logical explanation.

There were anomalies, he could admit that, but just because something didn't have an explanation *yet* didn't mean there wasn't one.

Like the explanation for how noise managed to travel three stories and two hallways to disturb him while he was trying to avoid—ahem, while he was trying to get in a bit of light reading.

Fine, *Bruno Dietrich's Historical Study of Population Migration Across Greater Svalta* wasn't exactly light reading, but it was doing the trick.

Until a feminine squeal told him that Elsie had caught something on fire again and Eoin was "helping her" to extinguish it. That or the baby was crying, Mara had spilled another tray of soup on the stairs, or *she* was making an unusual amount of noise.

Amos mentally scratched out the latter, knowing that it wasn't true. *She* was never making noise.

In fact, if he hadn't felt her in the flesh, Amos would think that she was a ghost.

A devastatingly beautiful ghost with an equally devastating set of daggers.

He wasn't sure which part heated his blood more.

That was exactly the problem. Lia had arrived on their doorstep only hours before the Soldiers of the Gods, claiming Eoin was in trouble and a rebel army planned to attack. Gannon had been skeptical as she explained what was happening to the clans in the mountains, but Amos was quick to convince his brother to trust the young woman.

What bothered Amos was that he didn't care if she was telling the truth or not. He wanted Gannon to trust her because that would make her stay.

Amos didn't recognize Lia, and he knew they'd never met, but there was something about her, some familiar scent or perhaps the shape of her face, which was driving him mad.

He didn't know her and yet he *knew* her. Knew her presence with such inexplicable familiarity that he was struggling to keep himself in check whenever she was near him. It wasn't appropriate to go touching a woman that he'd only know a handful of days, yet somehow that was all he wanted to do.

Constantly.

Her hair was like polished copper, and he wanted to unwind it from the tight braid she always tied behind her head to feel if it was as smooth as it looked. That was the most appropriate urge he felt whenever Lia was in the room. The others had him excusing himself to adjust the fit of his pants.

Amos wasn't the most experienced when it came to women. *Drakonmein* generally weren't since becoming too intimate with a woman could irrevocably bind her to them, for better or worse. That hadn't stopped the youngest Black brother from chasing any woman that so much as glanced at him, but Davin was an outlier.

Incorrigible, more like. Amos feared the day he would come home with a toothless tavern wench and sheepishly admit they were accidentally mated for the rest of their lives.

Gods, have mercy on his foolish little brother.

Davin was also part of the problem because his extensive knowledge of women meant he had no qualms about approaching Lia. He was quick with his flirtatious remarks, flicking the tip of Lia's braid between his fingers the way Amos longed to do.

Of course, that nearly earned him a dagger through the hand. Lia was a woman that could look after herself, and Amos was glad for it. If she hadn't reacted, he would have, and there was no telling what the result of that reaction would be.

Amos prided himself on being the most controlled of his brothers. He didn't have a hot temper, and he wasn't one to start fights. When necessary, he would finish them, and sometimes he gave Davin a well-deserved beating, but mostly he stayed out of his brothers' brawls.

No sense in provoking his dragon. That beast was feral. It wasn't some woeful title he'd given it for defying him, merely a matter of fact. Unlike his brothers, Amos couldn't control his dragon. At all. There was no camaraderie between them, no channel of communication.

Occasionally, Amos would feel pressure beneath his skin and know it was time to let the dragon free. He would travel deep into the mountains where the beast was happy to hunt and stretch his wings without bothering anyone.

The mountains were like home to the dragon. For as long as Amos could remember, he longed for them. Peace eluded him, of course, as dragons were not meant for such frivolous emotions. Only a mate would bring a dragon peace, or so it seemed, and Amos doubted he was destined for one.

How was he to know if he'd found her when the dragon was markedly silent?

Or was he?

Amos rubbed at his temples, feeling a tension headache coming on, and wondered if *this* was communication from his dragon. The first time it happened was at the tavern with his brothers and Elsie before she left for Brilend. His head was throbbing, and not from the drink.

The next thing he knew he was in an alley pummeling Eoin with no clear motivation. He didn't even remember how he got outside.

Those headaches persisted over the days that Elsie was gone, increasing in frequency when Lia arrived, and they were forced to fight a thousand men at the doorstep of his family home. He'd attributed it to stress. What was more stressful than seeing an armed mob descend on the people you loved, and watching them nearly die?

Elsie and Eoin would have both been taken from them if it weren't for Lia.

Lia who had vast knowledge about *drakonmein* and had yet to tell him how she gained that knowledge. Edgar was also not free from suspicion, he reminded himself. He might be mute, but that wasn't an excuse to keep secrets from his closest friends.

Where did a man—or woman—learn forbidden knowledge about a secret race of shapeshifters?

And was there a book they could loan him? Amos was painfully curious. Father never kept anything from them, but his knowledge was only as good as his father's, and his father's before him. Word of mouth became unreliable over time, and Amos suspected there was a great deal of history he would never know.

With a sigh he slapped his book shut. A quandary for another time. Reading about the history of Dunhill would not answer his questions anymore than pounding the insides of his brain with them would. There was an itch he needed to scratch, and he was coming to realize how fruitless it was to deny it.

The irritating pulse of his headache led him down the main staircase and to the dining room, where tea should have been served. He didn't expect there would be much company during teatime since they hadn't all had a meal together in days. It was hard to gather for dinner when Elsie was at risk of catching the drapes on fire, Mara was busy caring for Irene and the baby, Gannon was brooding because Mara's attention was elsewhere, and Eoin couldn't stop staring at Elsie with those creepy dragon eyes.

Not to mention the scales. It was one thing to see the dragon through Eoin's eyes—they were the window to the soul, after all—but his random outbreaks of black scales were unsettling. Amos hoped whatever condition his brother was suffering, he never encountered it himself. There was a solid boundary between man and dragon in his mind, and he liked to keep it that way.

Amos came through the doorway in the dining room, disappointment softening his shoulders when he found Davin seated alone, a stupidly feminine teacup in his hands. The floral monstrosity was one of their mother's keepsakes and they were all too sentimental to do away with it, though they all agreed that hulking dragon shifters looked ridiculous eating from plates painted with roses and pansies.

Sentimentality often won in a battle with pride in this family. That was why the Black Estate was filled to the brim with paintings, journals, out of style gowns, and Gods knew what trinkets and baubles. Four generations of Blacks had lived in this manor, and many more would follow. Someday he wondered if trunks of ancestral rubbish would be spilling out through the windows.

Amos disguised the odd grumble in his throat with a sigh, taking a seat next to Davin and swiping a cookie from his plate. Davin simply smiled at the thievery, black eyes twinkling in a way that made the hair rise on Amos's neck.

"Looking for something?" he asked with a smirk. "Or perhaps *someone*?"

Davin was the first to notice his brother's eager interest in their new guest, and he wasn't subtle with his teasing remarks.

"Yes, I was looking for you, dear brother. I've just been reading the most fascinating book—"

"Fine, fine, I'll tell you where she is," Davin groused. "My ears will bleed if I have to hear another lecture on *migratory populations*."

Two minutes later Amos was strolling into the stable, forcing his legs to move at a leisurely pace. They didn't want to move at any normal pace when Davin admitted that Lia was in the stable preparing her horse for travel, so the movement was awkward.

One foot in front of the other.

Fortunately being overly conscious of how he walked distracted him from the pulsing pain that was building behind his forehead. It travelled over the top of his skull, burning down his spine and making the place between his shoulder blades itch.

Suddenly he longed for the sensation of wings unfurling from that very spot.

"Good, you're here," Lia said, snaring his focus so thoroughly he forgot about his feet, his legs, and every other part of his body except the beating organ in his chest. "I was beginning to think you changed your mind."

"Yes," Amos answered dumbly. "I'm here."

She stood beside a stocky bay mare, fastening a heavy bag to the saddle. The horse shifted, snorting nervously, and Lia paused, glancing at Amos with narrowed eyes. "Are you unwell?"

"I'm wonderful, thank you."

Her stance was practiced, a warrior raising her guard. "Are you sure?"

Amos approached, putting a hand out to stroke her horse and startling when the animal stomped unhappily. He was accustomed to the horses that Edgar raised, hardy creatures bred to be around dragons. Perhaps Lia's horse sensed what most animals did and wanted to keep a healthy distance from him. Amos lowered his hand, frowning.

"Of course. Why?" He ran a self-conscious hand through his hair, glancing at the black strands to see if Davin had dumped crumps on his head, or worse.

"Your eyes," she whispered, sounding more awed than alarmed. "They're red."

Red like a demon's eyes. That was how his mother once described them. Not the most flattering description, and though she meant no harm, those words haunted Amos to this day.

He noticed it then, the shift in colors. The strange clarity his vision had when he was the dragon. Amos had shown the presence of his dragon a handful of times since coming of age and learning to control his urges, and it was only in the direst situations.

It was instinct to retreat, ducking his head and turning away from her. He pretended to study another horse dozing in her stall, sounding distant and disinterested when he said, "you're leaving, then."

"*I'm* leaving?"

"*You're* leaving?" He studied her in a sidelong glance. It was impossible not to stare at her. Copper hair braided carefully across her scalp to hang like a rope at her back, green irises painting the most beautiful contrast.

Lia propped her hands on her hips, sighing irritably. "Your brother didn't speak to you, did he?" Quieter, she mumbled, "dragons and their mates. Unbelievable."

"Which brother was supposed to speak to me about what?"

Teeth bared, she returned to saddling her horse a touch too rough. "Captain Black."

Eoin. That made sense. Eoin had scarcely spoken to him about anything since he brought an army to their doorstep and turned Elsie into a walking torch.

No, that wasn't fair. The Soldiers of the Gods were not Eoin's doing, and he was not responsible for what happened.

But it would have been nice of him to offer a more thorough explanation than, "a bunch of mad men decided the Gods want them to burn witches and wear ill-fitting clothes."

Amos was paraphrasing, of course.

"Eoin is a bit...distracted."

"Well, while he's busy *distracted* I have clans to protect," Lia snarled, causing her horse to jolt back again. "Are you coming or not?"

The clans. Right. Lia was a clanswoman, one of the few who chose to live deep within the mountains, abiding by the rule of the king only when it suited them. They were a wild people, undomesticated, some would say, and were known for the fierce warriors they raised.

Legend suggested that they were descended from dragons. Hard to say, since according to Lia, every last man in the clans was dead, and the *drakonmein* gift only passed down to sons.

Dead from the same war that left Eoin a shell of the man he once was.

"Yes," Amos said without considering what she was asking. He hadn't spoken more than a handful of words to Lia since she arrived nearly two weeks ago, but he understood how important this was to her.

These were her people, and they were under threat from the same men that would have burned the Black Estate to the ground on their hunt for some Gods promised dragon.

"There are many more where they came from," she'd told Gannon and Eoin when the battle was over. "This is only the beginning of a bigger uprising."

"It's not my war to fight," Gannon told her simply, choosing to turn his attention to the people under his immediate care.

Amos couldn't blame his brothers for refusing to get involved, but he also wouldn't stand by and watch a woman like Lia go to battle alone. She was an incredible fighter, but if the Soldiers of the Gods had numbers like she claimed, it would take more than swords to beat them back.

It would take dragon fire.

The trouble was that Amos wasn't sure his dragon would fight for Lia, or anyone. If he wasn't in danger himself, he would have no motivation.

Amos chose to deal with that concern later. The moment he uttered that one word agreement to join Lia on her journey north, his headache eased. The pain in his spine receded, and inside he felt a sense of calm. Of rightness.

"When do we leave?"

"Now," she said impatiently. "Immediately."

Amos glanced at his casual attire, and lack of supplies. "I'll need a moment."

"Yes, I think you will."

Edgar appeared from the shadow of the feed room, lifting his hands to explain, *"Your bags are already packed."*

So, Eoin told someone.

"Thank you, Edgar." Amos clapped him on the shoulder a little harder than necessary. "You could have warned me."

Edgar smiled, pale eyes crinkling. *"There's nothing I can do to prepare you for what's to come."*

He squeezed Amos's arm, stepping around him and leaving the stable without further explanation.

Amos looked between Lia and Edgar, feeling as if his world was about to change. He wasn't sure if the bubbling in his stomach was excitement or disquiet.

"Very well," Amos said, mostly to himself. "Let me fetch my sword."

THANK YOU FOR READING!

Ready for another fast-burn dragon shifter romance? Join my newsletter and download a Dragon Brides novella with new characters and a standalone story.

Thank you for reading Midnight Ruin! Would you help get my books in the hands of more readers by leaving a review?

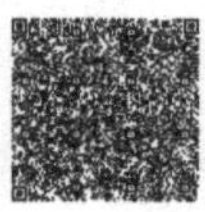